"But you promised. You promised you would love me.

"You can't break your word."

Her panic was his undoing. Brett had known Victoria Lancaster for four years—had lived with her for the last three of those years—and had never, not once, seen her lose control like this.

Panicked by what he had unintentionally caused, he pulled her into his arms, rocking her against his chest as he soothed her terror with a gentle hand.

"I'm sorry, baby. I'm sorry. Don't cry. Please don't cry. I never said I didn't love you. You're my world. You're my life."

She clutched at his arms, staring blindly into his face. At that moment he had the strangest feeling she was looking not at him, but somewhere deep in her mind.

*Watch for SHARON SALA's newest release,
coming in February 1999
from MIRA Books*

SWEET BABY

SHARON SALA

MIRA

ISBN 1-55166-416-X

SWEET BABY

Copyright © 1998 by Sharon Sala.

All rights reserved. Except for use in any review, the reproduction or utilization of this work in whole or in part in any form by any electronic, mechanical or other means, now known or hereafter invented, including xerography, photocopying and recording, or in any information storage or retrieval system, is forbidden without the written permission of the publisher, MIRA Books, 225 Duncan Mill Road, Don Mills, Ontario, Canada M3B 3K9.

All characters in this book have no existence outside the imagination of the author and have no relation whatsoever to anyone bearing the same name or names. They are not even distantly inspired by any individual known or unknown to the author, and all incidents are pure invention.

MIRA and the star colophon are registered trademarks of MIRA Books.

Printed in U.S.A.

I wrote this book for all the children who needed a Sweet Baby, but didn't have one.

I will say a prayer each night for the children who cry and no one hears.
I will say a prayer each night for the children who wake up hungry and go to bed the same way.
I will say a prayer each night for the children who are missing, and for those who are lost.
I will say a prayer each night for the children who suffer alone because they have no one who cares.
I will say a prayer each night for the children that no one loves.
I will say a prayer for the children.
I will say a prayer each night,
because when no one else is listening,
God still hears.

Prologue

Rural Arkansas, 1973

A rooster tail of dust billowed behind the bright yellow school bus as it rumbled down the Arkansas back roads, returning the children of Calico Rock to their homes.

It was dry for September. The narrow, two-lane road on which the bus was traveling was bordered on both sides with an abundance of dust-covered greens. Old trees, tall and angular, struggled for space among new growth in the constant act of taking root. On the ground beneath, bushes and scrub brush flourished, hanging on to their place in the mountains with fierce persistence.

The sky was pale, a blue so light it almost seemed white, and the sun beaming down on the roof of the bus sweltered the children inside like so many beans in a can. Sweat ran out of their hair and down their faces as they chattered away. They didn't care that it was hot, because it was Friday, and they were going home.

But though the noise level inside the bus was high, there was the occasional child, like six-year-old Victoria Lancaster, who sat alone in her seat, quietly contemplating the day's events and longing for the first sight of home.

Last night had been a first for young Tory in more ways than one. She and seven other little girls had spent the night at Mary Ellen Wiggins' slumber party. For Tory, it was the first time in her life that she'd slept somewhere other than beneath her mother's roof—and without her dolly, Sweet Baby. And she hadn't cried. Not even once.

As the bus began to brake, she looked up. The Broyles brothers were getting off. That meant she would be next. Her mouth pursed as she thought back to last night. She couldn't wait to tell her mommy about Mary Ellen's party. Roasting wieners and marshmallows and then telling ghost stories after the house was dark had been scary—but so much fun. Mommy would be so proud of her for not asking to go home.

The bus hit a bump, and Tory clutched at the brown paper sack in her lap. It held yesterday's dirty school clothes, as well as her nightgown. There was a ketchup stain on her dress and marshmallow on the front of her gown, but she wasn't too worried. Mommy never yelled at her for things like that. In fact, Mommy hardly ever yelled at all, and when she did, she was usually yelling at Ollie.

She sighed, remembering a time in their life when Ollie hadn't lived with them and wishing it could be that way again. Ollie was always teasing her about being a momma's baby. When she got home, she would show him. She'd spent the whole night away from home. Babies couldn't do that!

Right in the middle of planning what she would say to Ollie, a voice suddenly shrieked in her ear. "Tory's got a boyfriend. Tory's got a boyfriend."

Tory turned in her seat and stuck out her tongue, glaring angrily at the boy behind her. It was that stupid old Arthur Beckham. After less than six weeks of first grade, she'd already figured out that the older boys got, the dumber they became.

When he laughed in her face, she spun back in her seat, red-faced and a little bit shocked by her own temerity. When she got to be a fourth-grader, she wouldn't pick on little kids like Arthur did, of that she was certain.

Once more the bus began to slow. Tory glanced out the window as the brakes locked, then squeaked. When she saw the familiar rooftop of her home, she grabbed hold of the seat in front of her for balance, then stood. Arthur Beckham made a face at her as she passed down the aisle, but she was too anxious to get home to give him another thought. As she stepped off the bus, an errant wind lifted the hem of her dress, but she didn't care. The moment her feet hit the dirt, she began to run.

An orange-and-black butterfly fluttered just ahead of her, riding the wind current with delicate ease, and it almost seemed as if they were racing. The fantasy caught in her mind, and she shifted into an all-out stride. The afternoon sun caught and then held in the tangles of her long, blond hair. Had anyone been around to notice, they might have imagined they'd seen a halo above her head. But it was the end of the day, and had one been inclined to consider her an angel, she would have been a grubby one at best.

There was a skinned spot on her knee, a smudge from lunch on the front of her dress, and her shoes and anklets wore a light coating of dust as her little legs churned, making short work of the distance to the house. The brown paper bag she held clutched in one fist was torn at the top and about to give way, but it didn't matter now. She was almost there.

Just as Tory's feet hit the front steps, the butterfly darted off to the left. She laughed aloud, calling out to her mother as she grabbed the screen door and yanked.

"Mommy! Mommy! I'm home! You should have seen me! I was racing a butterfly and—"

She froze as the echo of her own voice moved from room to empty room, drifting like a bad memory that wouldn't go away. A draft of hot air came from somewhere before her, shifting the hem of her dress and pushing the fabric against her bare legs. Tory took a step farther, then another, and another, unaware when the brown paper bag she'd been holding fell from her fingers and onto the floor.

Everything was gone, from the faded blue curtains on the windows to the furniture that had been sitting on the floors. Her heart skipped a beat. Even though her eyes were seeing the truth, her heart would not accept it.

"Mommy?"

She cocked her head, listening for the familiar sound of her mother's voice, but all she heard was the faint grinding of gears as the school bus climbed the hill on the road beyond.

She called out again, her voice trembling. "Mommy? Mommy? I'm home."

The silence beyond the sound of her voice was insidious, amplifying the call of a bird in the tree outside the kitchen window. Somewhere within the house she heard a cricket chirp, and her heart leaped. Mommy hated crickets in the house. Any minute she would come racing into the room to get rid of it. She turned toward the doorway, her big blue eyes tear-filled and horror-stricken. But nothing moved, and no one came.

She called again. "Mommy…where are you?"

All she could hear was the thunder of her heartbeat, drowning out the sound of her own voice.

She ran toward her bedroom, the only sanctuary she knew. If she crawled onto her bed and cuddled Sweet Baby, Mommy would surely come home.

But it was as vacant as the rest of the house. And as she stood in the doorway, she started to shake. Sweat broke out across her forehead, beading on her upper lip. Her little bed—the one with the pale pink spread—was missing. Even worse, Sweet Baby was nowhere to be found.

Near hysteria, she began turning in a circle, her fingers knotting into tiny fists as she began to chant, "Mommy, Mommy, Mommy," as if saying the word enough times would make her mother appear.

Frantic, her gaze moved to the open closet door. Everything, including her new Sunday school shoes, was missing. Gone! Everything and everyone was gone!

She began to circle the four small rooms in the clapboard house, racing in and then out again as her hysteria grew, shouting her mother's name over and over until there was nothing left of Tory Lancaster but a scream.

The sound of a car going by on the road beyond sent her running to the doorway, but when it went past without a sign of slowing down, she backed up in sudden fear. Alone! She was alone! It was only after she'd backed herself into a corner of the room that she stopped, her eyes wide and staring, her expression blank. Tears were drying on her cheeks as she slowly sank into a squatting position, her gaze fixed on the door.

The afternoon turned into dusk, dusk into night, but Tory Lancaster never moved. She was waiting—waiting for Mommy to come home.

One

It was the faint but distinct sound of a closing door that yanked Brett Hooker out of a restless sleep and sent him reaching for the gun in the bedside table. In the few moments between sleepy confusion and the return of complete cognizance, he slid the gun back into the drawer, then pushed it shut.

She was back!

The wild thump of his heart began to slow down, returning to a regular rhythm. He rose up on one elbow, staring at the open doorway and accepting the weakness within him for putting up with a woman who was more gypsy than lover, wondering what it was about her that made it all worthwhile.

Something clunked on the living room floor, followed by a softly muttered curse. A few seconds later, another less distinct sound drifted down the hallway and into the bedroom. He tensed. She was moving through the apartment, toward the bedroom—toward him.

He lay back and closed his eyes, willing her to hurry. It had been so damned long since he'd held her that it hurt.

The heaviest of Tory Lancaster's camera bags had threatened to slide off her shoulder as she thrust the key in the lock. Without wasted motion, she'd hitched it higher and turned the key.

Silently, the door swung back as she stepped inside. She paused on the threshold, unaware she was holding her breath. Had she been looking in a mirror, she would have been surprised to know there was a faint look of fear on her face. Only after she heard the familiar night sounds of Brett Hooker's apartment did she shut the door behind her and relax. She slipped the camera bags off her shoulders and then eased her duffel bag to the floor beside them, breathing a sigh of relief.

Then she stood in the quiet, listening to a clock ticking on the kitchen wall, measuring the inconsistent drip of the faucet at the kitchen sink, savoring the hum of the refrigerator motor, feeling Brett's presence, although she had yet to see his face.

Unaware of the game her subconscious mind always played with her heart, the fear faded from her eyes and she began to calm. He was home. Just as he'd promised he would be. But there was always that doubt within Victoria Lancaster's heart that even time hadn't been able to erase. Although her intermittent absences from this man and his home were part of her life-style—part of her job as a freelance photojournalist—it was the manner in which she took leave of him each time that was the telling factor in Tory's inability to commit. He'd promised he would always be waiting, but subconsciously, she kept testing his word, testing his faith.

Inhaling deeply, she closed her eyes, savoring the texture of the air. It was warm and welcoming, and she shivered with sudden longing, opening her arms wide, then enfolding herself within the safety of these walls like rolling up within the folds of an old, familiar blanket. Down the hallway to her left, a bedspring squeaked, and a sudden urgency made her reach for the buttons on her shirt.

Brett!

It had been six weeks since she'd last seen him, but it felt like six months. The need to feel the tautness of his muscles and the strength of his body hammering between her legs made her weak with longing. She spun, and in the dark she stubbed her toe on the small table near the entry-way. A soft curse slipped from her lips as she reached to steady the vase rocking on its surface.

Once it was settled, Tory's hands went back to the shirt buttons, then her belt, then the button fly of her jeans. Within the familiar darkness of Brett

Hooker's home, she began to undress, leaving a trail of her clothing to mark her passing. When she stepped through the doorway to his bedroom, she was naked. The last thing she did was take down her hair. It spilled from her hands, sliding against her neck and then across her shoulders like a rich satin curtain, the ash-blond color a pale contrast to her smooth, white skin.

Shivering with a longing she would never have named, she stared at the sleeping man upon the bed, struggling with the ache of loneliness within her chest. Why? Why, if she loved him so much, did she keep leaving him behind? Tory closed her eyes and said a small, quiet prayer.

God, please don't let me mess this up.

And then she looked, and he was coming toward her through the shadows, his steps slow but measured, the tilt of his head a warning to the intent of his actions. When he opened his arms, she fell into them. And when he wrapped his hands in the long length of her hair and pulled, tilting her head back to meet his descending mouth, she sensed an unvoiced anger.

"Tory, Tory. My God, but I missed you."

His whisper shattered the silence in which they stood. Tears spiked beneath her eyelids as she gave herself up to his need. Her name on his lips was both a prayer and a joy. And then Brett picked her up and carried her back to his bed.

"I missed you, too," she said softly.

His voice was harsh as he pinned her beneath his hard, aching body. "Prove it."

She sighed, feeling the needy surge of him against her thigh. Now she was on familiar ground. She pushed at his shoulders, urging him to let her control the action. He complied with a reluctant groan. But when she straddled his legs and took him into her hands, she heard him groan again, then felt him relax. Only then did she know it would be all right.

Stroke after sensuous stroke, she stoked his passion until his control suddenly snapped. He rose up on one elbow, whispering promises to her, that, even after the three years they'd been together, made her blush. Before she could react, he had her flat on her back, his hand between her legs. After that, what was left of the night became a series of gut-wrenching climaxes that left her weak and shaking, then begging for more.

Somewhere among them, Brett shared one, taking her fast and hard, his control shattering along with what was left of her mind.

It was almost daybreak. Brett looked down at the sleeping woman in his arms and then back up at the ceiling, willing himself not to move. Just for the moment, the paradise of having her safe in his bed, of knowing that she was still alive and whole, was too precious to ruin.

And time passed.

Morning light was spilling into the room as Tory opened her eyes. For the moment, a smattering of chest hair and one hard brown nipple were all she could see, but it was enough for her to remember where she was. With Brett.

Stretching slowly like a waking cat, she closed her eyes and inhaled the essence of the man beside her, savoring the masculine smell that was uniquely his, as well as the lingering scent of their lovemaking that was still on their bodies. She snuggled against him as his deep, sleep-heavy voice broke the silence between them.

"It's about damned time."

By way of apology, Tory kissed his chin as she looked up. "It was a long drive, and you didn't let me get much sleep. I couldn't seem to wake up."

"I wasn't talking about the fact that we overslept. I was talking about the fact that you finally decided to come back."

Tory stiffened. This wasn't the way their morning-afters normally went. Then she remembered the anger she'd sensed in him last night. Old fear suddenly coiled in her belly, but she thrust it aside. With an easy smile, she reached up to cup his cheek, admiring with an artist's eye the shapely cut of his nose, the strength of his cheeks and jaw-line, as well as the near perfect conformity of black-winged eyebrows and lashes shading a shat-tering blue gaze. She traced the lower edge of his lip, testing the sensuous cut of it with the edge of her nail, then kissed the spot she'd teased.

"But I *always* come back."

Brett grabbed her hands and then rolled, pinning her beneath him.

"So far," he said harshly, hating himself for putting that fear in her eyes, yet needing to push, wanting her to say something that would take away the knot in his gut. The one that came from his own fear that one day she would leave him and never return.

Tory stifled a gasp, trying unsuccessfully to free her wrists from his grasp.

"Brett, don't!" she begged.

It was useless. He was too strong, and at that moment, too angry to hear anything but the sound of his own voice.

"You know, Tory, I'm curious."

She shifted nervously beneath him. "About what?"

"How long this is going to go on."

A quick shaft of unnamed terror moved through her mind. Her heart kicked out of rhythm as the blood began to drain from her face, but Tory didn't know how she looked, and if she had, she wouldn't have cared. Her entire focus was on the man above her and the subject of their conversation.

"How long is what going to go on?"

He almost sneered. "You know. This business of Tory calling all the shots and Brett taking the blows." His fingers tightened as his voice rose. "Goddamn it, Victoria, you assume a lot."

She couldn't speak, couldn't move. There was a sick lassitude spreading from the ends of her toes upward and she knew that when it reached her throat, she might die.

But Brett was too deep into his own rage to see the panic on her face.

"You know...sometimes you walk out without so much as a note to tell me where you've gone. Most of the time you don't bother to call, and when you do, you never ask what I've been doing, or even if I've been sick. Usually all I get from you is a pissant message on an answering machine."

He leaned over her, yanking open the drawer on the bedside table then thrusting his hand inside. Seconds later, a handful of tiny cassette tapes showered down upon her head.

"Do you know what those are?"

Tears were pooling in her eyes, shattering her vision of his anger. She shook her head.

"Your messages. That's what they are. About a

year's worth, actually. And do you know why I've kept them?''

She shook her head again, spilling a tear down her cheek.

His voice broke as he tossed the last of them onto the bed. "Because I can't bear to tape over the damned things for fear they'll be the last sound I'll ever have of your voice.''

"Oh, Brett, I'm sorry. I—''

"Goddamn it, Tory, why don't you keep in touch? Do you ever think about the fact that I could be dead and buried before you'd know it? One of these days you're liable to come home and I won't be here. Then what will you—''

When her eyes rolled back in her head, Brett choked on the last of his anger. The sound that came up her throat, then out of her mouth, was something between a scream and a shriek—a cry unlike anything he'd ever heard. He flinched at the sound, trying to find the Tory he knew in the high-pitched, childlike wail of despair. And in the midst of it all she kept saying the same thing.

"But you promised. You promised you would love me. You can't break your word, 'cause you promised.''

Her panic was his undoing. He'd known Victoria Lancaster for four years—had lived with her for the last three of those years—and he'd never, not once, seen her lose control like this.

Panicked by what he'd unintentionally caused, he pulled her into his arms, rocking her against his chest as he soothed her terror with a gentle hand.

"I'm sorry, baby, I'm sorry. Don't cry. Please don't cry. I never said I didn't love you. Of course I love you. You're my world. You're my life."

She clutched at his arms, staring blindly into his face. At that moment, he had the strangest feeling she was looking somewhere into her mind, rather than at him.

It took the better part of an hour before Brett had her calmed, and then she refused to look at him. He didn't know whether she was embarrassed by her outbreak or hurt by what he'd said. When she rolled over and away from him, a knot twisted in his gut.

"Victoria."

Her answer was little more than a whisper. "What?"

"I love you."

She rolled onto her back, wrapping her arms around his neck and clutching at him with a desperation he didn't understand. Moments later, she turned him loose as abruptly as she'd held him and then looked away. Brett sighed. Something was going on that he didn't understand, and she was obviously not in the mood to talk about it.

"I'm going to shower. Be back in a few minutes," he said.

She watched him intently as he moved around the room. When the bathroom door closed behind him, Tory stared up at the ceiling, her mind a total blank. Then, as if nothing untoward had occurred, she got out of bed and went into the living room to retrieve her bag. But she had a week's worth of dirty laundry inside and no clean underwear, so she came back into the bedroom, confiscating one of Brett's T-shirts and a clean pair of sweats.

She was tall, but her body structure was nothing like Brett's. On her, the sleeves of his T-shirt were inches too long and hung well below her elbows, and the pant legs of his sweats drooped around her ankles. Everything sagged in all the wrong places, but being inside something that belonged to Brett gave her a strange sense of peace. With a pair of his tube socks serving as house shoes, Tory gathered up her dirty clothes and headed for the kitchen. She would start her laundry while breakfast cooked.

A short while later, Brett came out, taking careful note of her empty duffel bag, as well as the tangled covers on the bed. He stood for a moment, anxiously listening for the sounds of her presence. It was the smell of brewing coffee that made him relax. Following it to the kitchen in the hopes of finding Tory, all he found was a pile of her dirty laundry on the floor by the washing machine.

"Tory?"

She didn't answer. He walked out of the kitchen, thinking she might be on the patio instead, but when he heard the familiar clunk of metal against metal he stopped. It was the lopsided sign hanging on the darkroom door that told him where she'd gone.

Do Not Disturb.

And it meant what it said. The significance of the closed door between them was more than accidental. Without thinking, Brett reached out, putting the flat of his hand against the surface of the door, then splaying his fingers across the wood, as if trying to hold on to Tory in the only way she would let him.

A few moments later he turned away with a weary sigh and headed for the kitchen. He needed coffee, and he needed to hurry or he was going to be late for work.

A day-old bagel with his last cup of coffee was breakfast. Then he headed for the bedroom, his mind already moving toward what he would do for the day.

As an investigator for the Oklahoma County District Attorney's Office, his job was never dull. And, for the last few days, the entire investigative force, as well as the Oklahoma PD, had been on the lookout for a missing witness for the prosecution in a murder trial.

Don Lacey, the county district attorney, was

bound and determined to win this trial and, in doing so, prove a long-suspected connection to a local named Romeo Leeds. Every cop on the force suspected Leeds was behind a large part of the area-wide criminal activities, but so far, they had yet to prove it.

Nailing Manny Riberosa, the man who was coming up for trial, was the best chance they'd had in years. A known thug who would do anything for money, Riberosa had long been suspected of being Leeds' right-hand man. And the murdered man had been Romeo Leeds' stiffest competitor. If they could prove that Riberosa was guilty of the murder for which he'd been arrested, then they would have the link they needed to pursue Leeds. And finding that link was part of Brett's job.

He took a clean shirt from the closet and then stood before the mirror to slip it on. But when he looked, he didn't see himself. He was looking at the reflection of the bed behind him and the condition of the covers, remembering the near-desperate manner in which he and Tory had made love. His jaw clenched as he tucked his shirt into his slacks; then he reached for a tie, slipping it on beneath the collar of his shirt.

This is one hell of a way to love a woman. Waiting and hoping she doesn't forget to come back.

He leaned closer to the mirror, making sure his tie was straight and his collar points buttoned. One more item and he would be out of here. He opened the bedside table and took out his gun. The Glock, an Austrian-made, double-action automatic, felt light in his hand as he slipped it into the holster, then fastened it to his belt. He picked up his suit coat and headed for the living room. But as he passed by the darkroom, he paused, staring intently at the door she'd shut between them. The urge to call out to her was great, but he respected her need for privacy too much to interfere with what she was doing.

With a heavy heart, he opened the front door and stepped out, closing it quietly it behind him.

Two

For Tory, being a photographer was like being a magician, only better. The darkroom was her top hat, the place where the magic was created, yet she produced no rabbits or doves out of the air. The magic came from the pictures she'd shot.

When the developing process began, the first images were little more than faint, ghostlike shadows. But as she watched, they became so lifelike that she could almost hear the sounds of laughter coming from them. It was then that she knew she'd captured the moment precisely. But unlike a magician, what she created wasn't illusion. When Tory was finished, she had something concrete to hold.

Each time she took a finished print out of the rinse, she would eye it carefully before clipping it on one of the lines strung about her darkroom, adding it to the dozens upon dozens of new prints drying above her head.

So engrossed was she in her work that she never heard Brett pause outside the darkroom door, and if she had, she wouldn't have stopped to respond. If someone had asked her how she felt about Brett Hooker, she wouldn't have hesitated to say she loved him. But if they'd asked her why she kept walking in and out of his life with little regard for his feelings, she couldn't have given them an answer. Even *she* didn't know why. All she knew was that the closer their relationship grew, the more intense her panic became.

She slid a new print into the pan of developer, eyeing the fuzzy image that began to appear, then watching with growing anticipation as the shadows became darker and darker until a complete picture had developed. It was a shot of a crowd taken at a fair somewhere in the Midwest. She looked closer, taking note of the old Ferris wheel in the background, and realized the photo was one she'd taken while following the broken-down rigs of Amherst Entertainment.

Her gaze went back to the crowd and the collage of expressions she'd caught on the people's faces. Excitement hit as she slipped it into the stop bath and then the fix. When she ran it through the rinse, her anticipation grew. She could hardly wait to look closer, and in better light. Instinct told her that this piece was going to be one of the best she'd done to date.

Step by step, she finished printing the last of the rolls that she'd shot. Only after she'd begun to clean everything up did she realize her back was killing her and her stomach was growling in protest of the fact that she hadn't eaten since four o'clock yesterday afternoon.

As she started to leave, she glanced back at the pictures hanging in her darkroom, a testament to the six weeks she'd been gone. With a weary sigh, she flipped off the safe light and closed the door.

"Brett?"

When he didn't answer, she glanced at her watch. It was almost noon. Her shoulders slumped. He'd been gone for hours, and she'd never even told him good morning, let alone goodbye.

As she wandered into the kitchen, her thoughts went back to last night and their lovemaking, and then to the unexpectedness of his anger. When she reached for a cup, to her surprise, her hands were shaking, but she attributed it to hunger, rather than nerves. Yet if Tory had been honest with herself, she would have had to face the fact that, for the first time in the three years they'd been together, she was afraid. Afraid of losing him and—even worse—afraid to care that it could happen.

Angry with herself and the situation, she put the cup back in the cabinet and decided to do her laundry. After starting a load, she went to the phone. She was in no mood to cook, and getting dressed to go out was out of the question.

I know. I'll order in a pizza.

She dialed the number, listening absently as it began to ring. Tonight she would make it up to Brett. She would fix all of his favorite foods, and after that...

Just thinking of the wild, uninhibited ways in which they made love made her flush. She closed her eyes, letting herself remember the feel of his mouth on her skin, the gentle rasp of his tongue against her belly as he moved lower and—

"Mazzio's Pizza, can I help you?"

Tory jerked, almost dropping the phone as she struggled to remember what she'd been doing.

"Uh...um, yes." She raked her fingers through her hair in an absentminded motion as she quickly gave her order.

About a half hour later, the doorbell rang. Tory bolted for the door with money in hand, assuming it would be the pizza delivery boy with her food.

"Here you—"

She paused in midsentence with the twenty-dollar bill still hanging from her fingers. Before she could react, Brett swept her into his arms, kicking the door shut behind him and grinning as her money fluttered to the floor.

"You can pay me later." And he stole a kiss.

The knot in her belly began to unwind. Brett was here, and he was no longer angry. Everything in her world was suddenly all right.

He began carrying her toward the bedroom.

"I ordered pizza," she said.

"You can eat later," he growled.

Just as he lay her in the middle of the bed, the doorbell rang again. Brett's eyes glittered. "Don't move," he said, and when she smiled, he added, "Hold that thought."

Tory listened to the exchange of polite conversation as Brett paid for her pizza. Then the door shut, and when she heard the unmistakable sound of locks turning, her pulse quickened and she closed her eyes, savoring the anticipation of what was to come. Moments later, the bed gave beneath his weight as he crawled on top of her.

"Tory?"

She opened her eyes.

"Who loves you, baby?"

A rare peace settled within her as she reached for his face. "You."

Brett growled beneath his breath, his mouth only a fraction of an inch from her lips. "And don't you forget it."

Tory gave herself up to his touch, relishing the weight of his body pressing her into the mattress, savoring everything there was about this man who was her world.

He tugged at the waistband of her sweatpants, grinning to himself as they all but fell off of her.

"These look vaguely familiar." He grinned again as he tossed them aside and then ran his hands beneath her oversize shirt. "And so does this," he added, pulling the T-shirt over her head and adding it to the pile on the floor.

"I like to wear your clothes," she said softly, stretching when he ran a hand up her belly, gently cupping her breast.

"Yeah, because all of yours are dirty," Brett said, then circled her nipple with his tongue until it began to harden and peak.

Tory locked her hands behind his head and pulled him closer, arching toward his mouth and that constantly seeking tongue.

"No. Because it's like being inside your skin."

Her admission startled him. To hear Tory admitting something that personal was rare. He raised his head, staring intently into her eyes. She met his gaze without flinching, and Brett couldn't help remembering the panic he'd seen there earlier.

"I know just what you mean," he said softly, and brushed his mouth against the curve of her cheek. "You've been under my skin for years."

She laughed softly.

"And I have to admit, having you there feels pretty damned good." He moved his hand to the juncture of her thighs.

She gasped and then sighed. "Ummm...Brett."

He grinned. "What, honey?"

"So does that."

* * *

The scent of pizza lingered in the apartment long after he'd gone back to work. Tory wandered through the rooms without aim, absently putting away her newly clean clothes and trying to focus on writing a grocery list. As always, after being gone on one of her trips, she'd found that Brett had let the stock of fresh foods dwindle. He said it was because it was more convenient for him to grab a bite to eat before he came home for the day, but Tory suspected it was because he didn't like to come home to the empty apartment and then eat alone.

She liked to cook, and when she was here, she spoiled him with an abundance of home-cooked food. Yet as long as she'd been sharing Brett's apartment, she wouldn't let herself think of it as home. She had her share of the closets and dressers, and Brett had willingly given up his office space in the apartment to her darkroom, but it wasn't her place, it was Brett's. And he was her lover, not her husband. The only permanent fixtures in Tory Lancaster's life were her cameras. They were the walls behind which she hid, the boundaries that kept her safe. They were her eyes to the world, and she never left home without them.

In spite of the dozens of odd jobs that needed to be done, she couldn't get her mind off the new pictures in the darkroom. She kept telling herself she needed to shop, but the closed door beckoned, and before she could talk herself out of it, she was inside and taking down the photographs.

A few minutes later she emerged with the stack of prints in one hand and a magnifying glass in the other. Like a child with a new toy, she crawled into Brett's easy chair near the window and began to go through her work.

The assignment she'd been on had been simple but hectic. It was a piece on carnivals. To keep up with their grueling schedules, she'd had to travel back and forth within a five-state area, taking pictures and getting the necessary information on two separate carnivals. One was privately owned and operated on a shoestring budget, the other was a corporately owned, five-star operation.

But the story she'd been sent to do had taken a different twist than the one the commissioning magazine had requested. Tory's story was no longer about carnivals. Two weeks into the project she'd realized the real story was in the people who came to them and the hard-earned money they were willing to spend for a fleeting moment of pleasure.

As she sorted through her pictures, her eagerness grew. She got out her notes, coordinating names with faces and places. She was as thorough with her paperwork as she was with taking pictures. When necessary, she had a file of signed consent forms from the subjects to go with the shots she'd taken.

After sorting through them twice, she picked up the stack on her right and began going through them again, picking out the ones she liked best, and the crowd shot she'd taken while traveling with Amherst Entertainment was one of her favorites. She had about a month until her deadline and would need every bit of it to do a proper job. For Tory, taking pictures was a snap. The real work began with the writing.

Sometime later, she glanced up and then dumped everything in her lap to the floor. Brett would be home before long, and she still hadn't gone to the store.

"Shoot," she muttered. Just when things got interesting, reality always managed to intrude.

She made a mental grocery list as she drove, and by the time she got to the supermarket, she had her trip down the aisles all mapped out in her head. In and out. That was what she was planning to do. Get in. Buy the food. Get out. It didn't get any simpler.

But things rarely go as they're planned.

Tory was in the middle of aisle five, trying to decide between a jar of dill pickle slices and one of dill pickle chunks, when she heard the unmistakable sound of flesh slapping flesh. Once. Twice.

Three times. The skin on the back of her neck crawled. When it was followed by a childlike voice begging someone to stop and then a high, plaintive wail, she lost it. With the inborn skill of a seasoned shopper, she spun the cart around on two wheels and began pushing it toward the end of the aisle, determined to find the source.

It wasn't hard. The child's muffled sobs and the man's angry voice continued to permeate the store. Tory wasn't the only shopper who'd heard, but she seemed to be the only one willing to get involved.

And then she saw them in the middle of aisle eight and turned down it like a woman possessed. The little girl was dirty-faced and shoeless. Her hair was greasy and looked as if it hadn't been combed in days. The shoulder seams of her T-shirt hung halfway to her elbows, and if she had anything on under it, it was lost beneath the voluminous folds of the hand-me-down shirt. She couldn't have been more the five, maybe six, but it wouldn't have mattered to Tory if she had been eighty. The tiny stream of blood running from her nose and the handprint on the side of her cheek were all she needed to see.

''Stop that snivelin','' the man snarled, and lifted his hand again.

Tory didn't think. She just reacted by grabbing his arm and yanking him around before the next blow could fall.

"Don't hit her again."

He spun around in shock. When he saw Tory, his face turned a dull, angry red, and he took a menacing step toward her.

He smelled like liquor and sweat, and she wanted to gag as he doubled his fist and shoved it right beneath her nose.

"Mind your own business, bitch. 'At's my kid, and I'll whup her any time I feel like it."

With him being drunk on his feet, and the lack of expression in his eyes, Tory knew a moment of fear. But the child's need was stronger than her own need to flee. She stood her ground, her voice rising in anger to match his.

"I said, don't hit her again," she repeated. "No child deserves to be beaten."

At that point, a store manager came running down the aisle. "What's going on here?" he cried.

The drunk pivoted, swaying on his feet, and took a swing at the manager, missing him by at least a foot. As he swung, he just kept going, falling headfirst toward a shelf full of baby food jars.

Tory grabbed the child, pulling her out of the way just in time to keep her from being knocked into the shelves beneath her father. Glass and baby food shattered and splattered as the manager groaned.

"Oh man," he mumbled, and reached for a two-way he had in his pocket. "I need some mops and buckets on aisle eight…and somebody call the police."

He looked up at Tory and then down at the child. "Are you with them?" he asked.

"No."

"What was going on?" he asked.

"Look at her," Tory said, pointing to the child. "I heard him slapping her from two aisles over."

The manager's face paled. The handprint on the child's cheek was still visible, and the steady stream of blood from her nose was evidence of the force of the impact. He shook his head.

"The world is full of crazies," he muttered.

Tory's eyes were blazing, her hands shaking from anger. "Unfortunately, some of them are parents."

She thought of her years in foster homes. Some of the people had been decent. Some of them had not. And when she'd needed help most, there had been no one to hear her cries. Ignoring this child's cry for help had been impossible. She fished a handful of tissues from her purse and then knelt by the child.

"Here, sweetie," she said softly. "We need to clean the blood off your face, okay?"

Too stunned to argue, the little girl stood while Tory swiped at her face. The sound of sirens could now be heard in the distance, and she knew within minutes the child would be gone. There was a panic within Tory, wondering if her interference in this child's life was going to make it better…or worse.

"What's your name?" Tory asked.

"Clydene."

"That's a pretty name." And then she added, "For a pretty girl."

The child smiled, and it was all Tory could do not to cry. By tomorrow, the child would have a black eye to go with the busted lip and swollen nose. Maybe she would remember that someone told her she was pretty.

The drunk was starting to rouse, so Tory pulled the child a bit farther up the aisle.

"Let's just move back a little bit more until they get through mopping up that mess, okay?"

The child nodded. "Daddy's gonna be pissed," the child said calmly.

Tory hid her shock. From what she could see, Clydene's vocabulary was well in keeping with her home life.

"The police will see that he doesn't hurt anyone else," Tory said.

The child shrugged. "He'll be pissed."

"Maybe not. Maybe your mother will be able to—"

"Ain't got one," Clydene announced.

A strong sensation of déjà vu rocked Tory back

on her heels. She could almost hear herself saying the same thing in the same monotone voice.

"I'm sorry," Tory said softly. "Did she die?"

The drunk rolled over on his back, groaning and cursing loud and long. The child gave her father a nervous look.

"Don't know," she said. "She's just gone."

Something nudged Tory's memory. Something old. Something bad. But before she could follow the thought, the store manager handed Tory another handful of wipes.

"Thank goodness," she said. "The police are here."

Tory looked up to see three uniformed officers coming down the aisle. She glanced at the child. There was a look of terror on her face that made Tory sick. Something told her this wasn't the first time the girl had seen them coming.

Within minutes, they were gone. Tory retrieved her basket and then stood in the middle of the aisle, staring down at the food and trying to remember what she needed to do. But her stomach hurt, and so did her heart, and she couldn't quit thinking about the look on Clydene's face as an officer carried her away. She hadn't been afraid. She'd just been resigned.

Because of what had happened at the store, Tory was certain that Brett would beat her home. But as she hurried into the apartment with an apology on her lips, the blinking light on the answering machine interrupted her anxiety, and listening to the message, she began to relax even more. She'd been given a reprieve.

"Tory, it's me, Brett. I'm going to be late. Conroy is taking a case to court tomorrow that just fell apart in his lap. I've got to find his other witness or the whole thing will have to be dismissed. See you later, honey. I love you."

Conroy was an assistant D.A. Tory rarely knew what went on at Brett's work, but she recognized most of the names of the people with whom he worked.

"I love you, too," she said softly, then headed to the kitchen.

Now she had all the time she needed to fix that special meal she'd been planning, but it was a toss-up as to when Brett would be home to eat it. She began to put up the groceries, her thoughts still lingering on a little girl named Clydene and the drunk who called himself a father. Then she frowned, giving herself a mental kick in the pants. She couldn't save the world, but she'd saved a child from a beating. At least for one night. And with that, she had to be satisfied.

Refusing to dwell any longer on whether she'd done right or wrong, she focused on the meal she was about to prepare.

"Okay, Hooker, you can be late, but you better be hungry when you get here." She opened a cabinet and took down a bowl. "First the cake, then the steak."

It was a couple of minutes shy of ten o'clock when Brett stuck his key in the lock. His steps were dragging, and the knuckles on his right hand were skinned and swollen, but he'd gotten his man. The fact that he'd had to go through a bouncer at a club on the south side to do it was just part of the job. And while he knew Conroy would be happy, he wondered how Tory's mood was going to be.

When he walked in the apartment, the scent of food beckoned, reminding him that the only thing he'd eaten all day had been that piece of Tory's pizza he'd confiscated as he was leaving. He glanced at his watch, then looked around for Tory. Food was still secondary to the need that had carried him through the day. It had been nine hours since he'd kissed his woman, and the urge to do it again was overwhelming. He shut and locked the door behind him, then started through the apartment, calling out her name as he went.

"Tory, I'm home."

When she didn't answer, his heart skipped a beat. The darkroom door was ajar. That meant she wasn't working. He glanced into the living room.

Pictures were scattered on top of the coffee table, and her camera bag was in the corner of the room near the sofa. He began to relax. Even if she was gone, she hadn't gone far.

"Tory...sweetheart, I'm sorry I'm late. I got—"

When he walked into the bedroom, the words stuck in his throat. She was sound asleep on the bed and hugging his pillow. There was a smudge of flour on her shoulder and a Band-Aid on her right index finger. A surge of emotion hit him belly high, and his legs went weak.

Ah, God, Victoria, you take my breath away.

He took off his gun, putting it in the top dresser drawer as he passed, then kicked off his shoes. When he got to the bed, he crawled in beside her, gently scooting his arm beneath her neck, then cradling the back of her head against his chest and cuddling her body into the curve of his own.

"I'm sorry I'm late."

She mumbled something beneath her breath, then reached for his hand and pulled, covering herself with his arm instead of a sheet.

Another wave of emotion hit him, bringing tears to his eyes.

"I love you, Victoria," he whispered. "I love you so damned much I hurt."

Tory sighed and turned, rolling until she was facing him. He watched her eyes begin to open, and when she saw him, she smiled a slow, sleepy smile.

"I baked you a cake."

His throat tightened with another wave of emotion. "I know, baby. I could smell it when I walked in." He cupped her cheeks and leaned forward, pressing a kiss in the center of her forehead.

Tory sighed with satisfaction. Brett was home, just as he'd promised. But he winced when she touched his hand, and she sat up with a jerk.

"What's wrong with your hand?"

He rolled over and then sat on the edge of the bed, slightly away from her gaze.

"Nothing. Just lost a little skin on my knuckles bringing in a reluctant witness."

Tory crawled toward him. "Let me see." She yanked at his shirtsleeve until he was forced to face her.

He held out his hand. "See, it's no big deal."

She winced. The knuckles were raw and bloody, and his hand was obviously swollen.

"Did you see a doctor? It could be broken."

In spite of the pain, the curve of her neck and the touch of her lips to the middle of his palm did things to him that a roomful of strippers couldn't have matched.

"It's not broken, it's fine. Come here, you."

He would have pulled her back down on the bed, but Tory would have none of it. Instead, she got up and headed for the kitchen, giving orders as she left.

"Get out of those clothes and get showered. I'll have your food warmed up and some ice for your hand when you've finished."

Brett rolled his eyes. "How am I going to eat if I've got my hand in ice?"

She didn't bother to answer.

A few minutes later he emerged from the bathroom wearing nothing but a towel and noticed that she'd laid out clean underwear and a pair of gym shorts. Her thoughtfulness touched him. No snaps, no zippers, nothing to fasten, thereby making them easy to pull on. And then the familiar odor of grilled steak drifted into the room, and his stomach growled in protest. He dropped the towel and began to dress.

Tory was at the sink when he entered the kitchen.

"Something sure smells good."

She dried her hands, then took a bowl of ice from the freezer and set it in front of Brett as he slid onto one of the bar stools at the counter.

She eased his hand into the ice cubes. "Maybe this will help the swelling."

The cubes gave way, shifting to make room for his hand, and he winced. "Ooh, damn!"

Tory frowned. The fact that Brett's job often put

him in danger was something she had yet to accept.

"Sometimes I absolutely hate your job," she muttered, and turned back to the stove to finish dishing up his food.

"Yeah, and I'm not real crazy about yours, either, but I'm willing to accept the choices you've made."

The unexpected shift of anger into their conversation startled her, but she knew he was right. She took a deep breath and then turned.

"I'm sorry. I spoke without thinking. I would never ask you to give it up. I only meant—"

Brett sighed. He hadn't intended to start this all over again.

"Let it go, honey. I'm just glad to be here with you, okay?"

She began to relax. "Okay." She took a plate of steak out of the microwave and added a serving of asparagus and another of carrots. "It might be a little dry," she said, apologizing ahead of time before he'd had a chance to taste the steak.

"Then that would be my fault and not yours," he said. "Besides, I'm so hungry even oatmeal would taste good."

Tory grinned as she set the plate before him. Brett hated oatmeal.

"I cut your steak for you."

"Thanks." He reached for his fork with his left hand.

"Are you going to be all right?" Tory asked.

Brett stuffed a piece of steak in his mouth and rolled his eyes in appreciation.

"I am now," he said, talking around the steak he was eating.

"Then I think I'll take my shower while you eat."

"Afterward, you can show me your pictures, okay?"

She beamed. There was nothing she liked better than to share that part of her life with Brett. In fact, it was the only thing she shared without thought.

"Okay," she said, but she remained, watching as Brett tried a left-handed attack on an asparagus spear. When it kept sliding off his fork, she picked it up with her fingers and aimed it toward his mouth.

"Here. Pretend it's a French fry."

He grinned, then opened his mouth as she popped it inside.

"Be back in a little while," she said, and headed for the bedroom.

He looked at the food on his plate and then shifted his hand to a different position inside the bowl of ice. "Don't hurry on my account. This could take a while."

A few bites later, he began to relax. By the time he had finished his food, his hand was numb and his belly was no longer grumbling.

"Hey, Tory, where's that cake you baked?"

"Just a minute," she called. "I'll be right there."

He got up from the bar stool and carried his plate to the sink, then rinsed it before putting it in the dishwasher. After giving his hand the once-over, he dumped the bowl of ice in the sink. Although his fingers were stiff and colorless from the cold, the swelling was noticeably less than it had been before he'd started his meal.

"Brett?"

He turned. Tory was standing in the doorway. A sideways grin tilted the corner of his mouth. She looked about thirteen years old. Her face was scrubbed clean of makeup, and her hair was still damp and hanging about her face in loose ringlets. Her long legs were bare, as were her feet, and from what he could see, the only thing she was wearing was another one of his shirts.

"You look a hell of a lot better in that than I do," he drawled.

Tory arched an eyebrow and blew him a kiss. "That's a matter of perspective. Now, save that thought for later while I get your cake." She opened the refrigerator, taking out a covered container. When she lifted the lid, he inhaled deeply.

She'd made his favorite, carrot cake with lots of cream cheese icing.

She paused in the act of cutting. "How much do you want?"

"What do you think?"

She thrust downward with force. "Your usual slab, right?"

He laughed. "For starters."

A few moments later, she slid the plate in front of him and started to hand him a clean fork when she realized the bowl of ice was missing.

"Let me see your hand," she ordered.

He held it out, palm down, then reached for the fork she was holding.

"Have mercy, Tory. It wasn't amputated, just banged up a bit. Now, may I please have my cake?"

"I suppose."

"Thank goodness for small favors," he muttered, as she relinquished the fork. The first bite was every bit as good as he'd expected. When he picked up the second bite, he offered it to her.

"Open wide."

Tory accepted the piece with delight. This was the Brett she loved. This calm, easygoing man who shared everything with her, including his food.

"Want to see my pictures now?"

He nodded. "I'd love to, honey. Lead the way."

He followed her into the living room and then

sat down on the sofa beside her, finishing off his cake while she began sorting through the photos.

"These are my favorites," she said, pointing to the ones she'd spread out. "But there are some good ones in that stack, as well. Tell me what you think. Maybe it will help me decide."

Brett couldn't help but stare. There was so much life in the expressions she'd captured. From the small boy with his face buried in cotton candy to the old woman astride a horse on the merry-go-round, riding side by side with a toddler. Despite the differences in their ages, the delight on their faces was identical. Brett whistled beneath his breath, then shook his head.

"Energy. That's what you caught. The energy."

Tory clapped her hands. "That's right! You understand! You really understand!"

He grinned wryly. "I understand a hell of a lot more than you give me credit for, Victoria."

Choosing to ignore what sounded like sarcasm, she continued to sift through the shots. When Brett reached across the table and picked one of them up, she didn't bother to hide her surprise.

"I really like this one," he said. "Where was it taken?"

"You know, that one is my favorite."

Brett sensed her surprise. The fact that he had zeroed in on something special to her was no big deal, but it never failed to amaze him that she was so obtuse about their relationship. Sometimes he thought he knew his woman better than she knew herself.

He handed her the picture. "Tell me why." Then he sat back, watching the changing expressions on her face as she started to explain.

"I'm not entirely sure, but it's such a collage of expressions. See...there. And there. And there. Look at their faces. He's disgusted. She's laughing. They're kissing. And look at the child near that man wearing overalls. She's so tiny, and she's clutching on to that hammer loop on his pants for dear life. It makes you look at the world from her point of view. All she sees are legs and backsides, so she's holding on to the only familiar thing within her reach, and that's the loop on her daddy's pants."

"Tory."

She looked up, her eyes alight with joy. "What?"

"I love you."

"Why?" she asked.

Her question startled him. "Why what?"

She laid the photo on the table, then gave him a long, intent stare. "Why do you love me? I'm not very reliable when it comes to considering your feelings...about anything."

Brett pulled her into his lap, ignoring the fuss she tried to make regarding his sore hand.

"Settle down," he ordered, and scooted her into a firm position in his lap. "You asked me a question. I'm trying to give you an answer."

She quieted, but Brett could see the intensity on her face as she watched him.

"Why do I love you? Hell, Tory, why does the sun come up every morning and go down every night? Why do babies cry and dogs howl at the moon? Because they can't help it, that's why, and God help me, neither can I."

He pulled her head down on his shoulder and cuddled her closer, unwilling to let a moment of Victoria Lancaster escape him.

"Do you remember the first time I saw you?"

She frowned, thinking back over the past four years. But before she could answer, he continued.

"Let's see, this is August, so it was four years ago last month. It was just after sundown, at that warehouse fire over on Reno. The police had roped off the area to keep bystanders at bay. Ambulance sirens were screaming, and patrol cars were parked all over the place with their lights still flashing. The fire was out of control, and the fire trucks kept coming. The heat from the day, as well as from the fire, was unbelievably intense. Instead of putting out the fire, the water they were spraying kept turning into steam."

Tory smiled. "It was just luck that I happened

on the scene. In fact, it was those pictures that later got me my first big assignment.''

"Yes, and they also nearly got you killed.''

She frowned. "Oh, I wasn't in that much—''

"Hell, honey, don't argue with me. You didn't see yourself, because you had that damned camera up to your face. I'm the one who nearly had a heart attack when I saw you emerging from a cloud of mist and steam. You didn't even know where you were or what you were doing. If I hadn't grabbed you when I did, that fire truck would have run over you.''

She flushed. Even now, she could remember the shock of being yanked backward and the anger she'd felt at missing the shot she'd lined up. But when she'd turned, her anger was nothing to the fury she'd seen on Brett Hooker's face.

"I remember you asking me if I had a death wish,'' Tory said.

Brett grinned. "Yeah, and then, about ten minutes later, I asked you out.''

"And I turned you down,'' she reminded him.

Brett nuzzled the spot behind her ear, smiling to himself when she moaned beneath her breath. "Yes, you did,'' he said. "Then and every other time I asked you for the next two months.''

"So why didn't you give up?'' Tory asked.

Brett caught her chin, then tilted it until she was forced to meet his gaze.

"For the same reason that I love you. I couldn't help myself. I knew I'd spend the rest of my life being sorry if I let you go."

He sighed, then lowered his mouth until their lips met. When her arms slid around his neck and he could feel her breasts pressing against his chest, he groaned, breaking their connection.

"You may not want to hear this, but it's time it was said. We belong, Victoria. Heart, body and soul, neither one of us is complete without the other. And if that scares you, and if you feel the need to disappear out of my life over and over again, then so be it. But face the truth of what we are. We aren't just lovers, baby. We love."

For once, the panic that Tory usually felt at any gesture of permanence just wasn't there. It was all she could do to keep from crying as she met his gaze. Her whisper was as soft as her touch as she cupped his face.

"I don't deserve you."

His grin was lopsided and his voice filled with emotion, but there was method in his madness as he stood with her still in his arms.

"Oh, yes, you do, baby. And I'm going to spend the next couple of hours showing you why."

Three

Tory slept curled beneath the shelter of Brett's outflung arm. His breath was warm and even against her shoulder, his body a wall between her and the world. But Tory was too lost in dream-sleep to know she was safe. For now, her subconscious was commanding her thoughts, and she was deep in a nightmare that was out of control.

The wind wailed, drowning out the small girl's screams. Night had come and gone twice, and she was still alone. From the back of the closet in which she was hiding, she could see the first hints of daylight beginning to show through the half-open door. She drew her knees up against her chest and hid her face. She'd long ago lost count of the hours that had passed since she'd crawled into the closet. All she knew was, in here, she felt safe.

Something scurried across the floor outside the doorway. She wrapped her arms tighter around her knees and squinched her eyelids shut, afraid to look—afraid to move. When her belly growled, she moaned and licked her lips. Hungry. She was so very hungry. She kept thinking of Mary Ellen's party and the marshmallows they'd had. Oh, how she wished she had some of them now. Another urge overrode her hunger, the need to relieve herself. Though she wiggled uncomfortably, she was unwilling to leave the safety of the closet.

The extent of her fear took everything she heard within the emptiness of the house and magnified it many times over: the sound of dry leaves blowing across the floor; the wind whistling through the half-open windows; even the sounds of cars going by on the road beyond made her panic. She didn't remember giving up hope, but there was an emptiness inside her now that had nothing to do with hunger.

Tory's legs jerked as she curled in upon herself, her breath coming in short, shallow gasps. Unconsciously, she pulled away from Brett as she was pulled deeper into the child in the dream.

There was a sound! Could it be...? And then she moaned beneath her breath and bit her lip. It wasn't a car that she heard, it was a motorcycle, and the moment recognition hit, she started to shudder. She knew who that was. He'd been here before. His clothes were black and shiny, and there were chains dangling from his belt, and from his boots and wrists. He'd laughed at her then, and all she'd seen were yellow-stained teeth parting the growth of his black, bushy beard.

When she heard him call out, she began scooting farther into the corner of the closet, all but holding her breath in an effort to hide.

"Hey, Ollie! Is anybody home. I came for—"

There was a pause, and she thought he'd gone until she heard him mutter.

"Son of a bitch. That sorry bastard skipped out owing me. It figures."

Quiet followed his outburst. Just when she thought he would leave, she heard him moving around. A sick dread began spreading within her. His voice had been loud and angry—just as she'd remembered. Afraid to move—afraid not to—she slowly stood, pinning herself against the farthest corner of the closet wall. Her eyes widened with fear as she stared through the half-open door, listening to the sound of his footsteps coming closer—closer!

Sweat beaded beneath her hair and began running down the back of her neck. She could see his arm, then his shoulder, now the side of his face. He turned and stared straight into the closet, as if piercing the darkness in which she was hidden.

As he reached for the doorknob, a warm, wet stream of urine began running down the inside of her leg. When his silhouette moved between her and escape, she started to cry, and when he reached for her, he was grinning.

She threw back her head and screamed.

Brett awoke just as a scream ripped from Tory's throat. She arched backward, all but ejecting herself from the bed. He grabbed her before she fell.

"Tory, baby, wake up! Wake up! It's me, Brett! It's a dream—a dream! You're having a dream."

She came awake within seconds of the sound of his voice, unable to stop sobbing. All she had left of the nightmare was a knot in the pit of her stomach and an overwhelming need to be held. She rolled over and into Brett's arms, choking on words that wouldn't come.

He cupped the back of her head and pulled her closer, rocking her against him as he would have a child.

"Sssh, baby, it's okay, it's okay. It was only a dream."

Clutching at his arms, she shuddered and buried her face against the wall of his chest.

"Brett?"

"Yes, baby, it's me."

"Dream... I had a bad dream."

He kept stroking her hair and her face in a slow, soothing motion. "But it's over, Tory, it's all over now. I'm here, and you're safe, okay?"

Tremors racked her body as she absorbed his presence. With a shaky voice, she pleaded with him in a soft whisper.

"Lights... Please turn on the lights."

He reached over her shoulder and pulled the chain on the bedside lamp, instantly bathing Tory in a soft, yellow glow. When she could see her surroundings, she began to relax, and when her sobs were down to an occasional sniffle, Brett began to relax, too.

And all the while he held her, he couldn't quit thinking how strange this seemed. Tory wasn't the kind of woman who suffered nightmares. She was so self-contained that he'd believed she was impervious to just about everything, yet twice now, within days of her homecoming, she had reacted in ways that were completely out of character.

The investigator in him was more than curious, but the man in him loved her enough to wait and let her do the talking, although he knew enough about her not to hold his breath. She kept everything to herself. If there was something she wanted him to know about her past, then he would be more than willing to listen, but it would have to come in her time, not his. And while he was thinking, Tory began to get restless. He rubbed her back in a gentle, soothing motion, then kissed the top of her head.

"Feeling better?"

Tory rolled out of his arms. "I want to get up. I don't want to lie in this bed anymore tonight."

Brett glanced at the clock. It was a quarter to five. He cupped her cheek.

"Honey, the night is gone. It's almost morning. So how about if I make some coffee and you dig out that cake?"

She almost managed a smile. "You'd find any excuse to eat some more, wouldn't you?"

Happy to see her focus shifting, he played along with the game and got out of bed, then turned and helped her up, as well.

"Come on, don't make me feel guilty. You like it, too."

She glanced toward the closet door as she stood. It was standing slightly ajar. A sudden chill made the flesh on the back of her neck crawl, and without thinking why, she slammed it shut. Ignoring the fact that Brett was watching her every move, she reached for her robe.

"Could we make hot chocolate instead of coffee?"

Brett was waiting, hoping for some sort of explanation for her odd behavior, but when once again it didn't come, he rolled with the change in conversation.

"I'll make whatever you want." And then he amended, "Short of anything that has more than two ingredients, that is."

Tory laughed, and he began to breathe easier.

He slipped an arm around her waist. "Laugh all you want. Just remember how my last attempt at cooking real food ended. The garbage disposal was stopped up for a week."

Tory was smiling as Brett guided her toward the kitchen. By the time hot chocolate had been made and the cake cut and served, the nightmare was all but forgotten. Within an hour the sun would be up. It was the start of a brand-new day.

Tory had pictures scattered on every flat surface in the apartment, picking through the ones she was going to use for the piece she was writing. After talking with her editor at the magazine, she had decided to take the story in two different directions, and she had the pictures to make it work. On the one hand, she had the jaded expressions on the carnival workers' faces, as opposed to the joy and anticipation of the carnival-goers. It was going to be a powerful piece. But first she had to choose the prints that would go with the text, and that was what she was doing today.

Every so often she would pick one up and add it to the small collage on the kitchen cabinet. When the photos began to tie into the piece in her head, she began getting excited, imagining how the accompanying story would unfold. The crowd shot she liked best was going to be the pivotal point, because it captured both angles of the story, depicting the carnival workers and the fair-goers alike.

As always, when there was a particular picture that caught her eye, she studied it for reasons why. As she stared at the crowd shot, it dawned on her that when she first looked at it, her gaze invariably focused on one particular face.

Curious, she carried it into the darkroom and then switched on the overhead lights. After shuffling through drawers, she found the magnifying glass she'd been looking for and held it over the picture.

When all she could see was the face of an older, nondescript man, she frowned with disappointment. His features were grim, and he seemed to be looking at a point beyond the eye of the camera, but the image was small; it was in no way a solution to the mystery of why she was drawn to his face.

Disgusted with herself, she went back to her work. Yet twice more she found herself returning to the shot and staring at the old man's face. At that point, she gave up in defeat. She knew herself well enough to realize that she wouldn't be able to work until she'd solved her dilemma. She picked the picture back up, staring intently for a few seconds longer.

"Maybe if I enlarge it—"

Intrigued by the idea, she put the picture down. It would mean a trip downtown to get some extra supplies, but it would be worth it. This was driving her nuts.

A few minutes later she was on her way out the door when the phone began to ring. She stood with her hand on the knob, waiting for the machine to pick up. The voice was one she recognized, but she let the caller talk without answering, adding guilt to her frustration.

"Hi, Brett, it's me—your mother. Remember me? I'm the woman who gave birth to you, the one who taught you to clean your first fish. The one you rarely call."

As she listened to Cynthia Hooker's voice, something inside of her began to shut down. Cynthia was still talking as Tory walked out of the apartment, quietly closing the door behind her. But instead of leaving, she stood just outside the door, listening to the rest of the message.

"Never mind the speech, that's not why I called. I thought you might like to know that you're now an uncle. Your sister Celia just gave birth to a beautiful baby girl—eight pounds, two ounces. Melissa Carol and mother are doing fine. Talk to you soon. I love you. Oh…and give Victoria our love, as well."

Tory's eyes narrowed as she headed for the stairs. Love. They were always saying that. Give

Victoria our love. It was kind of them to want to include her in their family life, but that wasn't for her. She didn't need other people to make her life complete. She'd learned years ago to be happy with less than everyone else, and she'd learned it well. If you didn't depend on anyone but yourself, then you had only yourself to blame if life let you down.

I don't need anyone. And then she thought of Brett and the anchor he represented in her life. *Except maybe Brett, but he doesn't count. He'll always be there for me.*

In spite of the confidence she had in the man and the love they shared, there was that niggling kernel of doubt that wouldn't stay put. *Why, Tory...why are you so sure about Brett?*

"Because he promised," she told the meddling little voice. "That's why."

A stray cat leaped from the ledge of a broken window as Brett pulled up to the Santa Fe Warehouse and parked. It was bad enough being down on this end of Reno Street on a good day, but an hour ago it had started to rain, and all the indigents would be looking for shelter. He glanced at his watch. It was a quarter to five, and for the last four hours, he'd been going from one abandoned building to another, trying to locate a material witness for his boss.

For most of the working citizens of Oklahoma City, it was almost quitting time, all except the investigators who worked for the Oklahoma County District Attorney's Office. Their hours coincided with the necessities of the courts, rather than convenience.

Don Lacey, the county D.A. and Brett's boss, was a power to reckon with, and while he was doing more than his part to convict the criminals the police arrested, he also had to deal with the laws as they were written. Sometimes, no matter how hard everyone worked, justice was not served. It was those disappointments that kept investigators like Brett on the streets, checking and rechecking everything the D.A. needed to make a case. And in this instance, that included finding a man named Harold Tribbey.

In March of 1995, Harold Tribbey had been working in a shop in downtown Oklahoma City. He'd been sitting on the loading dock behind the machine shop during his lunch break, savoring the last bite of a chicken-salad sandwich, when two men had come out of the building across the alley. Before he could swallow, one man suddenly pulled a gun and shot the other man point-blank.

Frozen by the horror of what he'd just witnessed, Harold had stared long enough to watch the shooter disappear, taken one look at the other man's blood and brains splattered upon the street, and proceeded to throw up what he'd just eaten. In the blink of an eye, Harold had become a witness to a crime.

Sometime later, he had picked a suspect out of a lineup, not knowing that the suspect was a hatchet man for one Romeo Leeds, late of Chicago and now making his home—and a bad name for himself—in Oklahoma City.

The identification of one of his men put Romeo Leeds in a precarious position. If his man went to trial, Leeds could very well go down with him. So he'd set his attorneys to the task, filing motion after motion to further impede the pending case from ever reaching trial. And while the wheels of justice were slowly grinding, the world as the people of downtown Oklahoma City knew it was suddenly changed forever.

On April 19th, the Alfred P. Murrah Building, and every building within a multiblock radius, including the machine shop in which Harold was working, was destroyed by a bomb. A few weeks later the owner went bankrupt, and Harold was out of a job.

And he, along with several hundred other people who'd survived the explosion, began suffering post-traumatic stress disorder. But Harold's problem was exacerbated by a condition most of the other survivors did not have. As a Vietnam vet, he'd had flashbacks for years. Now he couldn't sleep, couldn't eat, and his personality underwent a drastic change. He became angry and distrustful of everyone around him and found himself unable to hold a job.

After that, Harold Tribbey lost his wife, his house and his car. He was sick, both in body and in spirit, and nearly a year ago had taken to living in the streets. And while the crime Harold had witnessed so long ago might have faded in significance to him, it had not faded from the Oklahoma County court docket. Romeo Leeds' lawyers had run out of options and time. Luckily for them, the only witness to the crime had disappeared.

While Harold Tribbey had been coming apart, Leeds had not been wasting his time. He'd grown, both in power and in wealth, to the point of becoming nearly untouchable. There was nothing the D.A. would have liked better than to put away the shooter and put Leeds out of business, but unless Harold Tribbey could be located, the case would be thrown out of court.

Both the police department and the D.A.'s men were determined not to let that happen. Brett's assignment had been to help locate Tribbey, and he'd been combing the downtown area of Oklahoma City for days. About an hour ago, someone had tipped him off to the fact that Harold was partial to the Santa Fe Warehouse, especially when the weather was bad. Brett peered through the driving rain pounding on his windshield.

He glanced up at the building, taking careful note of the number of boarded up windows and doors, then picked up his cell phone. It was a personal thing, but he hated like hell to walk into a place like this not knowing if there was another way out. When the dispatcher at the country sheriff's office answered his call, he didn't waste words.

"This is Hooker. I'm at the Santa Fe Warehouse on Reno Street. I'm going in now. If you don't hear from me by five-fifteen, send someone to check on me."

He slipped the phone into his pocket as he exited the car, then ran a hand down the side of his jacket, making sure the gun and holster were secure beneath it.

Rain peppered his face as he ran toward the building. His jacket was waterproof, but his jeans were not. Within seconds, his pants and his boots were soaked. A swift gust of wind sent a blast of rain into his eyes, and he winced and turned away. When he looked back, he caught a glimpse of a man silhouetted in the doorway. Before he could react, the man disappeared.

Instinctively, Brett reached for his gun. Even though the man he was looking for was not in trouble, there could be others taking shelter from the rain who had more than a guilty conscience to contend with.

The Glock rested easily in his hands as he took a stance at the side of the doorway. But the rain was coming down too hard for him to distinguish one sound from another, and he got tired of waiting. He took a deep breath and slipped into the warehouse, then flattened himself against the wall while letting his eyesight adjust to the murky interior.

Somewhere beyond the doorway, a piece of metal fell onto the concrete floor, clattering loudly and shattering the rain-soaked silence. Brett jerked in reflex and turned just as three men came out from behind a stack of pallets and began running toward the back of the building. But when one of them suddenly stopped and spun around, the hair stood up on the back of Brett's neck, and without taking time to think, he hit the floor.

The impulse saved his life. Bullets splattered off the wall where he'd been standing, and then another half dozen passed through the barrels behind which he was lying, bouncing off the concrete near his feet.

"Hey," Brett muttered, then grabbed his phone and dialed 911. "This is Hooker with the D.A.'s office. I'm at the old Santa Fe Warehouse down on east Reno. Shots have been fired. I need backup."

Before he could move, there was a commotion at the far end of the warehouse and then silence. He shifted, getting to his knees and then his feet, moving in a crouched position along the wall with his finger on the trigger. Even before he heard the approaching sirens, he knew the trio was gone. When he found the boards kicked off of a window, he cursed.

After making a careful sweep of the area, he started back toward the front of the building. Moments later, he came upon a stack of wooden pallets and then the body of a woman lying facedown in a pool of her own blood. Brett cursed silently. Now he knew why they'd been running.

Careful not to disturb the crime scene, he backed away and then headed for the door. Two police cruisers slammed to a halt beside his car just as he stepped outside. As both officers exited with their guns drawn, he held up his hands and shouted his name. They eased off and ran toward him.

"You got a dead woman inside, but the shooters got out a back window. Call it in for me, will you?"

One of the officers nodded and headed back to his car, while the other holstered his gun.

"Hey, Hooker, don't you know it's time to go home?"

Brett squinted through the downpour, recognizing the officer as someone he'd known since their days in the academy.

"Come on, Ernie, you know Lacey, and you know me. We don't quit till it's over."

Like all police officers, when the call had come out that there were shots being fired at one of their own, their adrenaline had surged, but when it became obvious the danger had passed, they began to laugh and joke to relieve some of the tension.

"How did you get mixed up with what was happening in there?" Reynolds asked.

"Came looking for a witness and walked in on a murder in progress. They fired a couple of rounds off at me and then ran like hell. By the time I got down to that end of the building, all I could see out the window was rain."

"You okay?" Reynolds asked.

"I ducked."

"Shit, Hooker, you always were a little bit crazy."

Brett's laughter echoed as they walked back inside the warehouse. At least he had a dry place to wait for the coroner to arrive.

After they'd gone out the window at the Santa Fe Warehouse, Gus Huffman and his partners, Tony and Raul Gomez, had taken refuge in nearby Bricktown, the renovated area of old downtown Oklahoma City that was now the "happening" place to be. In spite of their sprint through the rain, they were no wetter than the rest of the dinner crowd at Spaghetti Warehouse who were waiting in line for a table.

Gus hated screwups, but today, thanks to the unexpected arrival of a stranger, what had started off as a simple hit had turned into a great big deal. The scent of marinara sauce and pasta drifted past his nose, and his stomach grumbled.

"Damn, Gus, this line isn't moving at all. Let's go somewhere else," Raul complained.

Gus shook his head. "It's after seven. There will be lines anywhere we go, and I'm not in the mood to get any wetter before I fill my belly."

Tony Gomez nodded in agreement and popped another stick of gum in his mouth. "Yeah, Raul, it's wet outside, bro, or haven't you noticed?" Then he snickered at his own joke and winked at the hostess.

Gus ignored the pair. They were shallow-minded men with little on their minds except getting paid and getting laid, and not necessarily in that order. He shifted nervously as a waiter sailed past them with a tray full of pasta. After this fiasco, he wasn't sure if they would ever get paid. Romeo wasn't going to be happy about this. The fact that they'd tied up one loose end of his life was unimportant considering the fact that they'd unraveled another. Although, to be fair, there was no way they could have known anyone would show up at that warehouse, and especially on a day like today.

Outside, the rain continued to pour, and Gus stared through the windows without seeing. His mind was stuck in a playback of the hit and of the man who'd walked in before they had a chance to get away. There was one thing for sure, he would know the bastard again if he saw him.

Gus glanced at his watch. "It's going to be at least another fifteen minutes before we get a table. I'm going to go call the boss."

He slipped out of line and headed for the men's room. There were two men inside, and he waited until they were gone before he took out his cell phone and made the call. The phone rang once. When he heard Romeo Leeds' voice, he took a deep breath.

"It's me, Gus."

"Is it done?"

"Yeah, no sweat."

"Good, come by the office tomorrow, we'll settle up then."

"Uh, yeah...okay, boss, but—"

Romeo Leeds had been in business too long not to hear trouble in Gus's voice.

"But what?"

Gus shuddered. The drawl in Leeds' voice was

deceptive, and he knew it. Romeo Leeds was not a laid-back kind of man.

"Someone came in before we had a chance to get away."

"Son of a—" Leeds' voice lowered. "Did he see you?"

"Yeah, but it was pretty dark. I don't think he got a good look at our faces."

Leeds' drawl deepened. "You don't think... You aren't sure... You don't know...." Then he exploded. "That's the kind of crap that can get you in deep shit, and you know it. Find out who he was and take care of it, do you hear me?"

Gus nodded, and then realized Leeds couldn't see him. "Yeah, boss, I hear you, loud and clear."

"Oh, and Gus..."

"Yeah, boss?"

"Don't bother coming after your pay until the job is finished. I don't pay for half-assed, understood?"

The Gomez brothers were going to be pissed, but there wasn't a thing Gus could do about it.

"Yes, boss, I understand, and I'll take care of everything. Don't worry about a thing."

Romeo Leeds hung up in Gus's ear. Gus didn't take that as a good sign. He got back to the front of the restaurant just as they were about to be seated.

"Damn, Gus, you got good timing," Raul said,

grinning as he slapped him on the back. "Come on, let's go celebrate."

"We'll eat, but it's not going to be a celebration," Gus said. "We don't get paid until we clean up the mess we made today."

Raul frowned. After the hostess left, he leaned forward with menace in his voice. "Listen, Huffman, you promised us dough. I want mine now."

Gus's voice lowered, and the glitter in his eyes was all the warning Raul was going to get.

"You get paid when I get paid," he said softly. "Now remember where you are and shut the fuck up. We came to eat. We're going to eat. When we're through, I want you out of my sight. Do we understand each other?"

Gomez nodded. In his neighborhood, he was a tough man. But compared to Gus Huffman, he was a beginner, and he knew it.

"No sweat, man," Raul said. "I was just talking. You know how it is. No hard feelings, okay?"

Gus shoved a menu toward him. "Shut up and order."

Raul did as he was told.

Four

A bolt of lightning streaked across the night sky, followed by a loud clap of thunder. It was raining again. Earlier this year Oklahoma had suffered one of the driest springs on record, and now that it was nearing fall, which was normally dry, they couldn't seem to get two good days of sunshine in succession.

When the thunder rattled the windows, Tory flinched and then glanced at the clock. It was after eight, and Brett still wasn't home. He'd called while she was out buying supplies, and from the short, distracted message he'd left, she could tell something unexpected had happened. All she could hope was that he wasn't directly involved.

When they'd first met, Brett had still been on the Oklahoma City police force, but after his partner was killed during a high-speed chase with some armed robbers, it seemed that he'd just lost the heart to continue. To make things worse, when the case came to trial, the perps were let go on a technicality. For Brett, it was the last straw. He'd

turned in his badge, taken an early retirement and
gone to work for the law from the other side of
the court bench. As an investigator for the district
attorney's office, he felt as if he had some control
in bringing justice to those who'd been wronged.
It wasn't much, but in Brett's mind, it was enough
to keep going.

The fact that Brett seemed to take each case
personally worried Tory. He put his heart and soul
into every one, and sometimes, when he pushed
too hard, he got in the way of trouble. All she
could do was say a prayer and hope that he made
it home in one piece.

Outside, the storm raged, belching one grumble
of thunder after another while she tried unsuccessfully to focus on her work. Her mind kept jumping
from Brett to the storm, to the hazards of his job,
to the pictures in her lap, to the notes she was
making.

The enlargement she'd made of the crowd photo
lay near her elbow. Periodically she would pick it
up and look at the man's face, as if willing him to
talk. Despite the intensity with which she kept
staring, no revelation came—no magic occurred to
answer a question she didn't know how to voice.
Disgusted, she finally tossed it aside and was about
to resume her work when a key rattled in the lock.
Relief washed over her in waves as she jumped to
her feet and headed for the door. Brett was home!

* * *

Brett was tired and hungry and couldn't remember ever being this miserably wet. All the way home he'd been thinking about a hot shower, dry clothes and Tory, and not necessarily in that order. Yet when he opened the door, he forgot about everything but her. The growl in his belly and the water in his boots became unimportant as she flew into his arms. He kicked the door shut behind him and just held her, lifting her feet off the floor as her arms slid around his neck.

"For a welcome like this, I'd almost be willing to go out and come back in all over again."

She sighed as the tension inside her began to unwind. "I was worried about you."

Although she would have denied it, Brett heard a hint of panic in her voice. He closed his eyes and tried not to think of the dead woman he'd found. Her hair had been blond, just like Tory's. On impulse, he hugged her a little bit tighter.

"I'm okay, but I'm getting you wet."

She pressed a kiss against the pulse in his neck. "I could care less. Why don't you go shower and then get into something warm and dry?"

Brett cupped her hips and then pulled her close to him, gently grinding himself against her until they were both more than a little bit achy.

"To hell with the shower," he said. "I can't be all that dirty. I've been wet all day."

"I made lasagna," Tory said.

His belly growled, and he groaned. "That's cheating. How can I concentrate on making love when you do things like that?"

Tory ran a fingernail down the front of his shirt, lightly tapping his belt buckle before letting it rasp along the zipper below.

"First things first, mister. Your food will be ready when you are."

Brett caught her hand and pressed it to the bulge behind his zipper. "I think I'm as ready as I'll ever be."

She grinned. "Hold that thought," she said, and headed for the kitchen.

He began stripping as he went, and by the time he got to the bathroom, he was naked. A short time later he was dry and dressed, and digging into a steaming helping of Tory's lasagna.

"Sit with me while I eat," Brett said. "Tell me how your work's going."

Tory smiled. "How about if I show you, instead?"

He nodded and took a mouthful of pasta, savoring the joy of food in his belly and his woman in his life. Right now, he would be hard-pressed to find something about which to complain.

Tory spread the photographs out on the table in front of him. "These are the shots I'm going to use."

"What's with this?" Brett asked, pointing at the enlargement she'd made of the crowd shot, then frowning at the face she had circled in red.

Tory shrugged. "It's nothing. I was just fooling around."

He could tell by the look on her face that the "nothing" was "something," but she was obviously not talking, and he wasn't in the mood to press issues tonight.

"Interesting face," he said, pointing to the man she had circled.

She shrugged. "I guess." And then she looked up. "To be honest, he sort of gives me the creeps."

Brett looked back at the picture. It was a rather innocuous face. The man needed a haircut, but other than that, he couldn't see anything remarkable about him at all. And then he looked closer. There was something on his cheek, below his right eye. He pointed to the small black spot on the photo with the tine of his fork.

"What's that, a tattoo?"

Something whispered in the back of her mind, like an ugly bit of gossip someone was trying to spread. Tory picked up the picture, staring even more intently than she had before.

"I thought it was a speck on the film."

Brett shrugged and took another bite. "You're probably right." And then he grinned. "You know me, ever the cop. You see dirt, I see tattoos and scars.''

But the idea had taken root in Tory's mind, and while Brett continued to eat, she got up without speaking and headed for the darkroom.

''The lasagna is great,'' he offered, and dished himself up a second helping, but she was already gone.

It cost Gus Huffman $255 to get the name of the man who'd caught them in the warehouse, and another two hundred to learn who he worked for. And finding out that the son of a bitch worked for the district attorney who was trying the case against Manny Riberosa, Leeds' right-hand man, made him nervous. Gus kept telling himself that things could be worse, but right now, he couldn't see how. It was all well and good that Romeo Leeds wanted his loose ends tied and clipped. But tying up these loose ends was going to take a little more finesse than normal. Brett Hooker was no ordinary citizen. He was a pro. Yes, Gus had his orders, but this had changed everything. He needed time to make a plan. They couldn't afford to screw up again.

The thunderstorm passed around midnight, leaving behind a clean, just-washed scent in the air. Brett stood on the balcony of his second-floor apartment, gazing up at the sky and watching the traffic passing by on the streets below. When he glanced back into the bedroom to check on Tory as she lay sleeping, his heart gave a tug. When he thought of how much he loved her, it made him weak.

Her sleep was restless tonight. He blamed it on the storm that had passed, but when he heard her mumbling, he began to frown. She never talked in her sleep. At least, she never used to. She'd never been prone to hysterics or nightmares, either, and she'd had an episode of each since she'd come home.

He turned back to the street scene below, but his mind was still on Tory. A couple of hours ago, they'd made love with a passion that had left him stunned. Afterward, he'd held her until she fell asleep, but for Brett, sleep wouldn't come. He could no longer ignore the fact that she seemed to be acting out of desperation. Every instinct he had kept telling him something was wrong. He just didn't know if the trouble was within Tory herself, or if it was something lacking in their relationship that kept triggering these episodes.

Tonight he'd tried more than once to bring up the subject of her past, and each time she had channeled the conversation in another direction. Brett loved Victoria Lancaster more than his own life, but he was beginning to wonder if the Victoria he knew was only a figment of his imagination. Was it possible to live with someone for the better part of three years, only to learn you'd never known them at all?

Somewhere off to the south, a siren began to sound, and he was struck by an urgency to move toward the emergency. And then he remembered that he'd given up that part of his life, and willingly. Call it disillusionment, call it burnout, call it fed to hell up with the system, but he wasn't sorry he was no longer on the force. The only thing he'd taken with him when he'd changed his life was Tory, and he wasn't about to give her up. Not now. Not ever.

"Ring around the rosey, pocket full of posies, ashes, ashes, all fall down."

The little girl laughed as her rag doll fell to the grass. The yellow yarn pigtails and the blue gingham dress were a splash of color against the dark, sweet green. Blue button eyes faced the sky, and the embroidered mouth wore a permanent smile at the games that the little girl played.

The child put her hands on her hips and pretended to frown. "Sweet Baby, you get up from that grass this minute, do you hear me? You're going to get stains all over your dress."

Cradling the doll to her breast, she skipped to the swing hanging from a big crooked branch on

*the sweet gum tree and plopped down on the seat,
absentmindedly humming a melody that had no
words. A sweat bee buzzed around the skinned
spot on her knee as a mockingbird scolded in the
tree overhead. The scent of freshly baked cookies
was in the air as the sound of laughter drifted out
from the house.*

*And then the hinges on the screen door
squeaked, and the little girl looked up. Someone
was standing in the doorway, calling out to her,
but she couldn't hear what was being said. She
stood up from the swing, and as she did, Sweet
Baby fell from her lap and onto the ground.*

*"I'm here," she cried, waving over and over,
but to no avail. It was as if she'd become invisible.*

*She started to run toward the house when she
remembered Sweet Baby and turned. But when she
looked, the tree was gone, and so was the swing
in which she'd been sitting. And when she looked
down, her dolly was nowhere in sight. She spun
back around and then froze. The house and the
cookies and the source of the laughter had disappeared, as surely as if they'd never existed.*

*The little girl began to run, circling the yard and
looking for something, but she couldn't remember
what. She ran and she ran, in an ever decreasing
circle, until her legs were aching and her bare feet
were bleeding and there was nowhere left to go
but the spot on which she was standing. She went*

hot and then cold, struck by a horror that had no name. Wringing her hands and sobbing now, she looked toward the horizon and the setting sun. Suddenly it was dark and she was all alone. With a wail of pure terror, she threw back her head and screamed.

Tory woke up screaming, then rolled out of bed before Brett could stop her.

"Oh God, oh God, oh God."

Her hands were shaking, and her face was wet with tears she didn't know that she'd shed. Her heart hurt in the way that it does when one has suffered great sadness, but all she could remember was an overwhelming fear and a sense of loss.

Brett was behind her within seconds and caught her to him, holding her trembling body close while his own heart hammered against his chest.

"Tory, sweetheart, you were just having another bad dream, okay?"

She clung to him like a child, unable to speak.

"Can you remember what you were dreaming?"

She shook her head.

"Are you sure? Whatever it is, you know you can tell me. Sometimes it helps to get rid of the feelings if you can just talk about them."

She continued to shake. "I don't remember.... I don't remember."

Her fear was palpable, and he would have done anything in this world to take it away, but he didn't know how, and she wouldn't help him.

"Maybe it was anxiety left over from the storm," he suggested, and then picked her up as if she were a child.

"Where are you taking me?" Tory asked.

"Trust me."

Tory flinched. Trust? Did such a thing really exist?

The living room was in shadow cast by the faint glow of the security lights coming through the curtained windows. Brett carried her to the recliner and then sat, cradling her against him. When her head was beneath his chin and her backside was warm in his lap, he started to rock.

"What are you doing?" Tory asked.

"Relax, Tory. We're just going to sit here for a little while and let it all go away."

The rhythm of the chair was soothing. And Brett's heart was beating strongly against her ear. The familiar scent of his body, the feel of his strength, as well as the way he cradled her against the night, gave her peace. An emptiness deep inside her began to fill. She closed her eyes, relaxing as the tears dried on her face.

Brett rocked into morning while Tory slept a dreamless sleep in his arms. But he hadn't been able to lose his fear as easily as she had. He couldn't turn loose of the notion that their lives were coming undone.

It was ninety degrees in the shade, but the digital thermometer on the bank across the street registered 102. In spite of the air-conditioned car in which Gus Huffman was sitting, he was sweating like a stuck pig. And, to make matters worse, he needed to pee. But to relieve himself, he would have to leave, and that meant he might lose track of Hooker.

The man was like a damned ant. It had been so easy to lure the woman to the warehouse. Why, he wondered, couldn't Hooker cooperate as easily as she had? One minute he was here, the next minute somewhere else. After what Gus had seen today, the plan he'd come up with last night was obviously never going to work. Hooker didn't stay still long enough for anyone to get a good look at his face, let alone take a clean shot. And Gus knew that when he took another shot, he'd better not miss. If he did, he might as well turn the gun on himself. Romeo Leeds did not give second chances.

And so he continued to wait, growing more and more uncomfortable by the minute. Thirty minutes passed, and a strange odor began drifting into the car. Frowning, he glanced down at the dash, and when he focused on the temperature gauge, he began to curse. It was all the way into the red. Before he could move, smoke began seeping into the interior.

"Son of a bitch! My car's on fire!"

He reached down and popped the hood before jumping out. The hood was hot to the touch, but nothing compared to the flare of flames when he lifted it up. A couple passing by paused to gawk.

"Call the fire department! My car is on fire," he shouted.

The woman ran into a nearby building, while the man stood by, watching Gus's misfortune as it continued to unfold.

"Man, look at it blaze," he said.

Gus glared. "You shut the hell up."

His behavior was so menacing that the man turned and ran after his wife, leaving Gus to watch the demise of his car on his own. To add insult to injury, at that moment Brett Hooker emerged from the building. Gus stood helplessly, watching as Hooker got into his own car and drove away.

By the time the fire department arrived, Gus's car was engulfed. Firemen piled off the truck in a rush and began hooking up to a hydrant. But when they turned the hose toward the fire, little more than a stream came out of the nozzle. Gus's first thought was, *Hell, I could have peed on it harder than that.*

* * *

Brett gave the burning car little more than a cursory glance. He was too busy trying to figure out how the call he'd just gotten figured into the Riberosa case Lacey was taking to trial. They'd identified the woman's body from the warehouse murder. It was Linda Tribbey, the ex-wife of Harold Tribbey, who was Lacey's missing witness. He was certain it was no coincidence that this woman had turned up where Harold Tribbey was supposed to be, but it made no sense to him. Getting rid of a material witness was one thing, but killing the wife of a material witness was another altogether. What purpose could it possibly serve except to drive Tribbey further underground?

He got in his car and had started to drive away when it dawned on him that, in a way, he'd just answered his own question. Brett couldn't be the only one looking for Tribbey. And it stood to reason that if Brett couldn't find him, then someone else might be having the same problem. Linda Tribbey's murder could have been nothing more than a warning for Harold to stay hidden.

But the identification of her body intensified Brett's need to succeed. If he didn't find Harold, then Leeds would be getting away with murder, not once, but twice.

The lead he'd gotten earlier from an insurance salesman who volunteered at a downtown mission on weekends could be the break he'd been waiting for. The salesman had identified Harold Tribbey's picture as a man who called himself Ratchet. There was another fact Brett had learned about Harold that might be the key to locating him. It was Saturday night, and there was a free country-and-western concert at the Zoo Amphitheater. Harold Tribbey was a big country-music fan.

Brett turned off the freeway and started for home. The concert didn't start until nine o'clock tonight. At least he could have dinner with Tory and spend some time with her before he had to leave.

It had taken some ingenuity, but Tory had accomplished what she'd set out to do. With the help of a friend and some high-tech computer imaging, they had picked the face from the crowd and then enlarged it repeatedly until the clarity was picture perfect. The black spot on his cheek had evolved clearly. She'd taken one look at the small black tattoo underneath his right eye and then shuddered before shoving the prints into a manila envelope. Profusely thanking her friend, she made a quick exit. She drove without caution, sailing through yellow lights, weaving in and out of traffic. There was a feeling of panic within her that made no sense. All she could think was to get back to the apartment. There she would be safe.

The panic disappeared when she walked in the

door, and she sighed, reveling in the cool, quiet atmosphere. It was a scorcher outside, a typical Oklahoma day after a storm. Last night's rain had turned the air into a sauna. Her clothes were limp, and the escaping wisps of hair from the ponytail high on her head were wet and sticking to her neck.

She kicked off her shoes and grabbed a cold drink from the refrigerator before going into the living room. The envelope burned a hole in her hands as she tossed it onto the coffee table. And while she wanted to look at the pictures again in the very worst way, there was a knot in her stomach that she couldn't ignore.

Why? Why is this happening to me?

She took another swallow of her drink and then set it aside. Wiping the moisture from her hands on the legs of her slacks, she took a deep breath and reached for the envelope.

One after the other, she let the photos spill out and onto the table. There were six of them in all, and with each progressive enlargement, the black spot on the man's face had become clearer and clearer, until there was no way to misinterpret the black tattoo. She touched it with the tip of her finger and was immediately staggered by an overwhelming sensation of déjà vu. The blood drained from her face, and in spite of the heat of the day, she broke out in a cold sweat. The room began to spin around her and she closed her eyes and leaned forward, letting her head drop between her knees until the wave of nausea could pass.

And that was how Brett found her.

"Hey, Tory, I'm—"

He broke off in midsentence and was at her side within moments of entering the apartment.

"Sweetheart! What's wrong?"

She looked up, and had to make herself focus to remember his name.

"Brett?"

"Yes, baby, it's me. What happened? Are you sick?"

She swiped a shaky hand across her forehead and tried to smile.

"I don't know. I think maybe I got too hot. I was just sitting here, and suddenly I got dizzy. Maybe I'm coming down with something."

Brett reached to help her up. "Come here, honey. I think maybe you need to lie down for a while. I'll fix us something to eat, and then you can have an early night, okay?"

Everything settled back into place as Brett led her toward the bedroom. For the moment, the photos were forgotten. He helped her undress and then turned back the bed. When she was tucked in and comfortable, he leaned down and kissed the side of her cheek.

"Call me if you need anything, okay?"

She nodded, then rolled over on her side and closed her eyes. The sheets were cool against her skin, and the knowledge that she was no longer alone gave her the peace of mind to relax. Within minutes she was dozing.

Brett stripped off his own clothes and took a quick shower. A few minutes later, he came out of their bedroom wearing nothing but a pair of old gym shorts and a worried frown. As he paused in the living room to check messages, he noticed the prints scattered on the table. Curious, he picked one up, then another and another, noting with some surprise that he'd been right, after all. That black spot on the man's cheek *was* a tattoo.

He tossed the photos aside and then headed for the kitchen, wondering as he went what would possess a man to want a scorpion on his face for the rest of his life. Halfway into the preparations he was making for dinner, he began to wonder why Tory had gone to all that trouble. And then he reminded himself. Maybe it was for the same reason he couldn't let go of a lead, even when it seemed to be going nowhere. Whether it was professional pride or professional curiosity, it was still something he understood.

"You outdid yourself," Tory said.

Brett grinned. "Hamburgers, Tory. I made hamburgers, not prime rib."

But she persisted, intent on letting him know how much she appreciated his thoughtfulness and concern.

"But they were wonderful hamburgers, done just the way I like them."

His grin widened. "Yeah, black on the outside—"

"—and black on the inside," she added, and they both laughed. Brett didn't eat anything raw, including vegetables.

"You look better," he said, eyeing her cheeks and the pretty flush she was wearing.

"I feel fine," she said. "It's like I said before, I think I just got too hot."

He kept staring at her, trying to convince himself that she was going to be fine.

"I wish I didn't have to go back out."

"Hey, it isn't every day you get to listen to toe-tapping music while you're on the job."

He grinned. "That's for sure." And then his grin faded. "If I wasn't working, I'd ask you to go. But there's no telling what could happen on this case."

"That's okay. I understand. Besides, I need to keep my nose to the grindstone or I won't meet my own deadline."

"I suppose."

"Think of this as a night out with the boys," she said.

He grinned. "Yeah, right, some boys. The concert is free, and it's hot as hell outside. There's bound to be a crowd. It will be nothing short of a miracle if I'm able to spot Tribbey."

Tory sympathized. Brett had been working on the same case for days now, trying to locate Lacey's witness. She didn't know the particulars, but she knew it was important. She slid her arms around his neck.

"You will find him."

Brett kissed her earlobe, then left a trail of kisses along the edge of her collarbone. "And just how do you know that, oh wise and beautiful one?"

Tory giggled and looked down. "Because you're good at what you do."

He laughed. Her double meaning was as obvious as the bulge behind his zipper. "Yeah, and I bet you tell that to all the boys."

Tory tilted her head back to look up at him, and as she did, her hair tumbled down from the clasp, covering his hands and arms.

Brett groaned beneath his breath as he settled his mouth on her lips. She was soft and yielding, and he'd never wanted anything as much as he wanted to take her to bed right now. He kissed her once more with feeling and then broke their connection.

"Victoria..."

She leaned into his embrace, adjusting her curves to the hard, flat planes of his body.

"Yes?"

"I need you to do something for me while I'm gone."

"Like what?"

He grinned. "Like...hold that thought until I get back."

She smiled, and he couldn't resist tasting that, too, tracing the shape of her mouth with the tip of his tongue before stealing another last kiss.

He was on his way out the door when he suddenly stopped and turned.

Tory, watching him from across the room, was at that moment stunned by the sudden depth of love she felt for him.

"I love you, baby," he said softly, and then winked as he shut the door behind him.

"Oh, Brett, I love you, too." But he was already gone.

Five

When Brett Hooker came out of his apartment, Gus Huffman breathed a sigh of relief. They'd identified Linda Tribbey's body. He'd heard that on the streets. Killing her had been a warning to her ex to stay lost. But there was no way to threaten this man to keep quiet. The only way to silence him was to put him out of commission... Permanently. The palms of Gus' hands itched. He wanted this job over and done with. He wanted his money and he wanted to leave town. After burning up one car and having to rent another, he'd almost given up and gone home. But the thought of facing Romeo Leeds had made him reconsider his options, and now he was glad that he had.

The side street he'd parked on was directly opposite Hooker's apartment complex, and the bushes in which he was standing were thick enough to give him plenty of cover. When Hooker came down the walk toward his car, Gus shifted his stance. Right now he had a perfect view of his target through the crosshairs of his rifle. Gus's finger moved to the trigger when Hooker reached for the car door.

And then, out of nowhere, a pickup full of teenagers came flying around the corner, coming to a skidding stop only yards from the bushes in which Gus was standing. He still had a clear shot at Hooker, but now there would be six other witnesses with which to contend. Cursing his bad luck and their timing, he had no choice but to watch Hooker drive away into the night. A few moments later the teenagers disappeared into a house across the way, and Gus made a break for his car. Within moments, he was flying down the side streets in an effort to catch up with his quarry.

Brett had been at the concert for nearly an hour, and, as he'd feared, the amphitheater was filled to capacity. The night was sultry, the air barely moving, and with the crowd that had packed into the outdoor setting, the night was fairly miserable. And yet the discomfort didn't seem to inhibit the concert-goers. They were jammed into every available space, obviously enjoying the entertainment.

Two hometown boys who'd made good were playing to a wild and rowdy bunch. Brett stayed on the move, constantly searching face after face as he passed through the crowd.

Now the need to find Tribbey had become urgent for reasons other than the trial. If Brett didn't find him first, there was every likelihood that Harold would wind up just like his ex-wife. If that happened, Manny Riberosa would walk, and Romeo Leeds would have once again gotten away with murder.

Suddenly everyone around him began shouting and clapping, and Brett turned to look. As he did, he caught a glimpse of an unshaven and stoop-shouldered man leaning against a nearby tree. His clothes were stained and several sizes too big. When he moved aside to let some people pass, Brett noticed a limp to his gait. The man Brett was looking for hadn't been wearing a beard, but the limp Harold Tribbey had earned in Vietnam wasn't something a man could disguise. Brett started toward the stranger, intent on getting a closer look at his face.

It had been years since Harold could remember experiencing joy, but tonight was special. He loved a good song as well as the next man. Once, in his youth, he'd even dreamed of becoming a country singer, but that was before 'Nam. After that, he'd never felt much like singing.

Truth was, he had given up counting on Lady Luck to control his fate. It seemed to Harold that every time he left his life to chance, someone would toss him the joker. He'd survived Vietnam, but for what point? He'd come home with nightmares he'd never been able to shed. Even after witnessing a murder years later, he'd done a fair job of maintaining control of his emotions. And then the bombing had occurred. After that, he'd come the rest of the way undone. The explosion had been the trigger for a war's worth of suppressed memories. He'd tried for a while to hold on to his life, and then he'd found it simpler to let it all go.

At first it had been hard, losing job after job, and even worse, knowing his friends were losing respect for him. After that, he'd lost respect for himself. Losing Linda was almost anticlimactic. He'd been expecting to fail for so long that when it finally happened, it was a relief. Life on the streets wasn't easy, but it was better than facing the challenges of the real world. And anyway, he'd been lost for so long now that he'd forgotten the way to go home.

There were days, even weeks, when he never thought of Linda. In fact, he rarely thought of anything more than what to eat and where to sleep. On the streets, Harold had finally achieved success. He'd done what he set out to do. He'd become anonymous, and at this point in his life, it was the only way he could cope.

Tonight he was happy, and he was so involved in the concert taking place that he didn't even see the man coming toward him through the crowd.

* * *

The moment Brett stepped in front of the man, he knew he'd finally found Tribbey. The face was older than the picture he had, and half hidden by a good week's worth of whiskers. But those dark, deep-set eyes and that thin, worried mouth were the same.

"Harold Tribbey?"

Harold jumped. The sound of his name from a stranger's lips was as near to a curse as he ever wanted to hear. His eyes widened, and he took a step backward, only to feel the hard, rough bark of the tree at his back.

"You got the wrong man. Leave me alone."

Brett took out his identification. "Mr. Tribbey, my name is Brett Hooker, and I'm an investigator for the district attorney's office. Manny Riberosa's trial is next Monday, and the D.A. needs you as a witness."

Harold started to shake. "I don't know what you're talking about."

He tried to run, but Hooker grabbed his arm and wouldn't let go.

"You witnessed a murder. Almost two years ago, remember? It was in an alley outside the machine shop where you worked."

Harold's eyes glazed. "It's gone," he said, and a line of spittle slipped out the corner of his mouth.

"It's all blowed up. Just like them people who died in the Murrah Building. It's all blowed up."

Brett's heart went out to the old, lost soul, and at that moment, he almost turned and walked away. Leeds' lawyer would take what was left of this old man apart on the stand. But it wasn't his decision to make. Don Lacey was calling the shots.

"Sir! Mr. Lacey needs you to tell about the shooting in the alley. Remember? It was before the bombing. You were in the alley on your lunch break, remember?"

Tribbey's eyes teared up. "Chicken salad. Lindie made me chicken-salad sandwiches every Friday." The tears began to roll down his face, leaving clean tracks on the dirty, unshaven cheeks. "I ain't been able to face chicken salad since."

Brett's voice was quiet but calm as he tugged on Harold's arm and began to move toward the edge of the crowd. "I can understand that."

"I can't go back," Harold said.

"You don't have to stay," Brett said softly. "But you need to tell what you saw. If you don't, a man will get away with murder."

"People die ever' day," Tribbey muttered. "I saw it plenty in 'Nam."

Brett felt like an executioner. His gut instinct kept telling him this would finish the old man off, but his dedication to duty wouldn't allow it.

"What about your wife? Don't you care about what happened to her?" Brett asked.

Harold stopped, and the look he gave Brett was suddenly clear and cold. "I don't have a wife," he said shortly, and then his voice cracked. "At least, not anymore."

"I know you were divorced, but I can't believe you're that blasé about her murder. We think they killed her to get at you."

Beneath all the whiskers and grime, Harold Tribbey went pale, and Brett suddenly realized the man hadn't known Linda was dead, let alone that she had been murdered. He dropped his grasp in regret.

"I'm sorry, sir, I thought you knew."

Harold started to shake. "Someone killed my Lindie?" Then he started to cry, soft choking sobs that broke Brett's heart. "She can't be dead. I'm the one who's dead." He held out his hands and then dug at his face. "See? See? I died years ago, but nobody would believe me."

Brett took him by the arm again and began moving through the crowd. Although few noticed their passing, he was breathing easier by the time they reached the parking lot. The shadows surrounding them were darker and deeper, but there was also more privacy here, and at the moment, privacy was what Brett needed. He could tell by the way Tribbey was behaving that he was going to need help.

He reached for his phone. If Lacey was going to use this man on the stand, he was going to have to get him some professional help first. Brett knew Lacey's home number by heart, and for the sake of justice, the man would welcome this call.

As Brett was punching in the numbers, an expression of sudden clarity crossed Tribbey's face.

"Murdered? You said she was murdered?"

Brett nodded.

Tribbey swiped at his nose with the back of his hand, then smoothed down the front of his shirt, although it would take more than a tug on the fabric to make him look decent.

"Who did it?"

"We're not sure, but we think it was meant as a warning to you not to testify."

"How did they...I mean where was she when they found her?"

Brett thought about not telling him, but the man was trying so hard to hold on to reality, and he had a feeling that truth was what Harold needed to hear.

"They shot her in the back of the head. I found her in the Santa Fe Warehouse down on Reno Street."

Harold blanched. "I know that place. I slept there more than once. I know that place. Oh God, oh God, my Lindie in that dirty old place." And to Brett's surprise, a strength came into Harold's voice that hadn't been there before. "Lindie didn't belong in a place like that. She was a good woman...a lady."

Brett's finger was on the Send button of his phone as he nodded. "Yes sir. Just give me a minute and we'll—"

Behind them, the crowd roared, masking the sound of Gus Huffman's rifle as it fired. Brett didn't hear the shot, but he felt the impact, and then the heat, as the bullet ripped through his shoulder. As if in a dream, he saw blood splattering all over the front of Harold Tribbey's shirt, and as he began to pass out, he realized that the blood was his own.

It was instinct left over from a long-ago war that made Harold Tribbey catch Hooker as he fell. He eased him down to the pavement, all the while wondering why he'd been destined to witness everyone's death but his own. He stared at the blood gushing out of Hooker's wound and blanched. He'd seen men die with less injury in 'Nam. Now in a crouch, he swept the parking lot with a frightened gaze, believing at any minute the next shot would be for him. It never came.

Brett moaned and opened his eyes. To his overwhelming relief, Harold Tribbey was still there by his side. He kept thinking there was something that needed to be done, but he was fading in and out of consciousness so fast it was hard to remember.

Tory! That was it! He couldn't leave Tory. And Harold Tribbey was his only hope of survival. There were too many things he hadn't done in this life to give up on it now. He wanted babies with Tory. He wanted to grow old with her. He wanted…

With his last bit of strength, he grabbed at the old man's arm, unaware that he scared Tribbey half to death. The old man had thought he was dead.

"My phone. Find it. Just push the Send button. Tell Lacey what happened. Tell them to send help."

Harold was wild-eyed and in an all-out panic. His first instinct had been to run, but he hadn't. He kept telling himself that was what he should have done the first time back in that alley. If he had, no one would be bothering him now to testify against anything. But he couldn't quit thinking about Lindie's face. The last time he'd seen her, she'd been crying because he was leaving. And now she was dead. He wanted to crawl in a hole and never come out. But then he looked down at Hooker…and the blood. Had Lindie hurt like this? Had she died afraid and all alone? And then the truth hit Harold like a slap in the face.

She died because of me.

He tried to focus on what Hooker was asking.
The phone. I need to find the phone.

He could almost hear Lindie urging him on.

Go on, Harold, you can do it. You can do it.

He shuddered. It was when he quit listening to Lindie that everything had begun to go wrong.

"You're right, Lindie, I *can* do it."

Harold began crawling on his hands and knees, looking for the phone Hooker had dropped. A couple of seconds later, he spied it on the ground near the wheel of a car. Moments later, the call went through, and Harold Tribbey took control of the rest of his life.

Tory had fallen asleep on the couch. At twenty minutes to eleven the doorbell rang, yanking her rudely awake. Disoriented, she sat up with a jerk and then glanced at the clock, unaware that it was the doorbell she'd heard. When it rang again, she staggered to her feet. All the way through the living room she kept thinking Brett must have forgotten his key. There was a sleepy smile on her face as she opened the door, but it faded when she saw the uniformed officer.

"Miss Lancaster? Victoria Lancaster?"

She frowned. "Yes, I'm Victoria Lancaster."

Then he flashed his badge. "Miss Lancaster, I'm Officer Ernie Reynolds. Brett is a friend of mine."

At that moment, clarity came. Brett. Something had happened to Brett.

"Miss Lancaster, may I please come in?"

Tory's legs wouldn't work. She could feel them, but she couldn't make her brain tell her feet to move. Inside her mind she was already screaming, though the sound had yet to be born.

"Has something happened to Brett?"

Reynolds took her by the arm and gently moved her inside, closing the door behind him. "Miss Lancaster..."

It hurt to breathe, and she kept trying to focus. Staying calm was important, because she needed to hear what the man had to say, yet at the same time, she didn't want to know. She blinked, and her voice was shaking as she spoke.

"Tory."

Reynolds frowned. "I'm sorry, ma'am? What did you say?"

"Not Miss Lancaster. Tory. Brett calls me Tory."

Reynolds sighed. There was no easy way to say this. "Yes, ma'am. I've been sent to tell you that Brett's been shot."

Tory swayed on her feet and then moaned. Reynolds caught her before she could fall. She grabbed at his hands in desperation, unable to ask what she needed to know.

Reynolds saw the question in her eyes. "Yes,

he's alive…but it's serious. The department sent me to get you, ma'am. He was on his way to surgery when I left.''

A knot began to form in the pit of Tory's stomach. She started backing up and then turning around. Her mind went blank as she started searching the room for her purse.

"I need to get my purse. I've got to go—'' She pivoted, panic etched on her features. "I don't know where he is. Where did they take him?''

"You just get what you need, Miss Lancaster. I'll take you to him.''

Tory spun around, and moments later exited the apartment on Ernie Reynolds' heels.

At least a dozen uniformed officers stood in a clump at the end of the hall. When the elevator doors opened and Officer Reynolds and Tory emerged, they all turned to look. Almost immediately, a slim-faced man with a stern expression and a full head of white hair emerged from the group. He was wearing jeans and a western-style shirt, minus his signature black string tie, but Tory would have known him anywhere. It was Don Lacey, the Oklahoma County District Attorney.

"Miss Lancaster, I'm very sorry this has happened. Brett's a fine man, one of my best. I want you to know that everything possible is being done for him. At the moment, he's in surgery, but if there's anything I, or my office, can do for you, all you have to do is ask."

Spoken aloud, the words were even uglier than the thought, yet Tory had to know. "Who shot him? Do you have someone in custody?"

Lacey's expression darkened. "We don't know the shooter, although we're pretty sure who's behind it."

Tory pressed her fingers to her lips and then closed her eyes. She kept thinking this was all a bad dream, that any minute she would wake up in Brett's arms, just as she had before. But the smell of disinfectant, the harsh glare from the overhead lights, and the sympathetic stares from the officers behind Lacey were almost obscene. What did they know of her terror? They were still breathing. Brett was the one who might die.

There was a compassion in Lacey's gaze that belied his lack of expression. He glanced once at Ernie Reynolds, as if assuring himself she was being cared for, and then lightly touched Tory's arm before walking away.

God help me...and God help Brett.

She wanted to rage at fate for tearing her small world apart. She kept telling herself that this couldn't be happening...not to Brett. He wasn't a police officer any longer. He'd told her over and over that his investigative duties for the D.A.'s office weren't dangerous. Anger surged past her fear. He'd lied to her, and maybe even to himself.

Like all the other officers who'd gathered, Ernie Reynolds felt sick for the woman. The day Brett Hooker had taken himself off the singles market, the men had known he'd found someone special, but he'd chosen to keep his relationship with his lady private. And while many of them knew her by name, this was the first time they'd ever seen her. Even after she'd moved in with Hooker, it hadn't taken long for word to get around that his woman came and went within his life to suit herself. And while they might not understand Hooker's willingness to live with such a strange relationship, after seeing Tory Lancaster, they could certainly understand his attraction. The woman wasn't just pretty, she was beautiful. And seeing her standing there in the middle of the hospital corridor in such obvious despair, there wasn't a man among them who wouldn't have volunteered to ease her pain. Ernie Reynolds was no exception.

"Miss Lancaster, is there anything I can get you? Would you like some coffee...maybe a soft drink?"

Tory swiped a shaky hand through her hair, tousling it even further. Her pupils were wide with shock, her expression still stunned. She kept fighting an overwhelming urge to throw up as she struggled with his question.

"No. I don't need anything." *Except Brett.*

Reynolds looked around, wishing to hell that some of the officers' wives would show up. When something like this happened, they usually did. Victoria Lancaster would surely be more comfortable with a woman instead of all of these men. And then he took a deep breath, reminding himself that if it was his wife, he would want someone to take care of her, too.

"Please, Tory, let's sit over here, okay?" He pointed to some chairs, then took her by the arm.

She stumbled.

Ernie moved his hand to her shoulder, and when she leaned against his strength, he cradled her against him.

"Ernie..." She looked up. "You did say your name was Ernie, right?"

He nodded. At that moment, she could have called him a jerk and he would have answered to it.

"Yes, ma'am."

The expression on her face was stunned, almost blank. "I can't live without him."

He felt lost. "Miss Lancaster, do you have a pastor or a priest you'd like us to call?"

Call. The word suddenly took on new meaning.

Stunned that she hadn't already thought of it, she grabbed at the officer's arm.

"His mother! I need to call Brett's mother."

Reynolds nodded. At last, something concrete that he could do.

"If you have her number, I'd be glad to—"

As badly as she hated to do it, it would be unforgivable if the news didn't come from her.

"No...but thank you," she said softly. "I just need a phone. I can take care of the rest."

At the age of sixty-two, Cynthia Hooker had lived long enough to know that any time the phone rang in the middle of the night, even if it was a wrong number, it was never good news. She reached for the phone and the light at the same time, turning on one and answering the other. As she struggled to orient herself on the edge of the bed, she noticed it was almost two o'clock in the morning.

"Hello?" Cynthia heard someone take a deep breath. Her heart stopped. "Hello, who is this?" she asked, and heard her own voice starting to shake.

"Cynthia, it's me, Tory."

For a moment Cynthia drew a blank. Her mind was racing through every person that she knew, and for the life of her, she couldn't think of a single—*oh, dear God.* "Victoria?"

Tory started to shake. She hadn't even accepted what had happened to Brett. How did she go about saying the ugly truth aloud? And then she thought of Brett's mother, of the fear she must be feeling, and knew she had to get through this with some sort of composure or it would scare the older woman to death.

"Yes, it's me. I'm sorry to call, but...Brett's been shot." Tory heard his mother moan, but she continued to talk, needing to get it all said before she came undone herself. "He's in surgery, and that's all I know."

Then her composure shattered. She began to shiver, as if she were freezing. A darkness hovered at the back of her consciousness, reminding her that she had no control of anything...including her life.

"Mrs. Hooker, I can't face life without Brett."

Cynthia Hooker heard the devastation in Victoria's voice. As for Cynthia, she had already buried her husband, she had no intention of burying a son.

"You're not going to have to. Where is he?" she asked.

"Saint Anthony's Hospital."

"Victoria, you listen to me. I'll let the rest of the family know what happened, although Celia won't be able to travel because of the new baby. Ryan's in Enid, so he's closer. He can get to you within a couple of hours, three at the most. You won't have to be alone long. We'll get there as soon as we can, but until then, you have to be strong. Can you do that for me?''

Tory took a slow, shuddering breath. "Yes, ma'am.''

Cynthia wanted to cry. This was the first time in over a year that she'd spoken directly to this woman, and they were still on a formal basis.

"Victoria?''

"Yes, ma'am?''

"My name is Cynthia.''

Tory closed her eyes, willing herself not to faint.

"Victoria…''

"What?''

"Are you terribly afraid?''

Tory swallowed a groan. Oh God, she was *so* afraid. "I've never been so afraid in my life.''

"Then pray, darling, pray.''

When the line went dead in Tory's ear, she dropped the receiver and turned her face to the wall.

Ernie Reynolds was standing nearby. When he saw her falter, he hung up the receiver for her and then touched her on the shoulder.

"Miss Lancaster, are you all right? Is there something I can get you?''

Tory shook her head and walked away to stand at the windows overlooking the city streets. It was then that she realized it had started to rain. Every time she turned around, it seemed as if a storm front was on the horizon, or just passing. But tonight, as she looked out the window to the streets below, it didn't feel like rain. It felt as if heaven were shedding tears. She leaned her head against the glass and closed her eyes. It had been a very long time since she'd prayed. If only she remembered how.

It was a quarter to four in the morning when Tory saw a man get off the elevator and start down the hall toward her. His jeans were faded but clean, his shirt and jacket about the same. His hair was black and in need of a cut, and even from this distance, she could read the stern expression on his face. The tennis shoes he was wearing made no noise as he walked, but there was something about the way he held his head and the length of his stride that she recognized. She'd never met any of Brett's family, but if she had to, she would guess that Ryan Hooker, brother number one, had just arrived on the scene.

God give me strength.

She took a deep breath and then stood.

Ryan Hooker was the wild card in the Hooker family. Five years ago his pretty young wife had chucked their ten-year marriage for an oil executive with a six-figure income and moved with him to L.A. Ryan had reciprocated by chucking a white-collar job that he hated, buying an auto parts store with a garage in the back and moving into the second-floor apartment above it. He'd hardened his heart to women and proceeded to make a small but tidy fortune in a business that should have bankrupted him. The family loved him in spite of himself, and he returned the favor. He'd spent the better half of his adult life worrying about Brett's occupation, and then, later, Brett's love for a woman who wouldn't stay put. More than once he'd passed his opinion on to Brett about a woman who would walk in and out of a man's life without so much as the common courtesy to call.

A few hours earlier, the phone call he'd gotten from his mother had rocked him in a way he wouldn't have believed. He wouldn't let himself think of Brett dying, and he'd driven like hell to get here. But he'd come for Brett, not the woman Brett slept with.

And then he saw a young woman get up from a chair at the end of the hall, and he knew before he got there it was her. She was slim and blonde, and like him, seemingly felt no regard for fashion. Her jeans were old, her T-shirt soft and clinging. But it was her face that staggered him. Sweet Jesus, Brett had said she was pretty, but that was an understatement if he'd ever heard one. From where he was standing, Victoria Lancaster was drop-dead beautiful. He hated her on the spot.

Tory was stunned. He looked so much like—

"You look like Brett," she blurted.

Ryan lifted his chin in a defensive gesture, but it was wasted, because Victoria Lancaster didn't behave as he'd expected. She didn't throw herself into his arms, or shriek and wail in some display of despair. Her eyes were red-rimmed, her expression drawn and haggard, ravaged by the long night of waiting. But it was her composure that was frightening, even unnatural.

"Yeah, I know. Where's Brett?"

"Surgery."

Ryan frowned. "Still?"

She nodded and then dropped back into her chair and closed her eyes, almost ignoring his presence. Again Ryan was taken aback. He didn't know what he'd expected, but this certainly wasn't it. He slid into a chair opposite the one in which she was sitting and then found himself staring at her face. The perfection of the shape, the cut of her chin, the arch of her amber eyebrows and the thickness of her lashes, was unbelievable. And then he caught himself looking at her mouth. She was biting her lip. To his horror, a small drop of blood suddenly appeared, and when he realized that she'd made herself bleed rather than cry aloud, his last defense went down.

"Victoria."

Tory opened her eyes.

There was no way he could ignore the depth of

the despair in her gaze. If she loved his brother, then it had to be enough.

"I'm sorry I was rude."

She almost smiled, and Ryan caught himself holding his breath, waiting for it to happen.

"It's all right," she said softly. "After all, we're nothing more than strangers."

Ryan shook his head. "Not anymore," he said shortly, and moved into the chair beside her. His words were clipped, his voice gruff, but there was no mistaking the sincerity of his words.

"If you get tired, lean on me."

Lean on me...lean on me.

The offer echoed over and over in Tory's head until she thought it would burst. A small spurt of panic came and went as she stared down the hall. She couldn't—no, wouldn't—let herself be caught up in this loving family thing. She'd been through that scene time and time again with foster parents. Some of them had been nice—some of them hadn't—but none of them had lasted. She'd learned a hard lesson early on—if you don't care, then you can't be hurt.

And so they sat in an uneasy silence, each lost in memories of a man they refused to give up. Tory was blind with exhaustion and all but falling out of her chair when Ryan Hooker suddenly stood. She looked up to see a doctor in surgical greens coming down the hall.

Brett! Please be all right.

"Are you the Hooker family? he asked.

Ryan nodded, and whether she liked it or not, slipped an arm around Tory. He didn't know whether it was to hold her up or steady his own shaking legs. But right now, he needed the connection.

The air was rushing past Tory's ears like the wind from a storm. She kept swallowing the same breath over and over, and still the words wouldn't come. All she could do was wait for the doctor to speak.

He didn't waste time by delaying their misery.

"He's in recovery. I won't lie to you and say he's all right, but he's alive, which, in itself, is a miracle. His main injury was blood loss. If he can maintain for the next forty-eight hours, he has a good chance. But for now, we just wait and see."

"Thank God," Ryan said, and then glanced at Tory as the doctor left. She still hadn't said a word, and her face was as white as a sheet.

"Why don't we—"

He never got to finish what he'd been about to say. Tory slipped out from under his arm and then walked toward the window. Ryan didn't know whether to go after her or leave her the hell alone. And then several uniformed officers came out of a nearby waiting area, anxious to hear what had been said. He gave Tory a last, nervous glance, and then turned to face them.

Six

The police had no idea why Brett had been shot. It wasn't unusual for something like that to happen in an open crowd setting. Tribbey was now under protective custody, and Lacey had opted for the "better safe than sorry" scenario and asked to have a guard posted at Brett's door, as well. At this point the doctor had him in a private room with an Intensive Care nurse, while the police had him under guard.

For Tory, the knowledge that Brett could still be in danger was secondary to her joy. He was alive. It was all that mattered. Meeting Brett's brother under such strained circumstances should have been awkward, but sometime during the early hours of the morning, they had come to an unspoken understanding. They both loved Brett, therefore, whatever they thought about each other was unimportant to the big picture.

Because of her reticence, she knew Brett's family was bound to have preconceived opinions about her that weren't necessarily good. Before, it hadn't mattered. But now, because of this crisis, she was being forced to face them, as well as old fears from her past.

Cynthia Hooker's first glimpse of the woman who'd stolen her son's heart came just before nine o'clock the next morning. Her flight from Denver to Oklahoma City had been turbulent, but Cynthia's fears had not been concerned with the weather. Until she could look at Brett's face—until she could touch the warm flesh of his body—she wouldn't be able to take an easy breath.

By the time she got to the hospital, her nerves were shot and her patience with them. To make matters worse, there was a guard at the door who refused to let her in.

"I'm sorry, lady, but no one's allowed in except immediate family."

"But I'm his mother!" she cried.

"I have no way of knowing that," he said.

For a mother who'd spent the most frantic night of her life, it was one roadblock too many. She reached into her purse for some identification and spilled everything onto the floor. It was the last straw. She started to cry.

Ryan eased his way into the empty elevator, punching the floor number with his little finger while trying not to spill the coffee and sweet roll he was carrying. He shrugged his shoulders, trying to ease some of the tension in his back as the doors slid shut. But it was impossible to relax. He kept thinking of Brett in that bed and wondering if he would ever get out of it again. And then there was Tory. Sometime during the early morning hours, he'd gained a whole new respect for his brother's lady. When they'd brought Brett up from surgery, the staff was adamant that no one but his nurse be inside the room. But Tory had been deaf to their orders and ignored their demands. She'd pushed her way past them and into his room. She'd looked at him once without speaking, then quietly pulled a chair as close to his bed as she could and crawled into it, curling up like a child in hiding. When they realized that she was not going to make a fuss or get in the way, they'd reluctantly relented.

And the hours had passed. The tension in her body was reflected in her eyes as she watched the readouts on the machines they'd hooked up to his body. She spoke only when spoken to and had yet to cry.

Ryan knew women, and this one was close to breaking. Since Brett was in no condition to worry about her, he considered it his brotherly duty to make sure she was still sane when Brett came to. And, as much as he hated to admit it, she seemed like the real thing. The least he could do was see that she was fed. God knew she wouldn't leave his brother's side to feed herself.

His mind was on one woman as he exited the elevator, but he quickly became focused on another. When he recognized his mother on her knees on the floor, his heart nearly stopped. His first and last thought was Brett. Coffee began sloshing out from beneath the plastic lid of the cup as he broke into a lope.

"Mom! What's wrong? Has anything happened to—"

"Ryan! Thank God," she sobbed, dropping the last of the items back into her purse. "They won't let me in to see him."

Ryan gave the guard a sympathetic look. "She's our mother," he said, and then turned to Cynthia. "Mom, just calm down. All he needs is some ID. Show him your driver's license."

"I was trying when I dropped everything," she said, blowing her nose loudly between handing the license over and then taking it back.

"I'm sorry, ma'am," the guard said. "But we can't be too careful. Hooker's a good man. I don't want to be the one responsible for getting him killed, understand?"

She blanched. Having the truth put to her in such a matter-of-fact manner put a whole new light on the situation. She dabbed at her eyes and then blew her nose again, suddenly ashamed that she'd lost control.

"I'm sorry. I don't know what came over me. I'm not normally hysterical."

"No, ma'am, I'm sure you're not," the guard said.

Ryan winked at the guard and then pointed to her suitcases. "Keep an eye on her stuff for a minute, will you, Ed?"

"My pleasure," the guard said, and shoved them against the wall near his chair.

"Are you okay now?" Ryan asked.

She sniffed and nodded. "I will be, as soon as I can see Brett." She eyed the food he was carrying. "And get some of that for myself."

"This is for Tory. If I'd known you were here, I would have brought more."

Her mouth firmed, not much, but enough for Ryan to know that his mother had just put up a guard of her own.

"Ease up, Mom. She's different, I'll give you that. But she hasn't moved from Brett's side. Whatever you think of her, just know that she loves your son as much as you do...and she's about at the end of her rope."

Cynthia Hooker reserved the right to form her own opinions, but as they entered Brett's room, her anger faded. A nurse was nearby, obviously keeping a constant check on her son's welfare.

That's a good sign.

And then she looked at Brett and everything he was hooked up to, and exhaled a shaky breath.

Dear Lord, what have they done to my son?

Her gaze then moved to the woman asleep at his side, and every concern she'd ever had about Victoria Lancaster ceased to be. Even though Brett was unconscious and Tory was asleep, their connection to each other was obvious.

She'd fallen asleep with her forehead resting against his bed and her hand on his leg, and while it was an unconscious movement on Brett's part, her hair was entwined through his fingers, as if he were holding on to her in the only way he could.

"Oh my," Cynthia whispered. "Oh, Ryan. Oh my."

"Told you," he said softly. And when his mother started forward, he added, "Hey, Mom."

She paused. "What?"

"She hasn't cried."

Cynthia nodded with understanding. "She's afraid to cry."

"But why?"

"Bad luck."

Ryan frowned. "Bad luck? That doesn't make sense."

"Yes it does," Cynthia said. "Crying is a part of grieving. If she lets herself cry, then she will be letting Brett down by not believing he'll pull through.''

Ryan shook his head. "And where does that bit of wisdom come from?"

Her chin trembled, but she met his gaze in her straightforward way. "Because that's the way I felt, right up to the moment I lost your father. After that, it was okay to let go of the pain."

Ryan looked away, unwilling to let her know how deeply he'd been touched by her words.

Then, before they could move, the monotonous beep of one machine momentarily broke rhythm and Tory's head came up from the bed as if she'd been slapped. She jumped to her feet, her gaze flying from Brett to the nurse at the end of the room. But when the nurse didn't react, and the machine regained a regular rhythm, she breathed a quiet sigh of relief.

"Thank you, God," Tory whispered.

"Amen," Cynthia Hooker echoed.

Tory spun around, only then aware that they were no longer alone. A flicker of panic came and went as she reminded herself that these people were Brett's family. They weren't the enemy. Smoothing her hand over her hair and then down the front of her crumpled T-shirt, she stepped around the chair and went to greet them.

"Mrs. Hooker, I'm Victoria."

Cynthia ignored her outstretched hand and

hugged her instead. "I do not shake hands with family," she said softly, patting Tory gently on the back. "How's he doing, dear?"

Family? It wasn't what she'd expected to hear. They belonged to Brett, not to her. Uncomfortable with the familiarity, she stepped out of Cynthia's arms.

"The doctors say he's holding his own." Her voice was shaking, and she tried to smile. "You know how hardheaded Brett is. He's going to get well just to spite everyone who says he won't."

Cynthia saw more than reserve in this young woman's eyes. She saw fear. Genuine fear, and the oddest thing was, she didn't think it had a thing to do with Brett's survival.

Ryan thrust the coffee and sweet roll toward her. "Here," he said gruffly.

Tory was touched by his thoughtfulness, but the thought of swallowing food made her sick. "I'm not hungry, but—"

"I didn't ask you if you were hungry. Just drink the damned coffee and eat the damned roll, okay?"

Cynthia watched the silent war of wills between the pair, then relaxed when Tory quietly accepted what Ryan had brought.

"Thank you," Tory said.

Ryan nodded. "You're welcome."

And the waiting began again.

* * *

Almost twenty-four hours after he'd come out of surgery, Brett Hooker woke up, more than a little surprised to find himself still alive. He had vague memories of blood, of Harold Tribbey's face, and of being afraid he would never see Tory again. And now he drifted within a cocoon of pain-killers, listening to the voices of those he loved best.

Ryan was here! He shouldn't have been surprised. Ever since their father had died, Ryan had considered himself the official head of the family. He heard his mother's voice, always a little breathless when filled with concern. Content with the half-light of consciousness, he kept listening, aware that there was one more person in his life who mattered. One more voice he had yet to hear. Victoria.

He lay without moving, without opening his eyes, still too weak to fight the lethargy claiming him. Drifting in and out of sleep, he kept thinking he would hear her voice, but he didn't. Somewhere within him, a knot of disappointment began to form. He drew a deep breath and then groaned from the pain.

At that moment there was a touch on his arm and sweet breath on his face, and the knot in his belly disappeared. He should have known. She'd been here all the while, keeping a silent vigil by his side. He heard his name on her lips, heard the urgency in her voice, and he opened his eyes.

Tory had been on her feet within seconds of hearing Brett groan. The nurse moved quickly to the bed and began an examination of his pulse and blood pressure. But Tory was already hearing an increased pulse rate from the machine to which he was hooked, and she'd seen his eyelids fluttering. It was enough for her to know he was on his way back. She called his name and then unconsciously held her breath.

"Brett…sweetheart…it's me, Tory."

He blinked and then reached for her arm. When her fingers closed around his hand, he relaxed even more.

"I got shot."

Ryan was suddenly at her side, as was his mother, but Tory's gaze never wavered from Brett's face.

"We know. It's okay, just rest."

But he couldn't rest. Not yet. There was something he needed to remember. And then it came. The old man. He'd found the old man.

"Tribbey…did they get Tribbey?"

"Yes, the police have him in protective custody. Mr. Lacey called this morning. Said to tell you when you woke up that you did a good job."

Brett inhaled carefully, easing the breath around the pain in his chest.

"I never heard the shot. Do they know who?"

"No," Tory said.

"Was anyone else shot?"

"No."

Brett sighed, trying to think. None of this was making much sense. It wasn't unlikely that several of the concert-goers could have been carrying, or that a fight could erupt between rival gangs, but it was unusual for a gun to be drawn without purpose. His thoughts were fuzzy, like the taste in his mouth, and he tried to focus on one thing at a time.

"Water... Can I have a drink of water?"

Tory looked at the nurse.

"Only ice chips," the nurse said.

Glad to have something positive to do, Tory slipped a small chip between Brett's lips. He was stunned at the effort it took just to swallow.

"Good...that's good," he whispered.

Tory leaned closer, speaking softly. "Brett, your mother is here."

Brett managed a smile. "Hi, Mom. Glad you're here."

Cynthia leaned over and kissed her son's forehead. "So am I, dear, so am I."

The nurse interrupted as Brett's doctor came into the room.

"He's had enough for a while. And the doctor needs to examine the patient. Would you please step out of the room?"

Brett's voice was weak, but they heard it just the same.

"Wait," he called.

They paused and turned. He reached for Tory. She grasped his hand and leaned down until their cheeks were nearly touching, and his words were for her ears only.

"I love you, Victoria."

The words brushed against her cheek, baby-soft yet strong enough to change Tory's world. With her control nearly shattered, she pressed her lips against his temple.

"I love you, too, Brett Hooker. More than you will ever know."

And then they moved out without argument, each lost in their own thoughts. Ryan wanted to shout with joy, while the knot in Cynthia Hooker's stomach began to unwind with relief. But Tory's reaction was taking a different turn.

The moment she stepped into the hall, her legs went weak. For the last twenty-four hours she'd been existing on sheer will alone, and now that the crisis had passed, there was nothing left on which to fall back. She wrapped her arms around herself and began to shake.

"Oh God, oh God," she muttered, rocking herself where she stood.

Startled, Cynthia saw Tory coming undone, but it was Ryan who caught her before she could fall.

Ignoring her resistance, he pulled her into his arms. His voice was gruff, but his touch was gentle as he enfolded her within his embrace.

"It's okay, kid. Let it all go."

And she did. In harsh, aching sobs that ripped up her throat. With shudders that racked her body and left her gasping for air.

Ryan held on tight, afraid of what might happen if he let Tory go. A mother's instinct to comfort moved Cynthia to join them. Between them, they held Tory while she cried.

Gus Huffman was worried. Twice now he'd screwed up, and Leeds was an unhappy man. But he kept consoling himself with the fact that he'd never seen a recent picture of Tribbey, so how was he to know that the old bum standing beside Hooker had been Tribbey himself? He damn sure hadn't looked like the picture they'd shown him. And the fact that Hooker was still alive made it worse. He'd failed miserably, and Leeds was not a forgiving man. If he didn't find a way to fix what he'd done, he might as well turn the gun on himself.

And because of his desperation, he was about to make a very risky move. Word on the street was that Tribbey was already in protective custody. The way Gus figured it, that was Leeds' concern. But Hooker was his. And there was no time left for plans. He had to get into Hooker's hospital room and finish what he'd started.

The hallway lights flickered, signaling the end of visiting hours. The guard at Brett's door was finishing off a cup of coffee when the nurse assigned to his room came out. The bag of fluids dripping through his IV was almost empty, and her patient was resting comfortably.

"Be back in a second," she said, and hustled up the hall.

Ed nodded, draining the last of his cup and then setting it on the floor by his chair. He leaned back and crossed his legs just as a doctor exited the elevator and headed his way. When he started into Hooker's room, Ed stood up.

"Evening," the doctor said. "I'm covering for Mailot tonight."

Ed frowned. That was Hooker's doctor, all right, but no one had told him of any changes. "Sorry, sir, but I'll need to see some identification. You haven't been in before, and I have orders to—"

But your orders don't coincide with mine. And Gus Huffman grabbed Ed by the throat, shoving his thumb in the carotid artery and pushing him inside the door. In a matter of seconds, Brett's safety had been breached. Ed was unconscious before he hit the floor.

Gus smiled to himself, pleased with the outcome

of his plan. He'd had no idea that Brett had a round-the-clock nurse, and it was just stupid luck that she was nowhere in sight.

He stood within the silence of the room, listening to the quiet but steady beeping of the monitors attached to Hooker's body and thinking there was no time like the present. He reached in his pocket and headed for the bed, his fingers curling carefully around the hypodermic syringe in his pocket. One quick dose of this in that IV and Hooker would never wake up.

He reached toward the bag, then frowned. It was almost empty. Any moment that damned alarm would likely sound and some nurse would come hustling in to replace it. Although luck had been with him, time was not on his side. Behind him, the guard on the floor began to moan, and Gus cursed. He should have killed the bastard.

"Okay, Hooker. Sweet dreams."

And he flipped the cap from the needle and thrust it toward the shunt on the tube.

Tory had taken advantage of the nurse's exit to make a quick trip into the bathroom. She didn't need to turn on a light to see what she was doing, and since the nurse was out of the room, she left the door slightly ajar, just in case Brett called out or some machine might sound.

As she was drying her hands, the door to Brett's

room opened suddenly, and she turned, expecting to see his nurse, not two men stumbling through the door. To her horror, the guard suddenly dropped to the floor without a sound, and the man who'd silenced him was heading for Brett.

Trying not to panic, she moved deeper into the shadows of the bathroom to give herself time to think, but when the man reached in his pocket, then started toward Brett's bed, she reacted without thought.

She stepped out of her shoes and then slipped through the half-open door, moving silently on bare feet until she was less than three feet from the man's back. Still unsure of what she should do, her decision to wait was taken away when she saw the syringe in the man's hand. And when he reached for Brett's IV, a blind rage swept over her. That was her Brett. He was her life. Her love. No one was going to hurt him again.

"Nooo!" she screamed. "Don't touch him!"

With no thought for her own safety, she made a dive for the backs of his legs, screaming all the way down.

To say Gus was startled would have been putting it mildly. Between the scream in his ears and the impact of dead weight against his knees, he was unable to save himself. He pitched forward. The needle he'd been holding flew out of his hands, and his chin hit the corner of the bedside

table. The crack echoed in his ears, and he had a
brief moment's awareness that he'd just bitten his
tongue, before everything went black. It was as
effective a coldcock as any boxer could have managed.

Ryan was in the hallway and only a few feet
behind Brett's nurse when Tory's scream rent the
air. Within seconds of the sound, the whole floor
seemed to erupt. People ran out of doorways,
nurses came out of rooms, everyone was standing
in the hallway, trying to get a fix on the sound.

But Ryan had seen something that everyone else
seemed to have missed. The guard was not at his
station. He started running.

"Call security," he shouted, and hit the door to
Brett's room with the flat of his hand.

When Ryan burst into the room he found, to his
surprise, that he was the only one standing. Everyone save Brett was on the floor. The guard was
rolling about and gagging, trying to breathe and
talk at the same time. And Tory was locked in
what appeared to be a deathlike embrace with a
doctor who was bleeding from the face.

He hit the light switch, instantly bathing the
room in full light, and then ran for Tory. It was
all he could do to make her let go.

"Tory! Tory! It's me, Ryan. What the hell happened?" he asked, as he pulled her to her feet.

She pointed to the man on the floor. "He tried to kill Brett."

Ryan groaned, thinking that she'd finally flipped. "My God, woman, that man's a doctor."

"No, he's not," she said. "He knocked Ed out. I watched him from the bathroom. And then he took a needle from his pocket and was about to put it in Brett's IV."

Ryan turned and stared at the guard, who was in the act of crawling to his knees. He ran to help him up.

"Are you all right?"

Ed nodded, his voice was little more than a croak, but he backed Tory up all the way. He pointed at the man on the floor.

"I don't know who he is, but he's damn sure no doctor."

At that point security burst into the room, coupled with two doctors and Brett's nurse. It didn't take long for Tory to repeat her story, and with Ed's corroboration and the syringe in question being produced, Gus Huffman was formally arrested.

However, it was thirty minutes before he came to enough to know it. And when he did revive, a real doctor was putting the last of six stitches into his chin.

"What hit me?" he groaned.

An Oklahoma City policeman leaned over him with a grin. "A real mad woman."

Gus groaned again. "I'm hurt. I need something for the pain."

"You better get tougher than that," the cop said. "You're going down for attempted murder."

Son of a bitch. Gus shuffled his thoughts to a different level. No sooner had the doctor finished with his stitches than the cop grabbed him by the handcuffs and hauled him off the table.

"Come on, buddy. We're heading downtown." He looked at the bandage on Gus's chin and grinned. "That's gonna look real pretty in your mug shot."

Gus began to panic as the cop dragged him through the hospital. Leeds' reach went farther than people knew. He wouldn't be safe even behind bars.

"I want to make a deal," he said.

The cop snorted beneath his breath as he opened the squad car and shoved Gus inside.

"Watch your head, sir, or you'll be needing some more stitches."

Gus ducked, then settled into the back seat with a thump. He might have a knot on his chin, but his mind was still working.

"You get the D.A. on the phone. Ask him if he's interested in Romeo Leeds."

Ryan hadn't been able to stop hugging Tory. Every time he looked at her, he had an overwhelming urge to thank her again. He kept thinking that if she hadn't been there, Brett would be dead.

Tory was still shaking from the adrenaline rush, and although the doctor had urged her to have an examination, she refused to budge from Brett's side. Ironically, Brett had slept through the entire thing, including her screams.

Ryan took a washcloth to Tory's face, wiping a small streak of blood from her cheek where she'd bitten her own lip in the struggle.

"My God, woman. You could have been killed," he muttered, as he tried to swipe at the spot.

Tory took the washcloth and wiped it herself.

"If he'd killed Brett, it wouldn't have mattered," she said coldly, and handed the washcloth back to him.

Ryan shuddered. There was a guardedness to this woman that he couldn't get past. He kept wondering what hardships had forged the wall behind which she stood. What had she endured to make her so tough? And then he abandoned the thought. It didn't really matter how she'd been raised. What mattered was that Brett was still safe and she was alive. And they'd doubled the guard on Brett's door.

Tory moved to Brett's bed, unable to stop touching him, needing to be reassured that he still drew breath. Her tenderness with his brother was impossible for Ryan to miss. He patted her shoulder, speaking softly near her ear.

"I was coming to see if you wanted some supper," he asked. "Are you hungry?"

Tory paused, considered the question and then turned. To his surprise, she grinned.

"Oddly enough, I am. I guess it was all that exercise."

Ryan grinned back. So, he thought. *She has a sense of humor.*

"Got any preferences?" he asked.

Her grin widened. "Anything but that vending machine tuna sandwich. It's deadly."

He glanced at Brett, then back at her. "Will you be all right until I get back?"

"Yes."

And he knew that she would.

Sharing space with people had never been Tory's long suit. Sharing an apartment with Brett had been a learning process, but she'd been so in love with him that it had been easy. Sharing the apartment with Ryan and Cynthia, and without Brett to run interference, was the most difficult thing she'd ever done in her life. But she would have had it no other way. They had gone out of their way to try to make her feel like part of the family. It wasn't their fault she didn't know how to coexist.

Today Ryan was going back to Enid, and that meant she and Cynthia would be alone together. One less person in the one-bedroom apartment should have been good news, but she was nervous. Cynthia Hooker saw straight through pretense. Tory supposed it was part of being a mother, although she wouldn't really know. She didn't remember anything about her own.

Tory was anxious to get back to the hospital, but she considered it her duty to wish Ryan a safe journey home. He was packing the last of his things while Cynthia hovered.

Ryan zipped his bag shut, then looked up. "That's it."

"Did you get all your shaving things from the bathroom?" his mother asked.

"I think so."

"Let me make sure," Cynthia said and headed that way, leaving Ryan and Tory alone.

Tory was quiet. In Ryan's opinion, too quiet. Even after she'd foiled the attempt on Brett's life, he still didn't know what made her tick. She was the most reserved, self-isolating woman he'd ever met. But she loved Brett, and Brett loved Tory, and for him, that was all that mattered.

Tory was immobilized beneath Ryan Hooker's stare. She resisted the urge to check her clothing for something undone, although she knew she was fine. Her jeans were clean. Her T-shirt was new and fresh. The laces on her tennis shoes were tied, and her hair was up and out of her face, pulled back in the neat ponytail she usually wore. And with all that, she still felt like a child who was about to be sent back to wash the egg from her face.

"Thank you for everything," she said softly.

Ryan grinned and tugged at a loose strand of hair that had escaped from her hairdo.

"You're very welcome."

Tory got the message and almost smiled. So, she'd sounded a little formal.

"Brett is going to miss you," she added.

"Thanks to you, he's going to be fine, remember?"

Tory nodded.

Ryan shifted gears. "He still doesn't know what you did, does he?"

"No," she said. "And I see no reason why he should. It would only worry him. Besides, the police think Leeds is long gone. Even if he's not, Brett will be the least of Leeds' worries. It's Gus Huffman's testimony that will put him away and I hear he's done plenty of talking."

"Yeah, I guess you're right. But sooner or later, Brett's bound to find out."

"We'll worry about that when it happens."

Ryan grinned. "A woman after my own heart."

Tory looked away, unwilling to let him know how pleased she was by his compliment.

"I'll just be glad to get him home," she said.

"If Mom starts driving you nuts, send *her* home."

Tory's mouth dropped. "Oh, I couldn't do that!"

At that point Cynthia came back into the room. "What can't you do?" she asked.

Ryan turned with a grin. "I just told Tory that if you start driving her nuts, she should send you home. She said that she couldn't."

Tory's embarrassment showed, but Cynthia Hooker's only response was a grin.

"You listen to me, Ryan Hooker, I know how to mind my own business...and my manners, which is more than I can say for you." And then she winked at Tory. "We'll get along fine. As soon as I know I'm not needed, I'll be gone."

"This is Brett's home. You're welcome to stay as long as you like," Tory said.

Neither Ryan nor Cynthia missed the reference to the apartment being Brett's home and not *their* home. They exchanged a look but remained silent.

A few minutes later Ryan was gone, and soon afterward, Tory left for the hospital, leaving Cynthia alone with her thoughts. She no longer worried about her son's recovery, but she couldn't help but be concerned about the extent to which

Tory Lancaster kept to herself. She had learned to care for the young woman, but she didn't want her son's heart to get broken.

Brett was in high spirits. He'd just gotten a call from the D.A.'s office that was better than a week's worth of antibiotics. Harold Tribbey had come through for them with flying colors. Manny Riberosa had been found guilty of murder, and Gus Huffman was still talking, although Romeo Leeds was nowhere to be found. While there was a warrant out for his arrest, Brett wondered if it would ever be served. Romeo Leeds had undoubtedly skipped the country. Brett leaned back on his pillow with a satisfied smile on his face. Sometimes the good guys *did* win. And then the door opened, and his smile widened.

"Tory, baby, I didn't think you would ever get here. Did you bring it?" he asked.

She glanced over her shoulder as the door swung shut and then pulled a white paper sack out of the bag on her shoulder.

"I saw a doctor down the hall. I think they're about to make rounds."

He reached for the bag, then grabbed her wrist instead, pulling her closer, then inhaling slowly as their lips met. The connection sent a heat wave of longing throughout his body. His fingers cupped the back of her neck, urging her closer, then closer still. He heard her gasp; then he heard her sigh. When she murmured his name between breaths, he physically ached with the need to be in her.

"I miss you," he said softly, and felt her tremble.

"Oh, Brett, I miss you, too."

This was getting too serious and way out of hand. Brett took a deep breath and a mental step back. No need starting something he couldn't finish.

"How about those doughnuts?" he asked, and dug into the sack, taking a big bite out of one with raspberry filling.

Tory smiled, but Brett's next question wiped it off her face.

"So how are you and the family getting along?"

"Did you know Ryan left today?"

Brett chewed thoughtfully, considering the fact that she hadn't answered.

"Yes, I know, honey. He called me before he left."

"Oh."

He took another bite. "What do you think of Mom?"

She smiled. "She loves her family very much, doesn't she?"

Again she'd circumvented his question by asking another, and he knew Tory well enough not to press.

"How's the article coming?"

She looked away, then back again. "I haven't done much since you...since we've..."

Brett dropped the doughnut back into the sack and took her hand. "Tory, look at me."

She did as he asked.

"I'm going to be fine. You know that, don't you?"

She nodded.

"And your deadline is, what...two weeks away?"

"More like one now."

He grinned. "Well then, get your pretty ass home and get busy. I don't need you to hold my hand while someone else pokes holes in my butt with a needle. There are guards on my door that I do not need, and I am no longer unconscious on an hourly basis. Do what you have to do, okay?"

Tory sighed. He had no idea how much he'd needed those guards, but she wasn't about to be the one to break the news. Besides, it was all she could do to go home at night. Leaving him alone during the day, too, would make her crazy.

"But I—"

"No buts, Victoria. I love you. When I come home, I'd like to think there was nothing standing in our way of making love but my mother, because

I can always send her home. At that point, I would like your undivided attention, at least for a while. Okay?"

She nodded and then kissed him again. This time, when she straightened, they were both breathing hard.

"Brett?"

"What?"

"Do you know when that might be?"

"When what might be baby?"

"When you might get to come home?"

He laughed and then winced as the stitches pulled. "These come out tomorrow," he said, tapping his chest. "And then a day or two in therapy. After that, I can come back on an outpatient basis for the rest of my rehabilitation."

She touched his arm. "I've been afraid to ask. Will you...I mean, will it..."

His eyes darkened. "I'll be fine. One hundred percent fine," he said, and watched her sigh with relief.

"Okay, then. I guess I'll go."

When she paused at the door then looked back, he blew her a kiss, then dug the doughnut out of the sack.

"Eat fast," she warned him. "The doctor is just one room down."

There was a smile on her face all the way to the elevator. When he'd stuffed the rest of the doughnut into his mouth, he'd left a trail of powdered sugar all over his belly. She didn't have the heart to tell Brett that when the doctor came in, he was bound to get caught.

Another thunderstorm was brewing on the horizon as Tory shut and locked the doors leading out to the balcony. Cynthia was taking a shower, and the television was off. The silence was a welcome respite from the endless chatter of a houseguest. She glanced at the pictures strewn over the coffee table and sat down heavily. As always, her gaze slid right back to the man in the crowd, and her heart gave a thump before it hit a regular rhythm.

"Why?" she muttered. "What in hell is so special about your face? Why can't I let you go?"

But there were no answers, either from the man or the picture. Not even from the enlargements that she'd made. All she had was the image of a used-up old man with a tattoo on his cheek—and a scorpion, at that.

She tossed the picture aside and picked up her notes. It was time to get down to business.

Rain fell from the sky without the usual accompaniment—no thunder, no lightning, no wind. It splattered upon roofs and flowed into gutters, washing away the heat of the day and the grime from the streets.

Miles away in the hospital, Brett lay without sleeping, listening to it rain and remembering another night and Tory's nightmare that had followed a storm. His gut clenched as he thought of her, alone in their bed.

Please God, watch over her while I can't.

And then he closed his eyes and gave in to sleep.

Cynthia Hooker slept comfortably on the living room couch, oblivious of the weather or anything else. Her rest was deep, her sleep, dreamless, unaware that in the next room Tory was wrestling with her demons, and this time, she was all alone.

The jumping rope slapped the hard-packed dirt like little dry bullets, churning up the dust as the child skipped to the beat of the rope and the rhyme.

"Pease porridge hot. Pease porridge cold. Pease porridge inapot, nine days old."

She didn't know what it meant, but everyone said it when they skipped rope, that's how she knew it was the right thing to say. And then she stumbled on the rope and missed a step.

"Shoot," she muttered, and flung down the rope, tired of the game. She gave the rope a final kick and then looked around, suddenly realizing

that Sweet Baby was no longer in sight. Her heart skipped a beat as she began to look around, unable to remember where she'd last had her dolly.

The back door slammed, and she looked up. Someone was standing on the porch and dangling Sweet Baby from the railing. She could see the yellow yarn pigtails and the blue gingham dress from here.

"Don't drop her!" she cried, and started to run.

She ran and she ran until her side started to hurt, and she was still no closer to the porch than she'd been when she started. She looked again and then started to cry. They'd thrown Sweet Baby up into the air.

She stopped, staring up in silent horror as the dolly reached the top of her arc and then started to fall, tumbling pigtails over heels toward the ground below.

"No!" she screamed. "Don't throw her away! Don't throw her away!"

The scream woke them both at the same time, and Tory knew before she got out of bed that Cynthia would be in the room within seconds. She was proved right when seconds later Cynthia burst into the room and turned on the lights.

"Victoria! Are you all right?"

Tory slumped to the side of the bed and covered

her face, unwilling for Cynthia to see the tears on her cheeks.

"I'm sorry I woke you. It was just a bad dream."

Cynthia had raised three children, and not once had she ever heard a nightmare with an accompanying scream such as that one had been. It had been a cry from the heart. A shriek of despair such as nothing she'd ever known. Her heart was still pounding as she sat down beside Tory and took her hand.

"Sweetheart, I know you're uncomfortable with me here." When Tory would have argued, Cynthia shushed her by gently smoothing the hair from her face and patting her arm. "No, it's okay. We both know I'm right." And then she tilted Tory's chin. "Look at me, Tory."

Tory did, but unwillingly. She didn't want this conversation to be happening. Once she'd had a foster mother who'd pretended to be nice, and the next thing Tory remembered, they'd shipped her off to another place because she was too much trouble.

Cynthia hardly knew where to start, but for Brett's sake, as well as theirs, the relationship had to start somewhere.

"You know that talking about bad dreams makes them go away."

Tory sighed. Brett had tried this, too. It hadn't

helped then, and it wouldn't help now. But Cynthia had no way of knowing that.

"I can't talk about them," Tory said.

"I've heard a lot of things in my life, and I can tell you that nothing surprises me anymore," Cynthia reassuring her.

"No, you don't understand," Tory explained. "I can't talk about them because, once I wake, I never remember them."

Cynthia frowned. Anything that would elicit a scream such as the one she'd heard couldn't possibly be forgotten. Either Tory was hiding the truth, or the truth was buried so deeply inside of her that even she didn't remember. She patted Tory on the knee.

"Do you have them often?"

"Only recently," Tory admitted, and then wondered why she hadn't thought of that before.

"Do you know what triggered them? You know…has something frightened you recently, or did you see something that made you remember something from your childhood?"

Tory shrugged. "I don't remember much about my childhood," she said. "Foster homes aren't all that memorable."

Cynthia had known about that part of Tory's life, but hearing the monotone timbre of her voice made her worry. No emotion. That was it. It seemed as if Tory were afraid to show emotion.

"What happened to your parents?" Cynthia asked.

Something whispered in the back of Tory's mind. A warning or a memory—she didn't know which—but the question brought her off the bed and onto her feet.

"I don't remember anything or anyone before the second grade. For all I know I never had any. All I remember are the foster homes. I think I'll make some cocoa. Want some?" She headed to the kitchen without waiting for Cynthia's answer.

Cynthia sat on the side of the bed, watching as Tory left the room. Even though she knew Tory was only going as far as the kitchen, she was moving too fast to be casual. Running. That was what it looked like to Cynthia. Tory Lancaster was running away.

Seven

Tory poured and measured the milk, sugar and cocoa without thought. When *had* the first nightmare come?

After I came home from the last trip.

How long after? Two days? Three? When had... then she paused, the spoon dangling from her fingers.

After I developed the film. That's when they started. After I developed the film!

The milk began to bubble at the edge of the pan, but she was still lost in thought.

Why then? Was it the carnival atmosphere? No. I'd been messing with them for six weeks. It couldn't have been the carnivals.

The milk continued to heat, now bubbling rapidly throughout.

Was it something Brett said? Was it something he did?

She remembered him coming home with his hand skinned and bruised from a fight at some bar.

Did that trigger some fear in me?

The milk started to scorch, but Tory wasn't aware. She'd just remembered something else.

The man from the photo. The one with the tattoo.

"Tory! The milk is burning!"

Tory blinked, then looked down. "Oh no," she muttered, and yanked the pan off the stove, but it was too late to save it from ruin.

Cynthia laughed. "That's okay by me. I'd rather have a good cold pop any day."

"Help yourself," Tory said, and began cleaning up her mess while Cynthia rummaged in the refrigerator. And even as she worked, Tory couldn't turn loose of the possibility that her guess had been right.

Could it be? Could that man's face have triggered my dreams? And if it did, then why?

But tonight was not the time to follow up on the idea, and truth be told, neither was tomorrow. Until Brett came home and Cynthia left—until her deadline was met and her world was back to normal—she had no time to dwell on herself. Afterward, maybe. But until then, Brett came first. With a sigh of defeat, she ran the pan full of cold water and turned.

"Cynthia, I'm going back to bed now, okay?"

Cynthia stepped back from the refrigerator with a can of pop in her hand, then set it on the counter and gave Tory a hug.

"Are you going to be all right?"

Tory nodded. "It was just a dream. It's over."

Cynthia smiled and then brushed a loose strand of hair from Tory's forehead. "You're a very brave girl, aren't you?"

Tory was embarrassed and tried to pass off the compliment by making fun of herself. "How so? By screaming into the night about dreams that can't hurt me? That doesn't sound very brave to me."

Cynthia shook her head. "You took on a killer with no thought for yourself, tackling him bare-handed at Brett's bedside."

"I could no more have stood by and let that man hurt Brett than I could have hurt Brett myself. Of course I tried to stop him. So would you, if you'd been there."

"Still, don't belittle your own accomplishments, my dear. What I'm getting at is, I think you suffer your wounds silently. That is a very brave thing to do."

Tory tried to smile, to laugh off what Brett's mother had said, but when she tried, she choked up instead.

Cynthia could see that Tory was having a difficult time accepting the praise, but she felt it had needed to be said.

"Run along to bed now," she said gently. "And sleep well. I'll be nearby if you need me, okay?"

Tory nodded and slipped away, thankful to be out from under the woman's scrutiny but inexplicably touched, as well.

A couple of Brett's old precinct buddies had just left, and the room was once again quiet. With the intensive care nurse no longer needed at his side, and the guards still sitting outside his door, his visitors were few and far between. And it was his own fault that Tory was absent. He'd been the one who'd sent her home so she could meet her deadline. He snorted beneath his breath and then winced as he stretched his arm to turn on the TV. Being noble had its drawbacks. He missed her like hell.

When the door swung open, he looked up in anticipation. Even the arrival of a lab tech was a welcome respite.

"Hey, Dracula. Did you come for more blood?"

The lab tech laughed and wiggled his eyebrows in a mock leer. "You can always tell when a patient is about ready to go home. They start getting a smart mouth."

Brett grinned. "So sue me."

The lab tech tied a thin strip of rubber around Brett's arm and then pulled it tight. "I'd rather draw blood."

Brett stretched out his arm. "Why am I not surprised?"

The lab tech smiled. "After everything that's happened to you, I don't think a vial of blood is much to bitch about."

A wry grin tilted the corner of Brett's mouth. "That's one way of looking at it, all right."

"Does that kind of thing happen often in your line of work?" he asked.

Brett frowned. "You mean, getting shot at? No, not really. At least, not since I quit the force."

The tech nodded. "Then you must feel twice blessed," he said. "Having two attempts made on your life in two days is pushing your luck, if you ask me."

Brett's frown deepened. "Two?"

"Yeah, you know. The guy who snuck into your room with that syringe full of poison. The way I heard it, if it hadn't been for your wife, you'd be pushing up daisies."

The blood drained from Brett's face, but the lab tech was too busy talking to notice. *Wife?* The only woman who came close to fitting that description was Tory. He had little or no memory of the first few days after surgery. Just what the hell had been happening?

"Well, adios until next time," the tech said, then took his tray and left.

Brett reached for the phone.

* * *

Tory hadn't been gone more than five minutes when the telephone rang. Cynthia reached for a towel, drying her hands as she reached for the phone.

"Hello?"

"Mom, it's me."

Her face broke into smiles. "Brett, darling, it's so good to hear your voice. How are you feeling today? Tory's on her way to the hospital now, and I'd planned to come over this afternoon. If you need anything, just let me know, okay?"

He shifted the phone to his other ear. "Yes, I need something," he muttered. "I need to know about someone making a second attempt on my life. I want to know what the hell Tory had to do with it, and why no one saw fit to tell me a damned thing about it!"

Cynthia sighed. When Brett got angry, there was never any reasoning with him.

"You'll just have to take that up with your doctors and Victoria," she said. "They decided you were on a need-to-know program of healing, and that you didn't need to know about something that you slept through anyway."

"Jesus Christ! What kind of cockamamy reasoning is—"

"Brett Hooker! Do not take the Lord's name in vain!"

He sighed. "I'm sorry."

"You nearly died, young man!"

His sigh deepened. Too late, he remembered he was yelling at the wrong woman.

"Yes, ma'am. So I've been told."

"The fact that you are still alive is entirely Victoria's doing."

He blanched. "Look, I just—"

"No, you look! She'll be there shortly. Whatever you have to say, you can take up with her. But if I hear that you've yelled at her, I'll deal with you personally later, do you hear me?"

Brett sighed. He might be thirty-six years old, but right now, he felt about six.

"Yes, ma'am. I hear you loud and clear."

Cynthia smiled. "That's good. Now...I love you, dear. Rest easy and have a wonderful day."

When she disconnected, Brett felt as if he'd just been given a reprieve. That was his mom. Tear a strip off of one side of a man's body while kissing the other for good luck. Meanwhile, Tory was on her way here, and his mom had been right about one thing. The last person he needed to be blaming was Tory. If the truth was anything close to the story he'd been told, he should be kissing the ground she walked on instead.

He picked up the phone again, this time calling someone he knew would tell him the unvarnished truth. When the receptionist answered, he was ready and waiting.

"This is Hooker," he said. "Is Mr. Lacey in?"

* * *

Traffic had been terrible. By the time Tory got to the hospital and parked, she was tired and tense, and the day was only a few hours old. The parking attendant called her by name, and as she walked through the lobby toward the elevators, a janitor grinned and waved, while another hospital employee called a hello.

As she paused at the elevators, waiting for a car to arrive, a volunteer came around the corner with a cart full of magazines and flowers. Tory shifted her purse to her other shoulder and stepped out of the way. But when the volunteer recognized her, she didn't seem inclined to hurry on.

"Hey there," she said, grinning widely at Tory. "If it isn't the Terminator."

Tory managed a smile. It wasn't the first time she'd been teased about taking on a hit man single-handedly.

"Good morning," she said, and wished to goodness that the elevator would hurry. She wasn't in any mood for chitchat, but obviously the other woman was.

"It's good to see how well your husband is recovering," she said.

Tory didn't bother to correct her about her relationship with Brett. She'd tried before. It was easier just to let the reference slide.

"Yes, ma'am. It's an answer to a prayer." And then she leaned closer to Tory, as if sharing a confidence with an old friend. "I was just up there a few minutes ago. He must be feeling real good this morning."

"Why so?"

The woman grinned. "You know how men are. The better they feel, the louder they yell."

Tory's face blanched. "Brett was yelling?"

"I could hear him all the way out in the hall." And then she realized she'd probably said more than she should. "But, of course, I couldn't hear what he was saying. I was just passing by, you know."

The elevator finally arrived, saving a thankful Tory from having to make any more polite conversation. But all the way up to the fourth floor, she kept wondering why Brett had been mad.

Brett's pulse accelerated when he heard Tory greeting the guards outside his door. He took a deep breath and made himself relax. *Calm. Stay calm. Take it easy. Don't overreact.*

And then she opened the door and came inside. The smile on her face was as welcome as sunshine after a week of cold rain. He'd been lonesome for her. Missing her laughter. Missing the sound of her voice and the touch of her hand. And the first thing he did was complain.

"When did you plan on telling me?" he growled.

Tory's smile slipped sideways. *Uh-oh.*

"Telling you what?"

"Victoria, don't play games. I'm not in the mood."

She panicked. *He knows.* And then her own ire rose as she shifted her stance.

"And I wasn't in the mood to watch you be murdered."

He blanched. Put like that, there was little he could say that wouldn't make him sound like a heel. He took a deep breath, then held out his hand.

"Come here." When she didn't budge, he added. "Please."

She dropped her purse on the chair by the door, and moments later she was in his arms.

"My God, baby, you could have been killed."

"You were worth the risk."

He closed his eyes and held her closer, letting himself absorb her by feel, rather than sight.

"If anything had happened to you because of me..."

She pushed herself out of his arms, making him face her, making him accept the truth.

"If I hadn't done what I had, there wouldn't be any you."

He sighed. "As stingy as it sounds, all I can say is thank you."

She smiled. "You're welcome."

He pulled her to him, urging her closer until she was sitting on the edge of his bed.

"Tell me what happened? Are you all right? Did he hurt you when—"

She stood up and did a quick turn. "I'm fine, see? No bruises, no scars." And then she grinned. "But you oughta see the other guy."

Brett's eyebrows rose. "What happened?"

"They had to sew him up before they could arrest him."

Brett began to grin. This was a side of Tory he hadn't known existed.

"You're feeling kind of frisky about the whole thing, aren't you?"

She put her hands on her hips, trying for a Wonder Woman pose. "Around here, they call me the Terminator now."

His grin widened. "Are you kidding me?"

She didn't smile back. "No, I'm not. After I'm gone, you just ask the first person who comes into this room. You'll see."

"But how?"

"Let's just say, if we'd been playing football, there would have been penalty flags all over the field."

Brett laughed. "How so?"

"I tackled him below the belt and from behind." Then she frowned. "Maybe I've got football penalties mixed up with boxing rules." She shrugged. "Oh well, you know me. I never was much good at sports."

Brett was still laughing when the door to his room opened. Tory turned just as another volunteer came in with a large vase of flowers. His room was already full of plants and bouquets from friends and family, but she never tired of the surprise of the arrivals. The woman smiled and waved as she left.

"Ooh, how pretty," Tory cried. "You have some more flowers. I wonder who these are from."

Brett grabbed her hand before she could get the card. "Come here," he begged. "I'm still waiting for my kiss."

She leaned forward, willingly going where he begged her to be. Their lips met, and the kiss began, lingering far longer than the welcome he'd intended.

"Umm," Brett groaned, when they finally parted. "That just makes me wish we were home alone."

She sighed. "We'd better think of something else to do besides that." Then she turned to the flowers. "Want me to hand you the card?"

"I know who they're from."

She smiled. "Don't tell me you're getting psychic on me now? How can you know who sent you flowers?"

"They're not for me," he said softly. "They're for you."

Startled, she looked deep in his eyes, to the love waiting there, and felt a lump forming in the back of her throat. She reached for the card, holding her breath as she slipped it out of the envelope.

"Thank you for loving me, Brett."

The lump was too big now for words to pass. She looked at him once. The guilt that was always within her was growing, choking off whatever brilliant remark she might have made. Loving Brett Hooker was easy. It was staying with him that was hard. Her voice was trembling, her heart so full of love for this man that it hurt to breathe. But, as always, he was waiting. Waiting for her.

"You're welcome, you know." She sighed. "You make it easy."

And then she was in his arms, her cheek near his chest, cherishing the steady beat of his heart beneath her ear.

Cynthia tacked up the loose end of the sign she'd just had made at a local copy shop and then stepped back to view her work.

Welcome Home Brett!

"There now. What do you think?"

Tory turned to look and then smiled at Brett's mother. "I think he'll get the message."

Cynthia grinned, pleased with herself and her work. "Is there anything else I can help you with? Do we have enough soft drinks? Should I get another loaf of bread?"

Tory shook her head. "No, I think everything's under control." *Except me.*

But Tory didn't voice her fears aloud. A woman as centered as Cynthia Hooker wouldn't understand.

Tory had counted on being the one to bring Brett home from the hospital, but Ryan had come back this morning, insisting that he be the one, and she'd quietly complied.

She'd also planned on bringing Brett home to peace and quiet, not a party. But Cynthia hadn't agreed. Added to that, Brett's sister, Celia, her husband and their new baby would also be here.

She kept thinking, if only she could be somewhere else when they got here, but she couldn't bear to miss seeing Brett walk in the door. A few weeks ago she'd feared that might never happen. After being reassured he would pull through, she'd lived for the day when he would come back to the apartment…and to her.

And the resentment she felt toward his family added guilt to the problems she was already facing. She didn't begrudge Brett his family, but she didn't want to be in the middle of it. With all of them here together, she felt an underlying pressure to belong, and she *didn't* belong—not even to herself. In the midst of her troubled thoughts, the doorbell rang. Before Tory could react, Cynthia headed for the door.

"It's too early for Brett. That must be Tom and Celia and the baby," she said.

Tory's stomach lurched. More family.

Cynthia had been right. Her daughter's family entered the apartment in a whirlwind of diaper bags and laughter, and as Tory waited for an introduction, she had a sensation of walls closing in on her, minute by minute. She heard Cynthia saying her name and made herself smile. There was nowhere to turn and nowhere to run.

Brett rode with ease, comfortable with Ryan's driving and the fact that he was finally going home. The day was almost balmy, unusual for this time of year. As they drove through the residential neighborhood leading to his apartment complex, he saw the world in which he'd been living and began to realize how much of life he'd been taking for granted. Everything was the same as it had been for the last seven years, but he was seeing it anew.

The flowers and shrubs bordering the walks and houses were vivid splashes of color against dark, green lawns. He saw children laughing and playing in the city pool they'd just passed, an old man walking his dog. His gaze centered on a young boy riding his bike, and he took a slow, deep breath, savoring the gift of life.

Ryan gave Brett a nervous glance. "You okay?"

Brett nodded. "Just happy to be here."

"No more than we are to have you, brother."

Brett looked away. He heard the emotion in his brother's voice. It would have been too easy to let his own emotions run away with him. But not today. Today was a day for celebration. Today he was alive and going home to Tory. The thought of her made him weak inside.

"Hey, Ryan."

"What?"

"How's Tory taking all this?"

Ryan frowned. "You mean, you getting shot?"

"No, I mean all the uproar at home."

Ryan looked nervous. The coming-home party was supposed to be a surprise. If it was ruined, Mom would blame him.

"What uproar?" he asked.

Brett grinned. "Come on, we both know Mom. And don't worry, I'll pretend to be surprised." Then he sighed. "I'm just worried about Tory. She isn't very big on gatherings of any kind."

Ryan's frown deepened. "Why the hell not?"

Brett shook his head. "I don't know. I think it has something to do with her childhood."

"You've lived with that woman for three years, and you still don't know her, do you?"

"I know enough," Brett said shortly. "Look, we're almost home."

Ryan heard the warning in his brother's voice and knew he'd said enough.

"Remember, I didn't say a word about this," Ryan muttered, as they pulled into the apartment complex and parked.

The closer they got to Brett's apartment, the more anxious he became. The sounds of laughter drifted down the hall toward them, and just for a moment he wished he were coming back alone. As much as he loved his family, he needed some time alone with Tory. His beautiful woman. His love.

He thought of her smile and the way she bit her bottom lip when she was concentrating. His stomach knotted, remembering the slow, deep breath she took as he entered her body. He remembered the shadows in her eyes—the ones that hid secrets she didn't know how to share. Tory. His Tory.

Ryan paused at the door and rang the bell. "We're here," he said. "Act surprised."

And then Cynthia opened the door and they were swept up in the moment.

* * *

Tory had her hands in dishwater when the doorbell rang. Before she could reach for a towel, someone else beat her to the door. Defeated before she'd had a chance to start, all she could do was watch as Brett's family engulfed him and try not to let her disappointment show.

"Welcome home! Welcome home!"

The shouts came at Brett from every direction, and accepted them gladly, smiling and answering the questions thrown at him as he pretended to be surprised, all the while looking for Tory. And then he saw her, standing in the doorway between the kitchen and the living room, a little apart from the rest of the crowd, as usual. Their gazes met and held. Brett exhaled slowly, only then realizing he'd been holding his breath. He gave his sister, Celia, a brotherly pat.

"Excuse me, sis, but there's one welcome home kiss I don't want to miss."

Everyone turned to look at Tory and then suddenly found something else that needed to be done. Before Brett could move, Tory was in his arms, touching his face, his chest, then taking his hand and holding it against her cheek. Her eyes were filled with tears she refused to shed, but there was a smile on her face.

"Welcome home," she said softly.

Brett groaned beneath his breath, then tilted her chin and kissed her. Her lips were soft, yielding to the demands of his own, and he wrapped his arms around her shoulders, enfolding her within an inescapable embrace.

"Be careful," Tory whispered, lightly touching his shoulder as a reminder of his injury.

Brett looked down at her and grinned. "No, baby, you're the one who'd better be careful. Something tells me you're in danger of being had. Do you remember what I told you just before I left here three weeks ago?"

She answered without missing a beat. "You told me to 'hold that thought.'"

He chuckled. "Good girl. You were paying attention."

She smiled. "I never forget the things that matter."

"I'll hold you to that promise later," he whispered, and put his arm around her, refusing to let her pull away as he headed toward the living room and the party that was going on.

Even as Tory let herself be led into the midst of his family, her own words began to haunt her.

Never forget the things that matter. Never forget. Never forget.

Then why couldn't she remember the tattooed man from the picture? It was obvious there was something about him that had triggered a memory from her past. So why...why in God's name, couldn't she remember?

* * *

The apartment was quiet. At Brett's request, Ryan had hustled the entire family to a nearby motel to spend the night, giving him and Tory some much needed breathing space. And now he stood within the silence of his home, aware of the sounds of the city beyond the walls, but even more aware of his woman within. He shrugged his shoulder, gently rotating the muscles to test for soreness, then winced when they pulled. The evening had been long and tiring, and he had several more weeks of therapy before he would regain full mobility. But he was filled with a sense of peace.

In the next room, Tory was taking a shower. She, too, had been exhausted by the events of the last three weeks. Her space had been thoroughly invaded, and yet Brett was surprised at how well she seemed to have adapted. Hope sprang in his heart as he headed for the bedroom. Even if they didn't understand her, his family genuinely liked her, and from what he could tell, she liked them, as well.

His thoughts were interrupted as the sounds of running water suddenly ceased. At that moment, everything else in this world became insignificant compared to the fact that he and Tory were finally alone.

Water droplets clung to the tips of Tory's hair as she stepped out of the shower, blindly reaching for a towel. Instead of terry cloth, her hand connected with the unyielding force of a hard, naked body, and her eyes flew open. Brett! Her gaze locked on the fire in his eyes and then instinctively moved to the red and healing wound on his shoulder.

"Don't," he said softly, and pulled her against him.

She closed her eyes, momentarily yielding to his insistence. "Oh, Brett, I'm afraid."

He nuzzled the lobe of her ear, licking the moisture from her skin in slow, sensuous strokes. "Of what?" he growled.

She reached toward his shoulder. "Of hurting you."

He paused, then guided her hand downward. "The only way you can hurt me is if we stop now."

Tory's fingers encircled him, taking in the fullness of his arousal. The need to be with him was strong within her, to feel alive again within this man's embrace. Her conscience told her they should wait, but her need for this man was greater as she let herself be led into the bedroom. As he urged her down to the bed, she remembered the clean sheets she'd put on it only this morning.

"Oh, Brett, I'm all wet."

He eased a hand between her legs and smiled

when she groaned. "Ooh, baby, you sure are," he whispered, and lowered his head.

Scratch. Scratch. Scratch.

The little girl hovered in the darkness, her eyes closed, her hands pressed tightly to her ears. But no matter how hard she tried, the sounds came closer and closer.

Scratch. Scratch. Scratch.

In terror, she opened her eyes, watching as they crawled up the walls and dropped from the ceiling. Black ones. Brown ones. Even long, blood-red ones. Little ones. Big ones. Their spiny-looking tails hooked over their backs as they scurried about on little claw feet.

One fell on her shoulder and then another on her skirt. In a panic, she brushed them away. There was nowhere to run and nowhere to hide. She began backing into the closet behind her, moving farther and farther, until there was nowhere left to go. She held her breath, pretending that if they couldn't hear her, they couldn't find her. But it was no use. The scorpions! They were everywhere...and they were coming for her.

Tory woke with a jerk and sat up in bed, swallowing the scream before it came out of her mouth. Sweat streamed from her body as she crawled out of bed and reached for her robe. Careful not to disturb Brett's sleep, she opened the sliding doors and slipped out of the bedroom and onto the balcony beyond. Outside, the air was heavy and still. She glanced up at the sky, wishing it would rain. Rain was good. Rain washed away all things ugly. She took a deep breath and closed her eyes. But instead of feeling better that she was no longer enclosed, she felt edgier. She was scared. Something was going on inside her head that she couldn't control. It was getting to the point where she dreaded the night. Every time she went to bed and closed her eyes, she saw that scorpion tattoo on that old man's face. Even when she was awake, her thoughts were never far from the image of his face in the crowd.

She glanced back into the bedroom behind her, watching Brett as he slept. Her beloved. She looked back to the streets and the city beyond, thinking back to last week and the day he'd come home from the hospital. She'd been ill at ease within the uproar of his loving family, and yet she'd so wanted to be a part of it.

His mother had been the last to leave, and even as she was bidding them both goodbye, Tory had felt herself pulling away from the love the woman offered. In that moment, a revelation came. Tory's breath caught in the back of her throat as tears filmed her view of the city by night.

Why won't I let myself be loved?

The sudden scream of a siren pierced the night, and Tory shivered. Somewhere, someone else was in danger...or in need.

God be with them...and those they love.

An urgency came over her, a need to reconnect with Brett. To touch him, to hold him, to know that his body was warm and alive and she was in his arms. She turned around and slipped back into the bedroom as silently as she'd come out, crawling back into bed with Brett, then sighing with satisfaction as he resettled himself up against her.

But even though she knew she was safe behind these walls and lying in the arms of a man who loved her, the anxiety within her wouldn't ease. She watched the night sky until it began to turn. Long before it was daylight, Tory knew what she needed to do.

Brett woke with a suddenness that startled him and he realized he was alone in the bed. Since he'd come home from the hospital, it wasn't uncommon for Tory to let him sleep in, but there was an emptiness within the house that hadn't been there when he had gone to sleep. He glanced over at the closet. The door was standing ajar, and he knew without looking that some of her clothes would be gone.

No, Tory. Not now!

He rolled out of bed and reached for his sweats, pulling them on with impatience as he strode toward the living room. It was as empty as the pit of his stomach. Anger surged within him as he searched the apartment, room by room, looking for a note, praying for an explanation. There was none. He barged into her darkroom, flipping on the lights as he went, and then stopped in midstep, too stunned to move.

They were everywhere—hanging from hooks, pinned to the walls, lying on tables, tossed aside on the floor. Dozens upon dozens of the same image: oversize blowups of an old man's face and the curl-tailed scorpion tattooed upon his cheek.

He picked one up, then another and another, swallowing a fear he couldn't name as he stood within the small enclosed space, imagining Tory in here, creating and recreating the same image over and over. But why? His hands were shaking as he looked into that old man's face.

"I wish to God you could talk, because Tory won't."

Then he tossed the pictures aside and walked out, closing Tory's devils inside.

He stood within the silence of his apartment, listening to the ticking of a clock and the echoes of a dying relationship. He didn't know what to do anymore. There was nothing left inside of him with which to fight. And even if there had been, he couldn't fight what he couldn't see. There was something within Tory that wouldn't let her believe—not in him—not even in herself.

Being shot was nothing to the pain inside him now. For three years he'd been living with an on-again, off-again love. And because he loved her, he'd taken what she was willing to give. But in the last few moments, Brett had had a revelation he could no longer ignore. He would never deny that Victoria Lancaster was the love of his life, but he was no longer convinced he was hers.

He looked around the apartment, noting what little bits and pieces of Tory had been left behind. A tortoiseshell hair comb on the coffee table. An empty film container in the trash. Extra prints of the piece she'd just written. Little things. Unimportant things. He sighed. It was always the same. Each time she left, she took everything with her that mattered.

And in that moment, the truth hit. Brett staggered to a nearby chair and dropped into it. He was part of what she kept leaving behind.

Oh God.

He leaned forward, then covered his face with his hands. Maybe he'd been going about loving Victoria Lancaster all wrong. Maybe he shouldn't have pressured her to move in with him all those years ago. Something was terribly wrong with this picture or she wouldn't keep leaving him over and over without so much as a word.

He stared at the floor without moving as the day began to pass. Noon came and went, and he ignored the hunger pangs in his belly, instead walking the floor and wrestling with his conscience and his heart. Night came, and he let it close in around him without turning on lights, taking what little comfort he could draw from the refuge of darkness.

Sometime during the early morning hours, he went to bed. His heart was heavy, but his reasoning sure. He knew what he had to do. He'd learned the hard way how precious and brief life could be. Even if it broke his heart into a million pieces, he was going to give Tory her space. The only way he knew how to do that was to be gone when she came back. The lease on the apartment was paid up until the end of the year, so her things would be safe here until she returned. He would leave his new address and phone number with the manager, in case she wanted to find him. Other than that, Brett Hooker was through playing games.

Tory drove without conscious thought, retracing her journey with the carnival circuit. From her notes, she had pinpointed the town in which the crowd shot had been taken. It was Dellpoint, Iowa. But she had no way of knowing if the old man in the picture had been with the carnival, or if he was a local. And she also had to face the fact that he could have been someone just passing through—a total stranger to everyone concerned. But the urgency to find answers kept her moving northward.

A stack of reprints of the old man's face was on the seat beside her. When she got there, she would start passing them around. Maybe, just maybe, she would get lucky.

She passed an Oklahoma highway-patrol car as she crossed the border into Kansas and thought of Brett.

I should have waited. I should have talked to him. He deserves to know what's happening to me.

And then she sighed in defeat. There wasn't anything to tell, because she didn't know what was happening. All she would do was make more trouble for him while he was trying to get well.

What could I say? I have dreams? Everyone has dreams. But I dream about bad things I can't even remember. How do I know they're bad? Because I wake up choking on my own sobs and screams.

She glanced down at the road map beside her and then back up at the highway as an emptiness seized her. She didn't know why or how she knew it, but somehow that old man held the answers to a life's worth of questions. But if she couldn't find him, then this time, when she went home, she would make an appointment to see a psychiatrist. Brett deserved a whole woman, not someone who was afraid to love. She shuddered. The thought of losing him was impossible to consider. He was the anchor in her world.

Dellpoint, Iowa, population 1,354, was corn belt country. An unlikely place for a man with a scorpion tattoo on his face to reside. Two days after leaving Oklahoma, she pulled up to the only motel in town, breathing a sigh of relief as she got out of the car. She would get a room, then call Brett. If he wasn't home, she would leave him a message.

The man behind the desk gave her a studied look as she walked into the office.

"Afternoon, ma'am. Be needin' a room?"

She nodded and slid a picture of the old man's face across the counter.

"No smoking room, please," she said, and then added, "Have you ever seen this man?"

He picked up the picture, tilting it toward the light for a better look, then shook his head.

"Nope. Can't say as I have." Then he added. "Are you the law?"

Tory looked startled. "No. Why would you ask?"

He shrugged. "No reason, I guess, 'cept that fella looks pretty rough. Didn't figure he was any of your kin, you bein' so pretty and all."

Tory didn't know whether to be pleased by the compliment or worry even more. Her memories went only as far back as the foster homes. Before that, it was anyone's guess. And the fact was not lost on her that if the old man's face had given her nightmares, there was every possibility that he was part of the past she refused to remember.

God help me, she thought, signed the register, pocketed her key, then picked up her picture and left.

Her room was this side of pathetic, which suited her mood perfectly. The urgency to connect with Brett was even greater than before as she dumped her bag on the bed and reached for the phone. The call went through, and she counted the rings, with each one expecting to hear the sound of his voice. When it rang seven, then eight, times and even the answering machine didn't pick up, she disconnected, telling herself he had probably gone out and forgotten to turn on the machine.

She glanced at her watch. It was just past three in the afternoon. Her stomach grumbled, a complaint about the peanut butter crackers and pop that had been today's breakfast and lunch. She was hot and sweaty, and her clothes looked as if she'd slept in them, which she had. As badly as she wanted to start her search, there were some priorities that needed to be observed. If she wanted to be taken seriously, she probably needed a bath, a change of clothes and then food.

She got up from the bed, undoing her clothes

as she walked toward the bathroom. Moments later, she was standing beneath the showerhead, massaging shampoo into her hair while the jets of hot water peppered her skin. As the water sluiced down her body, washing away the grit and the dust, she kept wishing it would be this easy to wash away the ghosts of her past.

Once she'd asked one of her foster mothers where she was from, and the woman had laughed in her face, telling her she'd be better off worrying about where she was going to wind up if she didn't hurry and finish her chores. After that, she had stifled her curiosity and focused on getting through life...one day at a time.

Eight

It took Tory less than two hours to cover the entire business section of Dellpoint, Iowa. One bank, one pharmacy, two grocery stores, three cafés, four convenience stores, five beauty shops and a barbershop later, she didn't know any more than she had when she started.

She'd faxed a copy of the old man's picture to Amherst Entertainment, the carnival she'd been shooting, but had little hopes of getting a favorable reply. She already knew that while some of the carnie crowd stayed in the business for years, many of the workers were transients who often left without notice. So when she headed toward her motel, her hopes were close to zero. There was a feed store on the outskirts of town that she had yet to visit, and a bar on the north side of the city limits sign that didn't open until six. Other than that, she'd *done* Dellpoint, and with no sign of the tattooed man.

When she got to the motel, she noticed that a bright red pickup truck pulling a matching but empty horse trailer had parked beside her car. The smell of horse manure was evident as she headed for her room. She wrinkled her nose and then dodged the cleaning lady's cart that had been left unattended outside the room next to hers.

Remembering the threadbare towels, on impulse, she snatched up an extra towel as she passed. She tossed her bag on the chair as she locked the door behind her, then flopped down on the bed in a dejected slump. A handful of the pictures had fallen out of the bag, and the tattooed man's face and his cold, blank stare seemed to be mocking her from a distance. She couldn't get past the idea that he knew something about her life that she didn't. In anger, she flung the extra towel onto the floor, smiling grimly with satisfaction as it landed on top of the pictures, covering them up.

Disappointed with her afternoon's effort, she reached for the phone and then paused. Maybe she should wait and call Brett after she'd gone to the bar tonight. Hopefully by then she'd have something positive to tell him.

A burst of raucous laughter, followed by a round of high-pitched giggles, came from the room next to hers. She remembered the abandoned cleaning cart and the shiny red truck and sighed. If she was a betting woman, she would be laying good money on the fact that the cowboy who owned the truck was having himself a real good time with the motel's cleaning woman.

"Just put it in there," Brett said, pointing to the first room on the right, down the hall.

The movers were almost through. Only a couple more trips back to the truck and then all his worldly goods would be in his new home. He walked from room to room, surveying the added space of the house he'd just rented. He wouldn't let himself think about why he'd decided on a house instead of another apartment. He refused to admit, even to himself, that when he'd seen the renovated family room next to the master bedroom, his first thought had been what a perfect office it would make for Tory's work, and that the roomy, connecting storage room would be a great darkroom. Those thoughts didn't belong in his world anymore. Not until he knew if she really wanted him in her life.

"That's the last one," the mover said, as he set down a box marked Kitchen.

Brett nodded and reached for his checkbook. A few minutes later the movers were gone. He stood in the midst of what was left of his life and realized he had never felt so alone. Then he took a deep breath and pulled out his pocketknife. Whether Tory remained in his life remained to be seen. Meanwhile, there were things to be done.

He opened the box marked Kitchen, pulled out a phone, then plugged it into the jack. The dial tone sounded in his ear. At least one thing had gone right today. His service was on.

He punched a series of numbers, then waited.

"Hello."

At the familiar voice, Brett gripped the receiver a little tighter, then started to talk.

"Hey, Mom. It's me, Brett. Got a pen and paper handy? I want to give you my new address and number. No, nothing's wrong. I just decided I needed more space."

When Tory woke up it was just after 8:00 p.m. She had a pounding headache and a pain in her side. She wasn't surprised about the headache. She had them often. But the pain in her side gave her pause until she looked where she'd been lying. She'd fallen asleep on top of her shoe. The irony of it was that she didn't remember even pulling it off. She yawned and stretched, then put her shoe back on before heading for the bathroom. If she was going barhopping, she needed to look her best.

But a short while later, as she entered the smoke-filled establishment known only as Dump's, she decided she could have saved herself a little hair spray. From the level of the lighting and the quality of the clientele, she could have been bald and it would have gone unnoticed.

"What'll it be?" the bartender asked, as Tory slid onto a stool at the end of the bar.

She reached in her purse for a picture. "I don't want anything to drink. I just want to know if—"

"Ain't nothin' free in here," the bartender growled. "Not even the talk. What'll it be?"

Tory sighed. The bartender's apron was dirty, and so were his hands, which didn't say much for the condition of the glasses sitting in a row on the counter behind him.

"Oh, how about a Coke...in the can," she added, unwilling to take her chances with the glasses.

The bartender popped the top, slapped a napkin down in front of her and all but dropped the can on top, sending a small spray of cola fizzing up into the air above it.

"'At'll be two bucks."

Tory's dander rose at the high-handed manner in which the man had behaved. Before she thought, she slapped a picture of the tattooed man on the bar and then laid a five dollar bill down on top of it. When the bartender reached for the money, she slapped her hand on top, and then leaned forward.

"As I was about to ask earlier...do you know this man?"

The bartender grinned at her gutsy move and leaned over for a closer look.

"Hmm, yeah, he looks familiar," he muttered, then pointed to the scorpion tattoo. "Once you seen one of them, you ain't likely to forget it. Know what I mean?"

Tory's hopes rose. "What's his name? Do you know where—"

"Whoa," the bartender said. "I said he looked familiar. I didn't say as how I knew him. Lots of people come and go in a place like this. I've seen him, all right, but it's been a while back."

Tory refused to be discouraged by the small setback. "Do you know where he lives?"

He shook his head, then glanced up and around the room, narrowing his eyes to see through the smoke and shadows.

"See that man at the back pool table? That big guy wearing jeans?"

Tory stared. Four of the five men standing around the pool table were wearing jeans.

"Which one of them?" she asked.

The bartender pointed. "The one with the bald head and the eagle on his jacket."

At that point, her heart sank. It would be that one. The man was a good four inches over six feet, with a face like a road map. Even from here, she could see the scars crisscrossing his cheek, and she didn't know what bothered her most—the ring in his ear or the one in his nose.

"Yes, I see him," Tory said.

"His name's Bull. If anyone knows your man, he will."

Tory stared at the rowdy crowd of men, and for the first time since she'd started this quest, she began to realize how quickly she could get in over her head. But there was too much riding on her need to know, and she'd come too far to back out now. Besides, she reminded herself, she was good at hiding her feelings.

Well, Bull, ready or not, here I come.

Like an animal on the hunt, the man called Bull sensed her presence before he ever looked up, and then, when he did, a feral smile broke the frown he'd been wearing. Instead of taking his shot with the cue stick he was holding, he used the end to lift a lock of her hair from her breast.

"Hey, sweet thing, old Bull don't like messy hair. I like my women well-groomed," he said.

Tory glanced at his bald head and then met his stare head-on. "Yes, I can see why you would," she drawled.

Bull looked startled that she hadn't backed down, then grinned when the other men standing around the pool table began to laugh. He took the point of the pool cue and circled her breast, tapping lightly on the end of the nipple.

"Something I can do for you, honey?"

Tory grabbed the cue stick and yanked, then

flung it aside. It fell to the floor with a clatter as she pointed at him.

"For starters, you can keep your damned hands—and your stick—to yourself." Then she reached in her purse.

Before she could pull her hand out, Bull grabbed her wrist.

"Take it easy, you feisty little bitch. Let's just see what you've got in there, okay?"

He eased her hand out, expecting to see a weapon, not the eight-by-ten blowup of the tattooed man's face.

"What the—" He yanked it out of her hand. "What are you doing with Stinger's picture?"

Tory forgot she was out of her element, forgot she was supposed to be afraid. At last she had a name to go with the face.

"What did you call him?"

Bull frowned. "Stinger. Stinger Hale. What are you doing with old Stinger's picture?" His frown deepened as he reached for her purse. "What the hell are you, a cop?"

Tory yanked her purse away. "No, no," she muttered. "I'm not a cop. I'm a photographer. Actually, a photojournalist. I'm just trying to find this man. Do you know where he lives?"

Bull took a step forward, but Tory held her ground. "Prove it," he said harshly.

"Prove what?"

"Empty your purse on the table. If there's no badge or gun in there, then we'll talk. Otherwise, get the hell out of Dump's before I throw you out."

"Oh, for Pete's sake," Tory muttered, and pushed past him angrily. Without thought for what she was about to do, she swept the game balls aside and dumped out the contents of her purse.

"Hey," one of the men shouted as the balls began bouncing off the sides of the table. "There was a hundred dollars riding on that game."

"This wasn't my idea," she said shortly, and then stood back with her hands on her hips, waiting for him to make the first move.

Bull dug through her stuff, even opening her lipstick and ballpoints as if they were some sort of secret weapons.

"It's not your color," Tory said, yanking a lipstick out of his hand as she began stuffing her things back in her purse. "I did as you asked, now it's your turn to talk, remember?"

He grinned. "What do you want to know?"

She pointed back at the picture. "Where I can find that man."

He gave her another long, hard stare. "If you're playing me for a fool...if I find out you went and got old Stinger in trouble, I'll come looking for you."

At that point, all the last few weeks of fear and

frustration came to a head. She shoved her finger against Bull's chest, her voice just below a shout.

"Damn you! I don't want to hurt him, I want to talk to him. And if I don't find that man, I'm the one who's going to be in trouble."

One of the bystanders took it upon himself to end the confrontation.

"Hell, Bull, tell her what she wants to know and let's get on with the game. I need to win my money back or my old lady won't let me in the house tonight."

Bull stared at Tory for several long, silent moments until he was satisfied that she was who she'd sworn to be.

"I haven't seen him in months. For all I know, he could have moved."

Tory bit her lip to keep from screaming. "Then tell me where he used to live. Let me worry about the rest."

"In Morrow."

"Where's Morrow?"

"About twenty-five miles that way," Bull said, pointing east. "I been to his house before. It's a rent house on the backside of some old lady's property."

Tory was scribbling frantically, making notes so she wouldn't forget a thing the man said.

"Do you remember the address?" she asked.

He snorted. "Hell, no. He's not on my Christmas card list."

Tory sighed. She would have to be satisfied with this.

"Thanks," she said, and started to leave when she felt that pool cue again, this time poking into the middle of her back. Her nerves were shot, and her patience was gone. She pivoted angrily.

"What?"

Bull grinned, then scratched at a spot just below the ring in his nose. "Turner Avenue. I think his house was on the corner of Turner and Fourth Street."

Anger faded. "Thanks," she said softly. "More than you will ever know."

By the time she got outside, she was shaking with relief.

"Oh God, oh God."

Her legs felt like rubber, and her heart was beating ninety to nothing. Without looking behind her, she sprinted toward her car. Only after she was safely inside, with all the doors locked and the engine running, did she take the time to take a deep breath. *Brett would kill me for that.* Then she put the car in gear and headed back to the motel. Tomorrow was a new day in the search for the tattooed man, but one thing had changed. Now she knew his name.

Stinger Hale.

It didn't mean anything to her, but maybe when she saw him, or when she heard his voice, maybe then she would have some answers.

Sunshine beamed on the little girl's face as she walked along the dusty road. A butterfly darted in front of her, and she laughed, then gave chase. Faster and faster she ran, trying to catch it, then trying to outrun it, but no matter how fast her little legs churned, she couldn't catch up.

"Wait!" she cried. "Wait for me."

A shadow passed over the sun. The air was beginning to cool as the butterfly disappeared. The little girl paused to look up, then gasped as she saw the dark thunderheads beginning to gather. It was going to rain! She had to hurry or she'd be in trouble if she got herself wet.

Ignoring everything but the house she could see at the end of the road, she began to run. She had to get there before the first drops fell. Her hair flew out behind her like a pale, yellow sail. The skirt of her dress was first plastered against her little legs, then bunched above her knees. With elbows pumping and her heart beating in a frantic rhythm, the distance to the house grew shorter and shorter.

The wind began to rise, wailing through the trees along the road in high-pitched shrieks. Just ahead, she saw someone, a woman, step out of the house. The woman was shouting her name, begging her to hurry...hurry...hurry.

And then the door swung shut, and just as her foot was about to hit the first step, the house disappeared. She pitched facedown on the hardpacked earth as the first raindrops began to fall.

"No! No!" she screamed. "Wait for me! Wait for me!"

Crying and begging, she scrambled to her feet and began to run in circles, looking for the house. It had to be here somewhere. If she could only find it, then she would be safe.

Rain was coming down harder now, plastering her hair to her face and her dress to her body. She looked down at herself, at the water running off her body and onto the ground. Lightning flashed above her, and in that instant, she looked down into the puddle in which she was standing and screamed. She couldn't see her reflection. Like the house...and the woman who'd called out her name...she was already gone.

Tory woke up to find herself standing in the middle of the floor, drenched in sweat and tears, and shaking like a leaf.

"Dear God."

With trembling fingers, she combed her hair away from her face and staggered to the bathroom. When she flipped on the light, she braced herself against the sink, looking deep into the eyes of the woman looking back.

"What's wrong with you?" she whispered. "What the hell is wrong with you?"

But the woman didn't answer, and Tory couldn't bear to look at the panic in her own eyes. She ducked her head and turned on the faucet, sluicing her face with the tepid water in a desperate attempt to wash away the memories of that dream. Instead of going back to bed, she crawled into a chair, curled her feet up beneath her and watched the sunrise through a crack in the curtain. Within an hour of the event, she was on her way to Morrow.

"Hey, Hooker, it's good to see you back."

"Same to you," Brett said, waving to one of Lacey's assistant D.A.s as he slid into a chair in the district attorney's outer office.

A few moments later, the door opened and Don Lacey exited with a briefcase in one hand and a black cowboy hat in the other. When he saw Brett, a slow smile spread across his face.

"I guess I shouldn't be surprised to see you," Lacey said. "And I'm not going to ask you what you're doing here, because I can see the look on your face. You're worse than a damned bloodhound, you know that?"

Brett grinned. "I want you to—"

Lacey interrupted. "My answer is no. Not until your doctor releases you."

Brett sighed. "Damn it, Don. Give me something to do. I'm going nuts sitting in that house by myself."

Lacey grinned. "With a woman as pretty as your Victoria, I could think of several things to do."

The tone of Brett's voice lowered, but his gaze never wavered. "Like I said...I need something to do."

Lacey saw past Brett's request to the pain in his voice. "I don't have what you need, Hooker." Then he touched Brett's shoulder. "The night you went into surgery, I never saw a woman as afraid of losing someone she loved as Victoria Lancaster was about you. And don't forget, she laid her life on the line when Huffman tried to finish you off. If she's gone, she'll be back. You can lay money on it."

Brett tried to grin. "I didn't think you were a betting man."

"A sure thing is never a gamble," Lacey said, and headed out the door. "And remember, until you get well, I'm shorthanded, so do as you're damn well told."

Tory had no problem finding Morrow. It was on the main highway. And she had no trouble finding

Turner Avenue. It was the third street just east of Main. But when she found out that Fourth Street didn't intersect Turner Avenue, she realized her troubles were starting all over again. It took her another couple of hours to locate someone who knew someone who recognized Stinger Hale's photo. At that point she was faint with exhaustion and sick to her stomach. By the time she realized she was only hungry and not coming down with something, she wasted another hour getting some food. At one-thirty in the afternoon, she pulled into the driveway of a neat, red-brick house and parked.

The house wasn't what she'd expected, and neither was the woman who came to the front door. It was obvious to Tory that LeeNona Beverly liked yellow, which, at LeeNona's age, was not the best of choices. It gave depth to her wrinkles she didn't need, and a sallow, washed-out tone to skin already dotted with age spots. In her prime, she had probably been quite a gal. But at this point in her life, she was an amazing fashion faux pas.

Tory got out of her car, trying not to stare at the bright yellow tights and the red-and-yellow striped baby-doll top LeeNona was wearing.

"Mrs. Beverly, I'm Tory Lancaster. I called a short while ago from the Realtor's office, remember?"

LeeNona waved her hand, scattering ashes from

the smoldering cigarette between her fingers. "It's Miss, not Mrs., and I'm old, not senile. Of course I remember."

Tory grinned. Darned if she didn't like Lee-Nona's attitude.

LeeNona took another drag from her cigarette, inhaling deeply, then jetting the smoke out her nose and mouth with a snort and a cough.

"Dammit, one of these days I'm gonna have to quit these things." She squinted through the smoke, eyeing Tory carefully. "So, Mayrene down at the real estate office said you are trying to find Oliver."

"Oliver?"

LeeNona frowned. "She said you had his picture. Do you or don't you?"

Tory yanked a copy of the picture from her bag. "This is the man I'm looking for. Someone told me he rents a house from you."

LeeNona glared at the picture, then turned aside and spat. "The rat. Yeah, he did rent from me."

Tory's hopes sank. *Did?* "Do you mean he's not here anymore?"

LeeNona spat again, then picked at the end of her tongue until she got rid of whatever it was she'd been trying to eject.

"No, he ain't, and I can't say as how I'm sorry to see him go. Oh, I'll admit we had our good times," she said, and fluffed at the bright yellow fuzz that passed for her hair. "But that was before he skipped out owing me two months back rent."

Tory wanted to cry. She'd been so sure that if she could only talk to him, her life would start to make sense.

"Do you know where he went? I really need to talk to him," she said.

LeeNona laughed, then choked and coughed, thumping her sagging breasts until she caught her breath. "He's in some jail but I don't know where. The stupid old fool tried to rob a liquor store. They caught him red-handed, and it served him right. But, I'm left with all his crap and nowhere to put it." She frowned and took another drag on the cigarette, inhaling and then blowing smoke out of the side of her mouth with the skill born of years at the job. "One of these days I'm gonna sell all that stuff in a garage sale and get my back rent."

Dejected, Tory turned and started to go, when she remembered something Brett had once said about investigations. Sometimes he got his best clues from the places people lived, rather than what he was told.

"Miss Beverly, I wonder if—"

"Hon, you call me LeeNona. That other way makes me feel old."

"Yes, ma'am," Tory said, and then grinned when the old lady gave her a frown. "Yes, Lee-

Nona. I was wondering if I could see where Mr. Hale lived.''

LeeNona shook her head. "Oh, I don't know about that. It don't seem quite right, him being locked up and all.''

"I'd pay his back rent," Tory offered.

LeeNona's face brightened. "Hon, you just bought yourself a truckload of junk.''

"I don't want his things," Tory said. "I just want to go through them. I have reason to believe that Mr. Hale could help me with the answers to some personal problems I've been having.''

The old woman cackled as she stepped off the porch. "Oliver Hale couldn't help himself fart, but it's nothing to me why you want to look through his things. Come with me, the house is just around back.''

Tory followed the old woman through a path between neatly trimmed shrubs, and was mildly surprised by the neatness of the tiny house behind LeeNona's home.

"When I bought this house, that was the garage. But I never did learn to drive, so what the hell do I need a garage for?" She brushed at a tube of ashes that had fallen on the front of her red-and-yellow blouse, then paused on the doorstep. "Ollie was owing me three hundred dollars when he got himself arrested.''

Tory froze, her hand on her checkbook, and

swallowed past a sudden knot of nausea. *Ollie? Ollie?* Somewhere in the back of her mind, she could hear herself shouting that name.

"Hey, dearie, are you all right?"

Tory leaned against the door frame and wiped a shaky hand across her face. "Yes," she said shortly. "I'm just tired. As soon as we get in out of the sun, I'll be fine." And before she could change her mind, she wrote LeeNona Beverly a check for three hundred dollars.

"It's good," she said, noting the hesitant look on the old woman's face as she handed it over. "If you want, you can call my bank."

"Oh, what the hell," LeeNona said, and tucked the check in the waistband of her tights. "Come on in and let's get this over with. I have a hair appointment in a couple of hours. I don't want to be late."

Tory followed her inside.

Over an hour later, Tory's hopes were just about gone. Oliver Hale's belongings were unremarkable and sparse, and not a thing among them had given her pause for thought. She dropped into a kitchen chair, staring around the small, compact kitchen, accepting the fact that she'd just wasted three hundred dollars. On the other hand, LeeNona seemed to be having herself quite a time going through Oliver's things.

"I remember when we bought this," she said,

holding up a chicken-head cookie jar. "We were at a flea market in Billings. Boy, Ollie sure does like them flea markets."

Ollie. Again, the name made her shudder. Tory nodded, and then had a thought.

"LeeNona, how long did Mr. Hale live here?"

"Oh, dearie, it seems like he's been here forever. Let's see, I had just bought this house. I guess it's been at least nineteen or twenty years…maybe longer. I remember he said he'd come up from Arkansas to work in the mills."

Tory sat up straight. Arkansas. The state of Arkansas had funneled Tory through its foster care system. This had to be more than a coincidence. And then she noticed a small, narrow door just behind LeeNona's left shoulder.

"Where does that door lead?" she asked.

LeeNona turned. "Oh! Why, the basement. Shoot, I'd forgotten there even is one. But I doubt if—"

"Could we see? We've come this far."

LeeNona glanced at her watch. "Okay," she said. "But make it snappy. I got to get my hair fixed, remember?" And then she led the way down the steep, narrow steps.

"Lord have mercy!" LeeNona shrieked, as they got to the bottom. "He's got hisself a still."

Tory had to smile. The setup was antiquated, but it had obviously done the job. There were several dozen quart jars full of some kind of liquid sitting on shelves. But she wasn't interested in illegal hooch and started digging through the boxes shoved beneath the old shelves.

In less than thirty minutes she'd gone through the entire lot, save for a small, brown trunk Lee-Nona had just kicked out of a corner.

"This is the last of it," LeeNona said. "Why don't you just take it with you, dearie? I really gotta go."

Tory eyed the dusty old relic, pictured it in her nice clean car and shook her head. "Wait. Please. It won't take but a minute to go through it."

She dropped to her knees and lifted the lid.

"Well, that don't surprise me none," LeeNona said, as a stack of pornographic magazines was revealed. And then she leaned down to finger through them. "But they're old. Maybe they're worth something."

"Feel free," Tory said, setting them aside as she continued to dig through the trunk. A few moments later, she rocked back on her heels with a sigh. "There's nothing left in here but a bundle of old rags." She picked them up, and as she did, something fell out of them and onto the floor at her feet.

She looked down, and as she did, the expression on her face shifted. A wail sounded deep down inside her mind, coming up from a place where it had long been lost. Her heart started to pound, and her legs went weak. If she hadn't been squatting, she would have fallen.

"Oh, oh, oh."

LeeNona heard Tory's whisper and turned in time to see the young woman blanch.

"Hey, dearie, are you all right? You didn't get bit by some spider or something, did you?"

But Tory couldn't speak, couldn't think, couldn't hear. Something kept pulling her down, down, down, into a dark, empty place.

LeeNona leaned over. "Well, would you look at that!" she said. "A little old rag doll. It's near about rotted, but you can tell the dress was blue. Blue gingham, don't you know? And look at that hair! I bet that yellow yarn was bright and pretty when it was new. I sure do love yellow."

Tory shook her head, unable to speak. She reached down to touch it, unaware she was holding her breath. The doll felt damp, and when she suddenly clasped it to her breast, she could smell the dust of the years on the fabric. A terrible pain racked her belly as tears blinded her eyes. She leaned over the dolly and started to moan, rocking to and fro on her knees as if she would never stop.

LeeNona looked around in a panic, suddenly aware that she was alone in a basement with what could be a crazy woman. She started backing toward the stairs.

"If you're getting sick, I guess I can call you an ambulance. But I'm not liable, you know. You didn't get hurt on my property, and I—"

With the instinct of a woman driven to get to her mate, Tory rose to her feet, staggering toward the steps leading up to the light.

Brett, my Brett. Something is wrong in my heart, and Brett will know how to fix it.

She walked out of the house and crawled into her car with the rag doll still clutched to her chest. Without conscious thought, she backed out of the driveway, somehow finding her way out of town.

She drove blindly, with no idea how fast she was driving, or how far she'd gone, stopping only when her body or her car refused to go any farther, refueling both and then driving again until she would fall asleep on the side of the road. The scent of the doll was in her nose and in her mind. The feel of the fabric against her fingers made her ache in a way she couldn't understand. With each passing hour, her world was growing darker and darker, closing in on her conscious mind and threatening to leave her lost inside forever.

Brett. Get to Brett.

It became her mantra. Her salvation. She had no concept of how long or how far she'd driven, only that she was going home.

Nine

It was eleven minutes past midnight when Tory pulled into the apartment parking lot, but time held no meaning for her. The only urgency in her life was the need to get to Brett. He would know why it hurt her to breathe. He would hold her and make everything bad go away.

She got out of the car with her keys in one hand and the rag doll in the other. Clutching the doll to her breast as if it were a shield, she started running and didn't stop until she reached the front door to the apartment. She dropped the key twice in an effort to get it in the lock, and each time she picked it up to try again, her anxiety grew. Only after the tumblers finally clicked and the door swung open did she take a deep breath and relax. She stepped inside the darkness, shouting his name.

"Brett! Brett! I'm home."

Her voice came back to her in an echo, but it didn't register. Her focus was on the room, and the room was dark. Darkness was not her friend.

She reached for the switch as she called out again, then choked in midsentence as the room was illuminated.

Bare. Bare walls. Bare floors. Everything was bare. Everything was gone. She started shaking her head from side to side in a childlike manner, refusing to believe what was before her eyes. Her purse fell to the floor, her keys beside it as she grabbed the doll with both hands, shoving it beneath her chin and burying her face in the faded fabric. From a long forgotten part of her mind she began to chant the doll's name, pretending, as she used to when she'd been small, that when she got to the end of the chant, whatever she wished would come true.

"Sweet Baby, Sweet Baby, Sweet Baby, Sweet Baby."

The words echoed around her. A draft from the open doorway in which she was standing pushed the fabric of her shirt against her back, and she shuddered as an ugly voice began to whisper inside her head, drowning out her Sweet Baby chant.

Again. Again. It's happened again. You aren't any good. That's why they don't stay.

She whimpered, clutching her doll closer as her voice rose in pitch.

"Sweet Baby, Sweet Baby, Sweet Baby, Sweet Baby."

But old echoes from her past persisted, growing

stronger with each passing second. She could hear them clearly now. Inside her head. Mocking her. Laughing at her. *Stupid…stupid…stupid. No good…no good…no good. Nobody wants Tory Lancaster. Nobody…nobody…nobody.*

"Sweet Baby, Sweet Baby, Sweet Baby."

But the chant wouldn't work, and no matter how many lights she turned on, the darkness inside her mind kept growing.

She began running from room to room and back again, shouting Brett's name in a frenzy. And with each trip, her terror grew, until his name was a scream with no beginning and no end.

When the phone rang beside his ear, Brett jumped as if he'd been shot. It wasn't as if he'd never gotten a phone call in the middle of the night. It was part of his business. But for some reason, this time the shrill urgency of the sound made him more than uneasy.

When he picked up the receiver, he knew he'd been right to panic. He could hear the woman screaming before he ever said hello. Although a dozen scenarios went through his mind in the seconds between answering, he was unable to focus on anything other than that unending, heart-wrenching scream.

"Who is this?" he shouted.

There was a scuffling sound in the background,

and then it sounded as if the caller was moving to another room in order to be heard.

"Mr. Hooker, this is Mel Roberts, your old landlord. I think you better get over here quick. Miss Lancaster came back tonight. She's uh... upset...as you can hear, and we can't seem to get her to stop."

Brett's heart stopped. "Tory? That's Tory I hear?"

"Yeah," Roberts said. "Something's wrong... bad wrong."

But Brett didn't have to be told to know that was so. He dropped the phone without bothering to hang up. Within moments of the phone call, he was dressed and grabbing his car keys on the way out the door. He couldn't think past the memory of Victoria's screams.

"God help me...and her," he muttered, as he backed his car out of the driveway.

A few minutes later he turned onto the Northwest Expressway, heading east. It was about a fifteen minute drive from his new address to his old apartment complex. He made it in just under seven minutes, with a city police car on his tail.

By the time he pulled into the complex, the cop had already run the plate, learned the identity of the driver, and was calling for backup. The way the officer figured it, if one of Lacey's men was in that big a hurry, there had to be a reason.

Brett started running toward the building before the police car behind him had come to a stop. There was no time to explain away his haste. Already he could hear Tory's screams, even outside the walls.

Every light in his old apartment was on, and the door was open. Some of the neighbors were standing in their doorways, their faces etched with worry, while others had gathered just outside his door.

"Get back!" he shouted, pushing his way through the crowd. "Let me through! Let me through!"

The landlord was just inside. His bathrobe was awry, and his hair was standing on end. It was obvious that Tory's screams had roused him from his bed, as well.

"I don't know what caused—"

Brett ran past Mel Roberts without waiting for his explanation. All he wanted was to get to Tory, to put his arms around her and never let her go. He ran into the bedroom, then stopped. She was nowhere in sight, but it was obvious from the sounds of her screams that she was in here somewhere.

"Tory! Tory! Where are you?" he shouted.

"In there!" Roberts said, pointing toward the closet.

Brett leaped, yanking back the door, intent on

scooping Tory up in his arms. But he wasn't prepared for what he saw. She was crouched in the back of the empty closet with her face on her knees. Her hair was matted with sweat and sticking to her arms and forehead. When he called out her name, it was as if he weren't even there. He knelt, touching her shoulder, then rocked back on his heels when she threw back her head in a shriek, exposing the tender white arch of her throat and the dirty rag doll clutched to her chest.

His heart sank. "Tory, sweetheart, it's me, Brett. Let me help you, baby. Let me help you."

She shook her head from side to side, unwilling to be touched. Slowly but surely her screams began to subside, not because she was calming down, but because she had cried herself hoarse.

Once more he tried to touch her, to help her out of the closet. She pulled away again with a frantic jerk, clutching the doll even tighter while murmuring something he couldn't understand. Defeated, he turned to the landlord, only to see a uniformed officer clearing the room.

"I need an ambulance," he said.

"Already done," the officer said. "Who is she? Do you know her?"

Brett looked back at the wild, sweat-drenched woman clutching that old rag doll and felt his life slipping away.

"I thought I did," he said softly. "But now I'm not so sure."

There were people coming to take her away, just like before. She smelled them, even before she saw their white coats. They smelled like hospitals. She didn't like hospitals. People went into hospitals, and sometimes they didn't come back.

"Sweet Baby, Sweet Baby, Sweet Baby, Sweet Baby," but the chant didn't work. The people just kept coming. She turned away from the doorway, hiding her dolly under her arm. She didn't want them to take Sweet Baby away again.

Someone touched her. She shut her eyes and flinched. "No, no, no," she begged.

A voice, deep and low, kept making promises. But promises were nothing but words. Words didn't mean anything, and neither did promises. There was a terrible pain in her chest, like a hole that kept tearing wider and wider with each passing breath. Someone was lost. She kept trying to remember the words to say, but they just wouldn't come. If she could only find out where they'd gone, she would be all right. But the problem was, she didn't remember who she'd lost.

A phone rang at the nurses' station just across the hall as the sound of voices and laughter drifted into Tory's room. Brett got up and closed the door, unwilling to disturb her uneasy slumber. He walked back to her bedside, staring down at her in the half-light, studying the way she clutched the rag doll beneath her chin.

She didn't know me.

Every time he let himself think it, his panic renewed. He'd tried to excuse it. He'd even tried to ignore it. But when there was nothing else to distract him, the truth of the fact was right there. She hadn't known him. She acted as if she didn't even known where she was. By the time she'd screamed herself hoarse, she wasn't saying much of anything.

Tory, baby, what happened to you out there?

He touched her face, then her hair, trying to find something of the woman he loved in this childlike creature curled up on the bed, but she was gone.

That damned picture of that tattooed man is part of this mess.

He had no facts on which to base the theory, but his instincts as an investigator told him he was right. When she suddenly shuddered, then sighed, Brett put his hand on her shoulder, wanting her to know that wherever she'd gone, she was not alone.

As he watched, her chin quivered, and a tear suddenly spilled down her cheek. Her lips were moving, repeating some word over and over. He leaned down, trying to hear what it was that she said, then frowned when he heard her whispering, "Mommy, Mommy, Mommy."

The word startled him. To his knowledge, Victoria Lancaster had never known her mother. It had been his understanding that she'd been in the foster care system from the time she was a baby. He leaned closer and kissed the side of her face, then whispered against her ear.

"Come back to me, Tory. I love you. I love you. Do you hear me, baby? I love you very, very much."

The little girl hated the dark, and it was dark now, just like she'd feared it would be. The house was gone. Sweet Baby was gone. Mommy was gone. There was no one left who loved her. There was no one left who remembered her name.

"I'll die now," she said, and lay herself down. As she waited, she could feel every part of her being turning in on itself, and she curled into a ball to make it easier to go.

But death wouldn't come. As hard as she tried to stop them from happening, the breaths still came. Inhale. Exhale. Over and over, the treacherous draughts of air continued, taking away her last chance for escape.

She lay without moving, waiting for it all to be over. Tired. She was so very, very tired. If she didn't move, maybe she would sleep forever.

And then she felt a touch, but that couldn't be. No one could touch her, because she'd been left all alone. It came again, on her face, on her hair, near her ear. She shifted uncomfortably. If she wasn't alone, then she wouldn't be able to die, and she was tired, so very tired, of fighting.

Then she heard the voice. Faint at first, and soft—so very, very soft. She listened harder, unable to believe what she was hearing. It came again, more clearly now, and her heart surged.

Oh! Oh joy, precious joy! There! Again, then again! Love? Someone was promising to love her? If only she dared to believe.

Sunlight was coming through the half-open shades when she opened her eyes. Brett caught himself holding his breath, afraid to hope, afraid to speak for fear of starting this nightmare all over again. In the few moments before their gazes met, he wished he'd taken time to shave, or at least comb his hair. But it was too late now, and he was afraid to move. So he waited, watching her eyes as they focused on first one object and then another. And then she suddenly jerked and began yanking at the sheets, searching for the doll that had slipped out of her hand.

"Here," Brett said softly, moving the sheet aside to show her where it lay. "There's your baby," he said softly.

When Tory felt the old fabric beneath her fingers, she relaxed. Then she looked up, and the hole in her mind began to close. Her voice was raspy and weak, but her words were clear and distinct, and they healed Brett's heart in a way nothing else ever could.

"Brett. I couldn't find you. I thought you were lost forever."

She knows me. Oh God...thank you God.

He put down the guardrail and picked her up in his arms, only then giving in to the tears he'd been holding back.

"Oh, baby, I thought I'd lost you, too."

Tory held the rag doll tight against her breast and rested her cheek against the rock-steady rhythm of Brett's heart.

"Don't let them take Sweet Baby from me, will you?"

He rocked her where they sat, holding her close, then closer still. "No, sweetheart, I won't let them take your dolly, I promise."

"You keep your promises, don't you, Brett?"

"Yes, Tory, I keep my promises."

"I want to go home now. Will you take me home?"

It had sounded like a plan to Brett, but her doctor had had other ideas. Relenting slightly only after he'd learned that she wouldn't be alone, the doctor had agreed to release her tomorrow, but not a moment sooner. They'd had to be satisfied with that.

Within the hour, the doctor had ordered a series of psychiatric tests and sent Brett home. On the way there, he'd made up his mind to do some checking of his own. Victoria had never talked about her past, and he'd respected her right to keep silent. But no longer. He didn't want to lose her, and to make sure that never happened, he was going to find out everything there was to know about Victoria Lancaster.

Brett had pulled out all the stops. He'd called in favors and ignored red tape that would have stalled a lesser man. It had taken better than five hours, but the file now sitting on his desk was everything that had been recorded of Victoria Lancaster's life to date. In Brett's opinion, it was little more than a continuing horror story, interspersed with just enough reality to make it convincing.

Abandoned...six years old...mother disappeared without a trace...three days...no food.

He took a deep breath, skimming through a psychiatrist's opinion to get back to the facts.

When found, was hysterical for six days...mute for four months.

When Brett read that, he felt sick to his stomach. He kept thinking about how coming back to their empty apartment had caused her to relive the hell of her childhood.

He turned a page, and then another and another, reading about the waste of a child's life and the promises made, and then broken, again and again. No wonder she didn't trust. No wonder she wouldn't let herself put down roots. Everyone she'd ever believed in had walked out on her or else given her back to the courts when her care became too much of a hassle. Victoria Lancaster hadn't quit on life. It had quit on her.

He turned another page, frowning as he read through the report. It was one doctor's opinion that she was withholding her anger by refusing to speak of her mother. It was another's opinion that she'd been so traumatized by the abandonment that she didn't even remember she'd had a mother.

Brett thought of his own childhood, of the constancy of his mother's love and his father's reassuring presence, of growing up with a brother and sister for companions, of never having to go hungry or cold, of holidays and birthdays and all the things that make a child's life sweet.

Dear God. In the blink of an eye, that six-year-old child lost every anchor she'd ever known in life, and then, unknowingly, I repeated her hell.

Blinded by tears, he shut the folder and covered his face with his hands.

"Oh God, Victoria, forgive me. I didn't know. I didn't know."

An hour later, he was at the hospital with the report in his hands. There were things in here that her doctor needed to know. Things that Victoria might not be able to tell him, not because she didn't want to, but because she didn't remember. Things that would help them heal her. He needed her well. He wanted her back—if she would have him. Just thinking about her loneliness made him angry all over again. So help him God, he would make sure no one ever hurt her again.

She was quiet on the way home. Brett kept giving her nervous glances as he negotiated the downtown traffic. Except for the presence of that rag doll in her lap, he could almost believe nothing had ever happened. When they stopped for a light, Brett patted her hand.

"Tory?"

She turned to him with a smile that lit his heart. "Hmm?"

"Are you all right?"

She sighed. Poor Brett. She didn't remember everything, but from the tests she'd taken and the things she'd overheard, she must have pulled quite a stunt.

"Yes, darling, I'm fine."

The light changed, and he moved with the traffic, still clasping her hand. But he couldn't stay quiet. There were so many things he needed to say.

"Tory."

"What?"

"I didn't move to get away from you."

Her smile was a little bit sad. "I know, but I wouldn't have blamed you if you had."

"I just thought if I gave you some space...if I let you..."

She squeezed his fingers, then lifted them to her lips.

"Brett. Stop. I'm the one who should be apologizing. I should have told you where I was going. I should have talked to you about finding Oliver Hale. If I had, maybe none of this would have happened."

He shook his head. "No, baby. I don't agree. I think it was only a matter of time before something inside you gave way. I'm just sorry I was the catalyst, that's all."

She nodded. "Apology accepted."

He glanced down at the doll in her lap and at the desperate grip she had on the fabric of the skirt. Other than asking him not to let them take it away, she hadn't mentioned the doll to him again. He decided to change the subject.

"I had all your things moved to the new house yesterday. You're going to love it. There's a lot more room and a great place for your—"

"I don't care where I live, as long as you're there, too."

He nodded, then gave her a lopsided grin. "*Now* you tell me."

She almost laughed. But when Brett turned the street corner and pulled into the second driveway on the left, she stiffened and clutched at the doll.

"Is this it?"

Brett nodded, holding his breath as he watched the expressions changing on her face, from unease at unfamiliar surroundings to a quiet acceptance of the simple red-brick house and the neat green hedges separating it from the houses on either side.

"I like it," she said.

He exhaled.

She slept in Brett's arms, clutching him as tightly as she'd clung to that doll. When bedtime had come, he'd waited, wondering if she would take it to bed, too, and had been more than surprised when she'd put it in her dresser drawer instead.

"You sure?" he'd asked, as she'd turned around to come to bed.

"If you promise not to snore. Sweet Baby never snores."

"Is that her name?"

Tory ran her hand across the surface of the

drawer and then nodded. "I think so. Anyway, it feels right."

"Was it yours...from before, I mean?"

She looked up, and the lost expression on her face broke his heart. "I don't know why I know it, but I know she's mine."

"Where did you find her?"

She closed her eyes, picturing the cellar and Stinger Hale's face. "In an old man's house."

Suddenly Brett knew which old man she meant. *I'll be damned. The man with the scorpion tattoo.*

"Was he related to you, honey?"

Her hand shook, and for the first time since coming home from the hospital, she felt a little afraid.

"I don't know. They said his name was Oliver Hale. One man even knew him as Stinger. But I don't remember anything about him."

"What did he do when he saw you?"

She dug her fingers through her hair in a gesture of frustration. "That's just it. I didn't get to see him. His landlady let me go through his things."

Brett looked startled. "Hell, Tory, that was dangerous. What if he'd come back and caught you?"

"Oh, no. It wasn't like that. She said he was in some prison. He owed her back rent. I paid it to get to go through his things."

He smiled at her. "Very resourceful, honey. I might have done something similar myself."

"I know. I remembered you telling me once that sometimes your best clues came from where someone lived, rather than what you were told about them."

"Good girl," he said, and patted her on the knee.

But Tory was too dejected to take the praise.

"Brett?"

"What, baby?"

"He had my doll. If he meant nothing to me, then why did he have my doll?"

"I don't know, sweetheart, but it's okay. When it matters, you'll remember." And then he changed the subject. "Come here to me. I'm needing a hug."

After that, there had been no more talk of Oliver Hale. And now she slept beneath the shelter of Brett's arm while he worried himself through the night. There were still too many unanswered questions to suit him, and he wasn't a patient man. Granted, Tory didn't remember the man from the picture, but Brett had ways of finding his own answers.

"You said Oliver Hale was in prison, right?"

Tory looked up from her newspaper and nodded. "That's what LeeNona Beverly told me."

Brett's mouth dropped. "Who?"

Tory frowned. "I guess I didn't tell you about her, did I?"

Brett shook his head. "Honey, up to now, you haven't told me much of anything. But if you want to find out what the hell's going on in your head, then I think it's about time that you did."

She tossed the paper aside and stood up. "You know, I think you're right."

She took Brett by the hand. "Let's go outside. I think better there."

He followed willingly, more than ready to hear what she had to say.

Hours later, he was still wrestling with the notion that what she'd told him hadn't clarified anything. In fact, it only served to confuse him even more.

What she remembered of her dreams were nothing more than bits and pieces of nightmarish horrors. And she'd learned nothing from LeeNona Beverly that really mattered, except maybe the fact that Oliver Hale had relocated to Iowa from Arkansas about the same time that Tory had been abandoned. Add to that an old rag doll that kept secrets better than the Pope and they weren't much better off than when they'd started.

At that point, he made up his mind. He was going to talk to Oliver Hale.

Ten

Tory stood naked before the full-length mirror on the back of the bedroom door. Her stare was appraising, almost judgmental. The woman looking back at her seemed wary, almost afraid. But of what? Tory wondered. The woman couldn't say.

Tory looked again, past the questions in her eyes to the face itself, looking for abnormalities that would echo the ones in her mind. Fortunately, Tory Lancaster's outer self gave away nothing of what was going on inside her head.

She lifted her arms, noting the firm tilt of her breasts as she stretched her fingers toward the ceiling. Then she turned, viewing herself first from one side and then the other. She sighed, dropping her arms to her sides, then running the palms of both hands across her belly.

Too skinny.

The whorl of hair at the juncture of her thighs was a thick, wheat-colored nest in which was hidden her womanly parts. She frowned. Secrets. Always secrets. Why did everything have to be a secret? Wasn't it enough that her own mind was keeping things from her? She leaned forward, pressing both hands against the face of the glass, staring deep into the wide blue eyes of the woman in the mirror.

Where did you come from? Who are your people? Why can't you remember anything about your childhood that matters?

She was still standing in that position when Brett walked into the room. She saw his reflection first, then turned, unashamed of her nudity. She stood without moving, watching the changing expressions on his face, recognizing his surprise, then his admiration, accepting his need as her own. Then she hesitated, suddenly too intimidated to make the first move. It took her a few moments to remember. Brett didn't judge.

She held out her hand.

He inhaled sharply, struck by a longing for this woman, yet afraid to move into an intimacy she wouldn't be able to handle. His voice was low, almost hoarse with longing.

"Tory...baby, what are you doing?"

"Waiting for you. Will you make love to me?"

"Willingly," he said softly, and reached for the top button of his jeans.

God, don't let me mess this up.

"Let me," she said.

She moved his hands aside, undoing the buttons,

then slipping her fingers inside, cupping him, testing the firmness of his body, savoring the thrust of him against the palms of her hands. When he groaned, she smiled. It had been so long.

He kicked off his jeans and then picked her up. There was a hesitancy in his voice as he brushed his mouth across the side of her cheek.

"Are you sure? The last thing I want to do is hurt you in any way."

She locked her arms around his neck and met his gaze straight on.

"I don't want to feel anything but you inside of me. I don't want to think of anything but coming apart in your arms. I don't want to hear anything but the sound of your breath against my face. Make love to me. Make me forget…forget everything but you."

Refusing Tory wasn't a thing he could do. He lay her on the bed, then followed her down, bracing himself above her. Loving Tory was easy. Making love to her was a pleasure he couldn't describe. But knowing how fragile her hold was on life and on trust made him scared. He looked at her and saw his world. But something inside of him knew that when she looked at herself, she saw someone that nobody wanted, nobody loved. It needed to be said now, before they became caught in the heat of the moment.

"Victoria?"

Her hand was on his arm, her gaze unwavering. "What?"

"Do you know how much you are loved?"

Something flickered in the backs of her eyes, like a shadow behind a half-drawn curtain.

"Do you?"

She shrugged, then looked away.

"That's what I thought."

Brett rolled, pulling her into his arms and holding her so close he could feel her heartbeat against his chest.

"I want you to listen to me, baby. And I want you to believe as you have never believed before."

He felt her sigh.

She finally answered. "All right."

"Do you promise?" he insisted.

"I promise."

"Victoria, do you know what I did the day I met you?"

She shook her head.

"I went home and called my brother and told him I'd met the woman I wanted to marry."

He felt her stiffen, but he kept talking, tired of playing games, tired of pretending things were all right when they weren't.

"I can't explain it, but I knew, even then, how special you would be to me. I live to hear your laughter—to feel the touch of your hand on my face. I draw easier breaths just because you're in the same room. I come undone in your arms, and I would willingly die for you—over and over again."

Tory started to cry. "I—"

"Don't talk, just listen," he said softly. "I'm only saying things I should have told you years ago. I guess I thought you knew them. I was wrong."

He began to caress her back, rubbing a wide, gentle circle between her shoulder blades until he felt her beginning to relax.

"Someday I want to stand in a church and watch you coming toward me down the aisle. I want to tell the world that you're mine and I'm yours. I promise I will hold you and keep you safe from the things that scare you. I swear on my life that I will never forsake you. Do you believe me?"

Blinded by tears, all she could do was nod.

"And someday, when you're ready, I would like to have a family."

She choked on a sob. "I know you would. I saw the way you were with your sister's new baby. You'll make a wonderful father. But I'm afraid. The only parents I remember were a series of strangers. What if I'm more of a monster than a mother?"

Anger for what she'd endured ripped through him.

"That's bullshit, Tory! There's not a mean bone in your body."

She put her hand on his face, making him focus on the seriousness of what she felt.

"You don't have to be mean to be a bad parent. Look at me now. Look at the way I treat you. I come and go with no regard for your feelings. I act as if I'm the only thing in this world that matters." She looked away. "Frankly, I don't know why you kept forgiving me. If the situation had been reversed, I wouldn't have forgiven you."

Again his thoughts went back to a little girl nobody had wanted. He kissed the side of her cheek, then her tear-stained eyes, then her mouth, each time leaving a little bit more of himself behind.

"Tory?"

"What?"

"You know what you said...about leaving without notice?"

She nodded.

"You know what I think? I don't think you were leaving me—ever. I think you were just testing me. To see if I would still be there each time you came back."

She grew quiet, absorbing what he'd said, and somewhere within herself something settled. What if he was right? She drew a shuddering breath, then looked up. She didn't give herself time to hesitate. There was only one thing left to say to him.

"Yes."

Brett frowned. "Yes what, baby?"

"Yes, I know how much I am loved. But..."

He grinned. "But what?"

"But I would a lot rather you showed me."

His grin slipped, replaced by a sudden need to be deep inside his lady.

"Now?" he asked.

She reached down and encircled him, feeling the power within herself as she felt him growing, and all because of her.

"Yes, Brett. Now."

He rolled, pinning her beneath him on the bed. The thunder of his own heartbeat was hammering against his brain. *Take it easy. Take it slow.*

But when she opened her legs and guided him inside, heeding his own advice was impossible. There was that instant of recognition, when he felt himself expanding within her, and the knowing of what was yet to come. And then he started to move, and every thought faded into obscurity. There was nothing that mattered but the woman in his arms.

Tory didn't know where she ended and Brett began, and for once in her life, she didn't care. When he took her to the edge of insanity, trust kept her with him every step of the way. When her blood thundered through her veins and every muscle in her body began to tense, it was faith in him that gave her the strength to let go—to follow the starburst of pleasure that comes from the joy of making love to your man.

And when it was over, she lay spent and shaking within his arms as a single thought kept repeating itself in her head.

I didn't know it could be like this.

Brett came out of the shower to find Tory sitting cross-legged on the bed with the rag doll in her lap. He paused in the doorway, watching the intent expression on her face as she touched its hair, then its face, rubbing the faded blue fabric of its dress between her fingers, as if trying to absorb memories from touch alone.

"What are you thinking?" he asked.

Tory jumped, then looked up. A corner of her mouth turned up. "That I wish she could talk."

Brett tossed the towel he was holding into the room behind him, then pulled on his sweats before sitting down on the bed beside her. For a moment he just sat, watching the gentle sweep of her fingers over the little doll's face.

"She's about to lose an eye," he said, pointing to a big blue button barely hanging by a thread.

Tory nodded.

"Want me to fix her?" he asked.

She looked startled, unable to picture Brett
Hooker with a needle and thread.

"Who do you think fixes my things when
you're gone?" he asked.

She flushed, then looked away.

Brett cupped her face, forcing her to face him.
"That wasn't a dig, sweetheart. Besides, my
mother made sure all her children were capable of
taking care of themselves."

Tory pushed at the big blue button with the end
of her finger, as if by pressure alone she could fix
the ailing feature.

"I'll be careful with her," Brett promised.

Tory's blush increased; she was embarrassed
that her reticence to turn over something as incon-
sequential as an old rag doll had taken on such
importance. But Brett wasn't laughing at her, and
she began to relax.

"I know that," she said, and handed him the
doll as if it were made of fine glass.

"Just let me get the stuff and we'll be in business."

Pleased that she'd trusted him to help, he began
digging through a dresser drawer. A few moments
later he joined her back on the bed and picked up
the doll, giving it a quick once-over before decid-
ing where to start.

Tory watched the careful manner in which Brett
picked up the doll and knew that he understood.

But when he thrust the needle into its face, she caught herself holding her breath, as if she needed to experience pain for a doll that was incapable of feeling it on its own.

Get a grip, Victoria, or you'll wind up back in the psych ward.

And then Brett began to sew, and she caught herself focusing on his fingers. They were long and strong, the ends wide-tipped and well capable of gripping. She swallowed, remembering how they felt on her body when they made love. As she watched him working, so intent on the task at hand, a phrase popped into her mind.

A man for all seasons.

That was Brett. And then she added a line of her own.

A man who makes promises and keeps them.

Unaware of Tory's concentration, Brett finished the job, then began to examine the doll, checking to see if there was any need for further repairs. Even though the doll was faded and dirty, it was evident to him that craftsmanship was the main reason it was still in one piece. The inside seams on the little dress had been finished to give them a clean edge. And although the yarn hair was tangled and fuzzy at the ends, it was still sewn tight to the doll's fabric head. He caught Tory staring at him, then held the doll up with a smile.

"Someone sure put a lot of time into making her."

Tory looked puzzled. "Do you think?"

He tilted the doll and then pulled up the side of the dress.

"I sure do, honey. Just look at the way the..."

As the skirt tumbled over the doll's head, a small, oblong label that had been stitched to the back of the doll was suddenly revealed. Brett paused, forgetting what he'd been about to say. He'd seen them before. Small fabric labels that crafters could sew inside their garments to personalize their project. But the significance of this one was deeper than most, because it was the first proof Tory would have that she'd once known her mother. He hesitated, remembering what the doctor had said about letting her remember things on her own. But she'd found this doll on her own and was bound to see it. He just didn't want her to find it alone. He looked up at her, wishing he could hear what she was thinking.

Tory waited for him to finish. When he didn't, her curiosity got the best of her. She reached for the doll. To her surprise, Brett didn't immediately relinquish it.

"What's wrong?" she asked.

"Tory, honey."

"What?"

"Do you remember who gave this to you?"

"No."

"What do you remember about it?"

She frowned. "Not much. Only that when I saw it, I knew it was mine."

"Look," he said, and handed it to her, pointing to the label.

The first line caught her by surprise.

Made Especially for You with Love.

When she read the last line on the label, an old longing swept over her that she couldn't control.

By Mother.

She looked up at Brett, her eyes wide with unshed tears.

"See, honey. I'm not the only one who ever loved you."

But she'd been hurt too many times, grown too callous to let herself care. She looked at the label once more and then tossed the doll aside, tension in every movement of her body as she got up from the bed. Her voice was shaking, her face flushed with anger.

"If she was so wonderful—if she loved me— then why can't I remember her?"

"I don't know," Brett said, and reached for her, but she dodged his grasp and stalked out of the bedroom, leaving him alone with the little rag doll.

Its legs were spraddled, and one arm was pinned beneath its body. But the mute, smiling face still stared up at him. He straightened it up and set it on her pillow.

"Tory was right. I sure wish you could talk." And then he followed her out of the room.

The little girl stood in the middle of a room, staring at the dolls. They were everywhere, surrounding her, closing her in.

Black dolls, brown dolls, white dolls, pink dolls. Dolls with long hair. Dolls with no hair. Dolls that cried. Dolls that stared. But no yellow-haired rag doll with a blue gingham dress and blue button eyes.

"Sweet Baby! Where are you?"

She ran from one wall to the other, searching through the inanimate little bodies, tossing first one and then another aside, searching for her own dolly. But the more she looked, the more the others seemed to multiply. No matter how many she tossed aside, there were still more waiting to be seen.

She glanced nervously out the window. It was getting dark. She had to find Sweet Baby before night. Sweet Baby was afraid of the dark.

She looked back at the dolls. Now they were all around her on the floor, stacking up in piles and closing in on the place where she stood. Her heart started to pound, and she wanted to cry. But she was a big girl, and big girls didn't cry just because they lost their dollies.

"Sweet Baby, oh, Sweet Baby, come out, come out wherever you are."

Nothing happened.

"Please, Sweet Baby. I promise never to lose you again."

But the dolls kept crowding, piling around her feet. She turned, frightened and unable to run. The shadows that had been upon the floor were getting longer, and there was still no sign of Sweet Baby.

Now the dollies were crowding her knees, piling up to her waist. She covered her face with her hands as the room went dark. When all she could feel were tiny plastic fingers poking into her flesh, she started to cry.

Tory was running when she woke up. Momentarily disoriented by the layout of Brett's new house, she stopped, then turned sharply. Brett caught her before she could speak.

"Tory, it's okay. I'm right here."

Her legs were shaking as he wrapped his arms around her. She relaxed, welcoming the feel of his arms around her, recentering her world around the sound of his voice.

"I had another dream. I'm so sick of this I could scream."

He stroked her hair and then kissed her. "I

know, honey. I wish I could help you, but I don't know what to do.''

''Neither do I,'' she muttered, and then ran her hand up his cheek, smoothing his sleep-mussed hair and loving the worry she saw in his eyes. ''I'm sorry about this. Did I wake you?''

Pressing her cheek against his chest, he combed his fingers through her hair in a gentle, soothing motion.

''No, baby. I was in the kitchen. I heard you running down the hall.'' He grinned wryly. ''I didn't think I was going to catch you this time. You were really moving.''

''I want this to stop.''

He frowned. The despair in her voice was impossible to miss.

''I know you do, sweetheart.''

''But that's just it. You don't know,'' she muttered, and tried to pull away from his embrace, but he wouldn't let her go.

''I'm not the bad guy here. Don't run away from me, too.''

She went limp. Brett was right. Why did she keep pushing away the only person who cared? She shook her head, disgusted with herself.

''I'm sorry. I'm not mad at you. I'm mad at myself. All the way to Iowa I was so certain that if I could just talk to the tattooed man, I would remember something...something important.'' She sighed. "And I need to remember."

At that moment Brett doubted the doctor's wisdom of letting her remember on her own. He'd seen her file. He didn't know everything, but he knew things about her that she didn't know about herself. It didn't seem fair. He was tired of seeing the panic in her eyes. He was tired of hearing her wake up screaming and crying. He glared out the window, past the defiant reflection of his face. This was bullshit! Doctors didn't know everything.

"Look, sweetheart, I have an idea. Maybe you can still talk to Hale."

She shook her head and looked away. "We can't. He's in prison, remember?"

Brett cupped her face, making her look at him. "I know. But I think there's something you're forgetting."

"What?"

"What I do for a living."

She stared as understanding slowly dawned. As an ex-cop and now an investigator for the D.A., he had access to a world of privileged information that would take a private citizen weeks to uncover.

"Do you think they'll let you? Search through the system, I mean."

When he spoke, the determination in his voice was impossible for her to ignore. "I'd like to see them try to stop me," he said.

For the first time in weeks, she felt hopeful. She threw her arms around his neck.

"Brett Hooker, you know what?"

He pulled her into the cradle of his hips, grinning as she snuggled. "What?" he muttered, trying to concentrate on what she was saying, rather than what she was doing.

"I love you forever."

He stilled, and his grin faded. "Thank you, baby," he said softly. "That should be just about long enough to last."

Oklahoma State Penitentiary, McAlester, Oklahoma

The scent of industrial strength soap, as well as the constant smell of hot steam and wet cotton, filled the laundry room in which a number of inmates were working. Some of them were old hands at the job, some of them just learning the ropes. And although they were trusted to some degree with the duties they'd been given, the ominous presence of armed guards was a constant reminder of their present position in life. The work was hard, the working conditions less than pleasant. Until they became acclimated to the steam and heat, it wasn't uncommon for an inmate to succumb to the atmosphere and faint. So when the old man at the dryers suddenly crumpled to the floor and was carried into a hallway beyond, where the air was less dense, they weren't expecting anything serious.

They laid him down, then rolled him onto his back while the guard was on his two-way, calling for help. The man's face was bloodless, giving the black scorpion tattoo on his cheek an eerie added dimension. His mouth was agape, and his eyes had rolled back in his head. A thin trickle of spittle ran out from the corner of his mouth, and there was a slight jerk and twitch to the muscles in his legs. The guard took one look at the old man and added an urgency to the message he'd already sent.

Within minutes they'd carried him away and someone else had been put in his place. The steam still boiled, and the scent of wet clothes and strong soap continued to drift throughout the area. In the grand scheme of things, one old man's presence in the laundry room of the state penitentiary was never going to be missed.

Meanwhile, his arrival at the health-care unit was causing a slight shift in their daily routine. He was transferred from a stretcher to a bed without his knowledge, and was stuck, poked and prodded before he ever came to. When Oliver Hale finally opened his eyes, the indignities of contemporary health care became secondary to why he was there. He didn't remember anything past the nausea he'd been fighting for weeks and a lassitude he'd been unable to shake.

"Mr. Hale, can you hear me?"

He stared up at the doctor leaning over him.

"How many fingers am I holding up?" Cal Levisay asked.

A surge of nausea bubbled at the back of Oliver's throat. He could see the doctor's hand just fine, as well as the fact that he was holding up three of his five fingers. But opening his mouth to talk right now could be risky.

"Sick," he muttered.

"Yes, Mr. Hale, you got sick. They brought you to the hospital from the laundry room. Do you remember?"

Hell yes, I remember, but can't you hear? I told you I was going to be sick.

Levisay frowned. The patient's behavior was suspicious, more in keeping with dementia after suffering a stroke. He leaned closer.

"Do you know what day this is?" he asked.

Oliver groaned. *The day you get to buy a new tie.* And answered the question by spewing everything in his stomach onto the front of the man's clothes.

"Damn!" Levisay cried and took several steps back. But it was too late to stop the damage from being done. "Run a complete blood workup on him," he ordered, and began stripping off his lab coat as he headed for the door. "Call me when the results are in."

"Can't believe he's so tough."

"Get me a new needle."

"He's badly dehydrated."

"We need to get a drip going now."

"Don't see how anyone in this kind of shape is still walking."

"He can't last. The tests are conclusive. He's dying."

The voices drifted in and out of Oliver's drug-laden mind, frightening him with their urgency, taunting him with their warnings. He struggled to come out of the shadows and tell the whole lot of them off. They hadn't told him anything he didn't already know.

Hell yes, he was dying. He'd been pissing blood for a month. After that, what else was left? And yet, he was a bit surprised with himself. He hadn't considered himself a man with constitutional fortitude, but it would seem that he had it after all.

Tough. They'd said he was tough. He tried to laugh, but he couldn't get past the thought. He'd had to be tough to survive the life he'd lived.

Damn! Felt like they were sticking him full of holes. If he could just get his wits about him enough to wake up, he would give them all a cussing they would never forget. Needles, needles,

needles. In his arms, in his hands, in his butt. Didn't doctors know how to do anything besides cut and poke?

"Mr. Hale, we're going to make you more comfortable now."

Like hell. You can't make wore out comfortable, and I'm plumb wore out. From the inside out. My innards are gone. My joints are wore. My body's quitting on me. Why the hell won't you just let me die? I'm not afraid to die.

"Maybe you better notify his next of kin."

There is no next of kin. No wife. No kids. No nothing. He wished he could laugh. Lord, but he would love to have himself a good belly laugh right now. They're wasting their time looking for someone who could give a shit. But who cares? Let 'em look. It'll give 'em something to do.

"Somebody called wanting to visit old man Hale. If they want to talk to him, they'd better hurry. He doesn't have many talking days left."

Oliver's finger twitched. It was the best he could do with what he had to work with. Yeah, and the same to you, babe. There's no one on the face of this earth who'd want to be visiting me.

And then he thought of LeeNona Beverly. The damned old bitch. He refused to wallow in regret. He'd made his choices and lived with them. And then a spurt of sadness hit him. Now he was going to die with them. He thought back to the early years. To the times when he'd planned to live forever.

Boy, wasn't life a pisser? Why hadn't someone told him he would get old and sick? If he'd known this was coming, he could have chosen a better way out. Now, here he was, tied to the damned bed, with buttermilk for brains.

"It's time for your bath, Mr. Hale. You're going to feel so much better after you're clean."

I'd feel so much better if I could stuff that washcloth up your ass. Dammit, woman, didn't anybody ever tell you a man's balls are tender? Oh damn. Oh hell. Don't tickle my feet. I'm ticklish you mule-faced son of a bitch. Oh. Oh. Oh. Well, you went and did it now. It's not my fault my bowels don't hold. You knew my bladder's gone. You should have figured this one out for yourselves.

Indignity after indignity pushed Oliver closer and closer to breaking. Just as soon as he could remember the way to wake up, he was going to give them all a good piece of his mind.

Eleven

Brett's new house had become a source of unending pleasure for Tory. There were nooks and cran-
nies to explore that the apartment had not had, and
the fenced-in backyard that went with it was the
best bonus of all.

A rose of Sharon hedge bordered all three sides
of the fence, enclosing the yard with the faint but
sweet odor spilling from the lavender and pink
blossoms. Dozens of bees fought with the occasional hummingbird for territorial feeding rights,
while a family of robins nesting in the old shady
oak in the middle of the yard had an ongoing quar-
rel with a mockingbird who also called the tree
home.

Tory was drawn to the daily drama going on
beneath her nose and had taken to spending the
day in the yard with a camera around her neck.
Using her favorite telephoto lens and high-speed
color film, she had captured the details of life that
most people miss. She didn't yet know what she

was going to do with the shots, but many were too priceless to ignore.

A cat doing a nosedive into the hedge after missing his chance at the mockingbird, who'd just taken flight. A bee and a hummingbird going nose to nose for the same blossom. A fat-bellied robin caught stealing a grape from the bowl of fruit she'd been eating. A squirrel doing a tightrope act on a limb too frail for its weight.

Two days ago Brett had come home with a surprise and hadn't let her look until he had it fully assembled. He'd bought her a free-standing hammock and set it up in the shade of the big oak. Now it was her favorite place to be. Lying on her back and looking up to the patchwork of blue sky showing between the branches and leaves was good medicine for a frail spirit. It made her thankful for what she did have, rather than sorry for what she'd lost.

It had become her practice to take the rag doll with her whenever she went into the backyard, and she wondered if she was repeating a habit she'd had as a child. As she would busy herself with the camera, the doll would be set aside. Then, when she would miss it and turn to see where she'd left it, she would be hit with a strong sensation of déjà vu. It didn't matter whether she found it lying in the flowers or propped up in the hammock with bits of sunshine dappling its face. Each time she bent to pick it up, a whisper of something long forgotten would hit her. It wasn't as strong as a memory, but it was more than a longing, and she knew that with each passing day, her mind was turning loose of the wall behind which it had been hiding. And she drew strength from each passing day, knowing that with Brett at her side, she could face anything.

It was midafternoon, the laziest part of a late September day, when Tory heard the familiar sound of Brett's car turning into the driveway. Surprised that he was home, she glanced at her watch. It was barely three o'clock. Before she could gather up her things to go meet him, he pushed aside the sliding glass doors and came out onto the patio. Only after he saw her did the tension in his face ease away, and it shamed her that she'd given him cause for so much pain.

"Hey, pretty girl," Brett called, and started toward her.

Tory smiled and waved, then bent to pick up her doll. When she straightened, she saw that Brett had stopped and was standing and staring at her. She had no idea that the halo of sunlight and flowers in which she'd been framed had taken away all his breath, or that he was fighting back a sudden burst of tears. All she saw was the love on his face, and she knew it was for her.

"What brings you home this time of day?"

You. Always you. Brett took a deep breath, stunned by the beauty of the woman before him. Her hair was flyaway clean and pulled away from her face, and the dress she was wearing hung loose upon her, sheer pink-and-white gauze that teased the viewer with vague shapes and suggestions of the body beneath. She stood barefaced and guileless beneath the heat of the sun, holding her camera in one hand and that doll in the other. He was struck by an urgency to capture the moment.

"Don't move," he ordered, and took the camera from her before stepping back several paces.

"You'll need to reset the—"

"Just be still, Victoria. The rest will take care of itself."

She laughed, and that was how he caught her, with her head thrown back to the world, laughter spilling out of her mouth, and a ragamuffin baby doll clutched to her breast. Even after the shutter had clicked, he kept staring at the image before him, knowing that for the rest of his life, he would remember her this way, full of life and just happy to be here.

"Here, let me," she said, and forwarded the film, readying it for the next shot.

Brett's heart was still in his mouth when he swung her off her feet and into his arms.

"You're going to hurt yourself," she cried, reaching for the place he'd been shot.

"Victoria, do shut up," he muttered, and swooped for a kiss.

He started for the house.

"Don't drop me!"

"Only onto the bed." He grinned when she blushed.

It was an hour and a half later before they came up for air, and only then did Tory realize he still hadn't told her why he'd come home. She rose up on one elbow and ran her finger down the length of his arm, testing the tensile strength of muscles cording beneath her touch.

"Careful," he warned her, and then pounced, rolling her onto her back and pinning her to the bed with both hands. "Didn't anyone ever tell you to let sleeping dogs lie?"

She laughed. "Yes, but my mistake was in not recognizing that you fit into the canine category. Brett, darling, are you really a dog?"

He grinned. "Baby, there isn't a man walking who doesn't have a tiny bit of the dog in him. Why else would we screw up on a regular basis and never even know we're wrong?"

She laughed again, looping her arms around his neck and pulling him down until he was stretched out on top of her, chin to chin, toe to toe. She sighed, relishing the feel of him against her skin.

"You know what I love more than anything else in this world?" she said softly.

"What, honey?" he asked, then started to move, afraid he would crush her with his weight.

"No, don't," Tory begged, holding him in place on top of her.

"But I'm too heavy," he protested.

"No, I like it," she said, and then hushed when she realized that to say more would be giving herself away.

Brett rose up to gaze down at her face. He cupped her cheek, feathering tiny little kisses across her mouth until she was gasping for breath and yearning for more.

"Tell me why?"

Lost in what he was doing to her pulse rate, she'd almost forgotten what they'd been discussing.

"Why what?" she murmured.

"Why you like me to lie on top of you like this."

What she was about to tell him would be very revealing. But it was time she was honest with herself, as well as with him.

"Well, first because it's you, and because I love you," she said.

"And...?"

She fought an urge to look away as she met his gaze. "Because it makes me feel safe."

His shook his head, almost laughing at her answer. "Safe? How can me squashing you halfway into the mattress make you feel safe?"

Her chin quivered. "Because when I'm holding you like this, I don't feel vulnerable. You lie between me and the world."

Oh, Tory. He was too full of emotion to speak. Instead, he lowered himself back down on the bed, feeling the imprint of her body against him and letting himself be where she needed him to be.

"Always," he whispered, and held her close.

Tory closed her eyes and gave herself up to the man who was her life. It was only later, when Brett had gotten up to answer the phone, that she realized she still didn't know why he'd come home. When he disconnected, she poked at his bare backside with her toe to get his attention.

"Hey, you."

He looked over his shoulder and grinned.

"You're awfully feisty for someone who just flew over the rainbow."

Her mouth dropped. "Why, Brett, that's a beautiful analogy for making love."

He grinned. "Yeah. This old hippie I know says it all the time."

She threw a pillow at him and then laughed. "You're such a mess," she muttered, then reached for her clothes. "And hey, by the way, you never did tell me why you're home in the middle of the day.''

Because she was pulling her dress over her head, she didn't see him tense, and by the time it had fallen into place, he was grinning again.

''That's right, I didn't. Meet you in the hammock in two minutes, okay?''

Her eyes lit with delight. A surprise? She loved surprises. Without waiting for him to continue, she raced toward the door.

''You forgot your shoes,'' he yelled, but she was already gone.

He shrugged and headed for the kitchen. If Tory wanted to go barefoot, then barefoot she could be. The way he figured it, she hadn't done nearly enough things in her life just for fun.

Just before he started out the door, he yelled, ''Close your eyes.'' Then he hurried across the yard, juggling a carton and two spoons. When he got to the hammock, he stuck one of the spoons in the carton and dug deep.

''Okay,'' he said. ''Now open your mouth.''

Tory groaned. ''Oh, Brett, you know how I hate to be tricked. Please let me look. I can't open my mouth unless I know what you're going to put in it.''

''Trust me, baby. You're going to love it.''

She shuddered but did as he asked; then, when she felt the cold sweet taste of strawberry ice cream melting on her tongue, her eyes flew open in delight.

"Ice cream! And it's strawberry—my absolute favorite."

"Hold this," he ordered, handing her the carton and both spoons while he slung one long leg over the hammock and then settled himself into place facing her, with the carton of ice cream between them.

She handed him a spoon, then helped herself to another bite.

"It's going to melt," she said, giggling between bites as a thick film of condensation began to form on the outside of the carton.

"Then eat fast."

She grinned and did as he suggested.

They were down to the bottom of the carton when Tory threw up her hands in defeat.

"I can't eat another bite," she said, and leaned back in the hammock with a groan, rubbing her tummy and thankful that her dress was loose at the waist. "But it was wonderful. Thank you so much for my surprise."

"You're welcome," Brett said, licking his spoon. Then he set the carton onto the grass beneath the hammock.

His conscience was bothering him. She looked so content, and he was about to ruin what was left of her day.

"Tory."

Replete from her feast, she lay motionless, her eyes half-closed from the glare of the sun lowering toward the western horizon.

"Hmm?"

"You know when you went to Iowa?"

"Umm-hmm?"

"If you'd found Oliver Hale, what were you going to ask him?"

For a long moment she thought back, trying to remember what she'd been thinking. But so much had happened since then that she drew a blank.

"You know what? I'm not really sure. I think I was just planning to play it by ear."

"What if he hadn't recognized you? What if you'd gone all that way for nothing?"

She met Brett's gaze. "I was going to come back and make an appointment with the first psychiatrist I could find."

Her answer startled him. He hadn't realized she'd thought it all through so thoroughly.

"You're really serious about getting to the bottom of your nightmares, aren't you, honey?"

"Wouldn't you be?" she asked.

He nodded and began absently rubbing at her ankle as they rocked face-to-face in the hammock.

"You know how much I love you, don't you, baby?"

She smiled. "Yes."

He paused as he considered how to word what he had to say next.

"So, knowing what you do now...I mean, having found the rag doll and all...what would you say to Hale now if you saw him?"

She looked straight in Brett's face and then stiffened. *He knows something.*

"I found him," Brett said, confirming what she already knew.

God help me.

Her expression stilled, and Brett could have sworn he watched her spirit slide behind a blank wall. But there was an urgency in her voice as she leaned forward, her fingers clutching at the fabric of his pant legs. "Where?"

"As luck would have it, if you can consider anything about this mess lucky, he's incarcerated here in this state."

She repeated her question. "Where?"

"Oklahoma State Penitentiary in McAlester."

"I need to talk to him. Will they let me talk to him?"

Without waiting for his answer, she rolled out of the hammock and bolted toward the patio before he could stop her. Midway between the tree and the house, she turned to wait for Brett, who was close on her heels.

"Oh, Brett, I'm scared."

He pulled her into his arms, nestling her head beneath his chin and holding her close.

"I know, Tory, but I'll be with you all the way."

She drew back, needing to see his face when she asked, "They'll let me see him?"

"I don't see why not."

"When?"

"I'll make a couple of calls. We should know something by tomorrow, okay?"

"Okay."

Then he remembered the carton they'd left under the swing. "Give me a minute to clean up our mess and I'll meet you inside, where it's cool."

He went back to the hammock as Tory disappeared inside. When he bent down to pick it up, he noticed a small green worm floating in the bottom of the carton. He turned the carton upside down, spilling the melted ice cream, as well as the worm, onto the ground.

All the way back into the house, he couldn't help wondering how symbolic that might have been. By finding Oliver Hale for Tory to meet, he could very well be opening up a real can of worms. And then he shook off the thought. It couldn't matter. She needed—no, deserved—to know the truth, no matter how frightening or ugly it might be. As he dumped the carton in the trash and the spoons in the sink, he kept remembering one of his mother's favorite phrases.

The truth shall set you free.

"Or make you crazy," he muttered, and went to look for Tory.

She slept in a tangle of bedclothes, her body curled tightly within the sheet, her hands tucked beneath her chin like a child in prayer. Lightning flashed in the sky as a storm front moved across the northern half of the state, but she didn't see it. She was too lost in the dream playing out in her mind.

The child rode the swing hanging from the sweet gum tree, her little legs pumping as she hummed a made-up tune. Now and then the hem of her dress would billow, revealing white cotton panties and little brown legs. All around her was sunshine and light, but she was safe and cool here in the shade, in her swing.

Her fingers were curled tight around the rope as she flew high toward the overhead limbs. Then, swinging backward in a 180 degree arc, she would give herself an added pump before rocking back down. Higher and higher she flew until she could almost touch the leaves and the sky and the clouds. Overjoyed with just being, she burst out in a cry of delight, "Look at me! Look at me!"

Behind her, a door slammed abruptly, and as she continued to swing, she heard a voice suddenly cry out, "Be careful! Oh, sweetheart, be careful!"

No sooner had the words been uttered than her fingers slipped from the rope. The wide, open smile on her face turned into a shrill scream, and she tumbled head over heels into the air before landing on her back in the ankle-high grass.

Shocked, and with no breath left to cry, she lay stunned and gasping and wondering if she was dead. The sound of running footsteps was loud in her ears as she turned to look. Someone was coming toward her and calling out her name in a high, frantic voice. She reached up, trying to speak, but her lungs were still filling with much needed air, and all she could do was gasp painfully.

"Oh dear, oh dear, are you all right?"

Someone was kneeling beside her. She looked up, expecting to see the face of her savior, and was blinded instead by the sun. Instinctively, she blinked, and when she looked up again, there was nobody there.

Tory woke suddenly, realizing afterward that she'd been holding her breath. She inhaled deeply, taking much needed air into her lungs, thankful that, for once, she hadn't awakened Brett, as well. Then she closed her eyes, letting herself back into the dream and experiencing a moment of frustration that she'd awakened too soon. There was a knowing within her that if she could have stayed with the dream, she would have seen the face of the person who kept calling her name.

She sighed. This whole business was making her crazy. It was obvious that her subconscious was trying to tell her something, but for the life of her, either she couldn't or wouldn't let herself understand.

Maybe...just maybe...Oliver Hale will have the answers I need.

Having to be satisfied with that, she rolled toward Brett, taking comfort in the fact that he was there.

The scorpion was almost lost in a wrinkle of the dry, burning flesh of Oliver's cheek. He grimaced with pain as he bumped the IV needle in the back of his hand and wished to God he hadn't tried to hold up that liquor store in Ponca City. It had seemed like an easy way to make himself some quick money. That night there had been no customers in sight and only one old clerk. Who would have thought that run-down place had a silent alarm, or that the clerk was a salty old man who was willing to shoot back?

He moaned, drifting in and out of consciousness and willing himself not to be sick again. Damn, but he hated to throw up. Vaguely aware of someone standing at his bedside, he tried to wake up enough to tell them he hurt, but they kept giving him stuff that put him out like a light. He had yet to connect the two in his mind.

He didn't know that the doctors were well aware of his suffering. It wasn't often that someone in such an advanced state of disease was still walking, let alone enduring his misery without benefit of medication.

He thought of his place back in Iowa, with all his worldly belongings. LeeNona, that damned old hen, was probably mad as all get-out by now. But the way he looked at it, it was partly her fault he was in this mess. There had been a time in their relationship when he had been living with her, not out back in that little shed of a house. But she'd gotten on her high horse some years back and booted him out of her bed.

After that, their arrangement had become commonplace. Life hadn't been spectacular, but it hadn't been all that bad. And then he'd lost his job at the mill and fallen behind on his rent. He still couldn't believe she'd threatened to have him evicted. The bitch. She never would cut a man any slack. It was his last conscious thought for several long hours.

Sometime during the night he came to again and was instantly engulfed in a wave of nausea and pain. A monitor started beeping. It took several moments for him to realized it was connected to him. He moaned, trying to call out, but there was no need. Footsteps sounded on the tiled floor. Someone was already coming. Moments later, a blessed lassitude began spreading through him from the inside out. His fingers relaxed as he rode the morphine into unconsciousness.

Brett hung up the phone and then cursed beneath his breath.

What the hell else can possibly go wrong?

He heard a car slowing down and glanced out the window, relaxing only after it had passed. It wasn't Tory. At least he still had some time to figure out how to give her the latest bad news. How was he going to explain that he'd promised her something he might not be able to deliver? But who could have known this would happen? Who could have predicted such a far-fetched possibility?

He gazed around the room, thankful that at least she'd fallen in love with this house. When he let himself dream, he could almost believe their world was normal—that she was an everyday lady with an everyday life. Then something would happen—something like the phone call he'd just received—and he would be reminded how fragile their world really was, and how much of their happiness was hanging on the word of a stranger.

A car door slammed, and he looked up. Damn. She was back. He gritted his teeth and headed for the door. Procrastination was not one of his faults.

"Hey, baby, did you buy out the store?"

Tory looked up, then grinned. "Make yourself useful," she said, and handed him a bulging grocery bag in each arm, then took the last one herself and headed for the front door. "I've been hungry for pot roast for a week. And you'll be glad to know I got all the ingredients to make strawberry cheesecake."

Watching the sway of her backside as she stepped up on the porch, Brett lost focus on what she was saying and groaned beneath his breath. Without trying, she was the sexiest woman he'd ever known. And right now she was happy. It made him sick, knowing he was about to ruin her whole day.

He set the bags down on the counter, then took the one she was carrying and set it aside, as well. But when she started digging into the sacks, he stopped her with a touch.

"Tory, we need to talk."

"In a minute. Some of this stuff needs to be refrigerated as soon as possible."

"It can wait a minute, okay?"

The tone of his voice was beginning to soak in. She paused and then turned to look at his face.

Her heart dropped. She'd seen that expression too many times before.

"What's wrong?"

"It's Hale."

She straightened, as if bracing herself for a mortal blow.

"What about him?"

"I don't know if we're going to be allowed to talk to him or not."

"But why? It's not as if we're going to hurt him."

"I know, honey, but he's—"

"I wouldn't cause a fuss, I promise. Can't you tell them that I just want to talk?"

"It isn't that, Tory. The problem isn't in what you want to say to him, or even that you want to see him at all."

She doubled her hand into a fist in frustration. "Then what?" she cried. "What else could there possibly be?"

Brett took a deep breath. "He's no longer in lockup. As of a few days ago, he was moved into the prison hospital."

Her expression brightened. "Then that's okay," she said. "I don't mind waiting. After all, I've waited all these years, right?"

"No, honey, it's not okay, and neither is Hale. I just got a phone call from the warden, denying your visit. Hale isn't suffering a temporary ailment. He's dying."

Twelve

Stunned, Tory walked out of the house without saying a word. Brett started to follow her and then changed his mind. After having pinned all her hopes on finding this man, she needed time alone. If a woman had ever needed a break in life, it was Tory. He stood at the window, watching as she crawled into the hammock. When she rolled herself into a ball, he frowned. Pulling away. She was pulling away from everything, including him. He thrust his fingers through his hair in frustration.

"Dammit! This isn't fair. There has to be something else I can do."

And then he paused. *What if...*

He headed for the phone. If the warden wasn't sympathetic to Brett's appeal, maybe he would listen to Tory's doctor.

A day later, they drove into McAlester at a quarter past two in the afternoon. Tory was white-lipped but determined to take advantage of the warden's change of heart. She knew Brett had pulled some strings to make this happen, but she didn't care. She just needed to see Oliver Hale's face and hear his voice. After that, if no bells rang, then so be it. At least she had been given the chance.

She touched Brett's leg. "I don't know how you did this, but I will be forever grateful."

He dodged a jaywalking pedestrian with a dog on a leash, muttering beneath his breath at the near miss. When he braked for a red light, he glanced at her.

"Let's hope you still feel this way after it's over."

She shrugged. "I only want some answers. I don't believe in miracles."

Brett reached for her hand. Her fingers were cold, her skin clammy. In spite of her bravado, he could tell that she was scared to death.

"No matter what you do or don't learn today, remember I love you."

She sighed and leaned back against the seat. "I know. I keep thinking that all this hell is worth it for that reason alone."

He frowned. "No way, baby. I know all I need to know about you. Whatever you learn is for you, not me. Understand?"

She nodded. "Understood."

Within the hour they were being escorted, under guard, into the hospital area of the penitentiary, past the main ward, where normal convalescent care took place, and into the twelve-bed unit housing the critically and terminally ill.

The moment they passed through the doors of the critical care, Tory sensed the atmosphere changing. She caught herself holding her breath, as if unwilling to share the same air with so much despair.

A man in a white lab coat met them at the doorway.

"Good afternoon," he said. "I'm Dr. Levisay. The warden told us you were coming." He looked to Brett. "I was told you came to question Oliver Hale? Am I right?"

Brett shook his head. "I'm only here as an escort. This is Victoria Lancaster. She's the one who wants to see Hale." He looked around the ward. "Where is he?" he asked.

But Tory had already seen him—in the bed against the far wall. Even though his face was drawn and pasty, the tattoo was impossible to miss.

"There. He's there."

Brett looked, then groaned inwardly. He'd seen less wiring on a jet than they had hooked up on that man—and jets could fly.

"You do understand that he might not be able to talk?" Levisay said.

Tory heard him but refused to consider the possibility. They'd come so far. Surely fate wouldn't be this cruel.

"I'll see if he's awake," Levisay said, and moved toward the bed, his lab coat flapping at the backs of his knees as he walked.

Tory began to follow.

"Tory, honey, maybe we'd better wait until—" He gave up. She obviously wasn't listening to him any better than she'd listened to Levisay. At this point, she wasn't about to be deterred by a sleeping man, even if he was dying.

Levisay read the monitors at a glance as he leaned over his patient. Hale had recently been sedated. Chances were it would be a couple of hours before he was lucid again, but there was no harm in giving it a try.

"Mr. Hale, you have some visitors." The man barely stirred. "Mr. Hale, do you hear me? You have some visitors."

Oliver's eyelids fluttered as his mind began to focus on the doctor's voice. Although the words were faint, he could hear him fine. But he wanted to sleep more than he wanted to listen.

The doctor turned. "I'm sorry, but as you can see, he's out. If you care to come back in a couple of hours, he will probably be more cognizant than he is now."

Once again Tory's hopes fell, although she

could see for herself that communicating with him was impossible.

"May I just wait here a moment?" she asked. "I won't bother him, but I would like to take a better look."

The doctor frowned. "I'm sorry, but I was under the impression that you knew him."

"I don't know whether I do or not," she said. "I don't have any memory of my childhood."

"Then why—"

Brett interrupted. "It's a long story, Doc. Trust me when I tell you she's been cleared to ask Hale anything she wants."

Dr. Levisay shrugged. "Fine. I have no problem with you being here, as long as you don't endanger my patient's health."

Brett took the doctor aside, giving Tory the opportunity she wanted to look more closely at Hale.

"Look, Doc. Hale's dying, right?"

Levisay nodded.

"Then cut her some slack. She had a hell of a childhood, and Hale may very well hold the key to why she can't remember anything about the first six years of her life."

"No, you look, Mr. Hooker. Three-fourths of the inmates here had miserable childhoods. The other fourth are just miserable human beings. I'll give her the chance she needs, but it's not up to me, it's up to Oliver Hale."

* * *

Oliver was floating. The sensation was so real that when he suddenly found himself standing in a corner of the room, he wasn't surprised. Weightless. That was what he was. Weightless. He looked back at the body lying still on the bed and shrugged. Man, but it felt good to be mobile again. He wanted to laugh. Look at them, standing around his bed like they were at a wake. *Not yet!* he crowed. *I ain't done for yet.*

He moved toward them, curious as to who they were and why they'd come. Visitors, the doctor had said. It wasn't likely. He didn't have any family, and he damn sure didn't have any friends like them. The woman's hair was long and blond, just like LeeNona's had been when they'd first met. He moved closer, frowning as he overheard them talking.

Dying. Hell yes, I'm dying. If your liver was as eaten up with a cancer as mine, you'd be dying, too.

His attention strayed to the nurse on the other side of his bed.

Damn, but she has some pretty tits. I'd give a whole lot just for the strength to squeeze them. But it ain't gonna happen. There ain't even enough juice left in me to spit.

Again Hale's attention was drawn toward the young woman standing by his bed. He couldn't see her face, but she sure had pretty hair. He looked at her hands, at the tilt of her head. She reminded him of someone, but he couldn't think who. That frustrated him. He hated being weak. He hated not being able to remember. Then he sighed. And dammit, when he thought about it real hard, he hated the idea of dying.

Religion had never been part of his life before, but he'd been thinking real hard on it now for days. Ever since he'd heard them whispering over his bed when they thought he was unconscious. Dying, they'd said. The old man is dying. Well, okay. It comes to everyone. But what was bothering him now was what comes after. Is it all over when you draw your last breath, or do angels really come to retrieve your mortal soul?

Hale looked back at that shell of a man and felt like crying. What if there really was an afterlife? If there was a heaven, then that meant there was also a hell.

Oh God, if you're there, I'm sorry...for a whole lot of things.

Hale was waiting for God to answer when the young woman turned around. And when he saw her face, he knew he'd been right. There *was* a God. And He'd sent this woman to sit in judgment on Oliver's fate. His conscience smote him.

I am going to hell!

And then he remembered a time from his youth

and a night when he'd sat in the back row of a church and listened to the town whore reciting her sins. They'd said she'd been saved. He remembered thinking that night that they hadn't saved her from nothin', cause there hadn't been anything there to hurt her. It had been years later before he'd understood the term. And now he found himself in the same predicament. He tried to remember what the town whore had done. Oh yes. She'd confessed. That was what he needed to do. He needed to confess. But he was out here, and the old man was there. This would never work. He had to go back.

As Tory stood at his side, the old man started to moan. She spun around. "Doctor! He's waking up."

They didn't know it, but Oliver Hale wasn't just waking up. He'd come back to beg for forgiveness and plead for redemption.

Hale reached out, grabbing Tory's wrist before she saw his intention, and clinging with a strength she wouldn't have believed.

"Sorry...sorry. Didn't mean...should have stayed...loved you...loved you."

Levisay was stunned. He couldn't believe the old man was awake, let alone talking. He had enough painkillers in him to fell an ox.

Brett took one look at Tory's face and moved

to her side. He didn't know what was going on, but her expression was fixed on the old man's face as if her life depended on it him.

Levisay glanced at the heart monitor. It was going wild. He turned around. "I'm sorry," he said. "But you two are going to have to leave. He's—"

"No!"

Stunned, they all turned to look. No one could believe the cry had come from Oliver Hale's mouth. Levisay reached for Hale's arm, but the old man wouldn't turn loose of Tory's wrist.

"Nurse, get them out now!" Levisay shouted.

Oliver struggled to remain conscious. If she left before he got a chance to apologize, he would go to hell.

"No! Don't leave me." And then he pulled Tory close, whispering his plea to her alone. "Please, little girl...don't go."

Tory froze. That voice...calling that name. Something shifted inside her mind and started trying to come out. Something old and forgotten. Something bad. Something that hurt. She forgot that she'd come for answers and tore herself free from Hale's grasp. In a panic, she started backing up. If she got far enough away, it couldn't find her. But when she tried to run, she found herself unable to move. Something had hold of her arms. Someone was calling her name. She shuddered, then sighed, letting the panic subside. It was Brett. Only Brett.

Hale could see her clearly now. He'd been right. She'd come to point blame. He'd lied once to save himself, but if he wanted to save his soul, it was time to tell the truth.

"Doctor...gotta listen...tell her...sorry. She's gotta understand."

Brett couldn't stand idle any longer. No one was asking the right questions, and from the looks of the old man, he could go at any minute. He hadn't brought Tory this far just to let her watch a man die.

"Understand what, Hale? What does she have to understand?" Brett asked.

Oliver sighed. At last. Someone was listening.

"Didn't mean it. You gotta believe me. I didn't mean it."

Brett kept thinking back to what he knew from Tory's file. Could Hale have been in on the abandonment of Tory? Was he part of the reason a six-year-old child had been dumped?

"Mean what? What didn't you mean to do?" he asked.

Barely able to lift his arm, Hale pointed at Tory, his hand trembling.

"Kill her. I didn't mean to kill her."

Oh, hell, Brett thought, as Levisay interrupted.

"He's out of his head," Levisay said. Then he

glanced at Tory. "I don't know what you came to hear, but I'm sorry. I told you he might not be lucid. You're obviously not dead."

But Oliver kept talking, spilling his secret to cleanse his soul, uncaring if they listened our not.

"You shouldn't'a got mad at me," he mumbled. "You always got mad at me."

Tory's eye were huge, fixed in disbelief upon the old man's mouth. With every word he uttered, a new image flashed in her mind. It was like looking at hundreds of still shots, one right after the other, but unable to remember where they'd been taken, or by whom. Yet the longer she stood, the more certain she became that the child in the images was her. With Brett beside her, there was a calmness within her that hadn't been there before. And she looked at that scorpion and at the old man's face and she remembered it all, right up to the day they'd left her alone. *Oh, God.*

"Are you my father?"

He groaned. "No."

She fired another question at him, her voice ripping through the silence surrounding the bed. "Why did you take Sweet Baby?"

Hale's voice was fading. "You told me to pack it all."

"I didn't tell you anything," Tory said. "I wasn't even there, remember? You and my mother left me behind."

Hale gasped and choked, his breathing more and more ragged with each passing inhalation. Then he closed his eyes.

Tory leaned down. "Don't you do this!" she shouted. "Don't you die on me yet!" She grabbed him by the shoulders. "Why didn't you take me with you?"

Levisay started to intervene when Brett held him back.

"Dammit, man, let her talk. In the long run, it's not going to matter."

Hale kept mumbling, spitting out words as they came from his mind. "Fight...you fell...didn't mean..."

Tory was shaking, awash with a lifetime of suppressed memories. She was hearing Hale's answers, but he wasn't making sense. She kept asking him one thing; he kept answering another. Bordering on hysteria, she screamed in his face.

"You and my mother left me to come home to an empty house. I stayed in a closet for three days and nights, afraid to come out. Didn't you think of how terrified I would be?"

Hale's head was rolling from side to side on the pillow. His color was ashen, his voice barely above a whisper.

"Not closet...tub. I put you under the tub." His eyes widened, and it looked as if the scorpion on his cheek had just flicked its tail. He inhaled a ragged breath, struggling to pull air into his lungs, but he was so weak. Seconds passed as he stared straight into Tory's face. "Ruthie...forgive... didn't mean...kill. Why didn't you stay dead?"

Tory froze.

Ruthie?

She tried to breathe and heard herself choking instead.

Ruthie?

Brett was talking to her now, telling her that she was going to be all right.

Ruthie?

An image flashed in her mind, an image of a woman with pretty brown hair and laughing eyes, a woman who smelled like roses and soap and who made up her own special songs to sing her little girl to sleep.

Hush little Tory, don't say a word.

Mommy's gonna buy you a honeybird.

A tear ran down the side of Tory's nose. Honeybird. Hummingbird. Sometimes, when you're only four, one word is as good as another.

The room was beginning to spin. She grabbed Brett, desperately holding on to the only solid thing in her world, but it was no use. She looked up, trying to focus on Brett's face, and all she could see were those dark blue eyes, swimming in tears. Brett. Her Brett. He was crying...crying for her. That meant he understood.

"Oh, Brett, he killed my mother…didn't he?"
She fainted before he could answer.

It was midnight when Brett pulled into the driveway and parked. Although the street was well lit, the house was dark. He wished he'd had the foresight to leave a light on when they'd left this morning. And then he glanced at Tory, who was still sleeping in the seat beside him. This morning? Surely it had taken longer than eight hours for their world to take this big a turn?

Gently, he lifted a tendril of hair from her eyes and slipped it behind her ear. Poor lost little girl. Being left behind and believing it was because she was unworthy of love.

And Hale. Fate had given him the perfect out. He hadn't been married to Ruth Lancaster, therefore he did not abandon a child, therefore the state was not looking for him. And if Oliver Hale was to be believed, after the accident in which Ruth Lancaster had died, he'd panicked and hidden the body in a pretty obscure location. Beneath a bathtub, of all places. It would be hell trying to serve an arrest warrant on a woman who was no longer alive.

Even as they'd been leaving the prison, Hale's doctor had still been hedging his bets, not fully convinced that the old man had known what he was saying. But Tory had been certain, and that was enough for Brett. Now all they had to do was alert the Arkansas authorities regarding Oliver Hale's deathbed confession and see what happened next.

He reached over and touched Tory's arm. "Tory, baby...we're here."

She sighed and then blinked. "What?"

"We're home. Are you awake enough to walk?"

She sat up and looked out the window. Beneath the glow of the streetlights, the concrete walk leading up to the porch looked like a bright white path. A path that showed the way home.

She looked at Brett. "I can walk. When I was little, I walked home by myself every day."

Brett's heart was so full of emotion that he didn't trust himself to speak. It was the first time since he'd known her that she'd spoken of her childhood. He reached for her hand and then cleared his throat.

"Tory?"

"Hmm?"

"You don't have to go home by yourself anymore."

It was ten minutes after eight the next morning when the phone rang, startling Brett and waking Tory. They both rolled toward the sound, wanting it to stop. Brett grabbed it first, and his voice sounded more like an angry growl from a bear whose slumber had been disturbed than a man who'd just awakened.

"Hello?"

"It's me, Ryan. What the hell's going on up there?"

Brett sat up, combing his hair with his fingers and rubbing sleep from his eyes. "I don't know what you're talking about, and good morning to you, too."

"Turn on the television—now!" Ryan ordered. "Channel four. Victoria is all over the news."

Brett's heart did a flip-flop, and he hit the floor running, taking the portable phone with him as he headed for the living room.

Tory sat up in bed. Something was wrong!

"Brett?" He didn't answer. "What's wrong?" When he kept running, she jumped up and followed him. The last thing she expected to see was her picture being flashed on the morning news.

"Oh, my gosh."

She stared in disbelief.

"According to unnamed sources, a deathbed confession from the state prison in McAlester yesterday could be the answer to an unsolved mystery that began years ago at a rural house just outside of Calico Rock, Arkansas.

"Victoria Lancaster, a local photojournalist of national renown, was abandoned at the age of—"

She took the remote from Brett and hit the mute button. Dumbfounded by this turn of events, she didn't know what to do.

"How did they find out?"

He snorted rudely. "How do they find out about anything? Somebody talked for money, that's how."

"But what am I going to do?"

He handed her the phone. "For starters, talk to Ryan. I need a cup of coffee."

She stared, first at Brett's bare backside as he walked away, then down at the phone. She sighed and put it to her ear.

"Good morning, Ryan, how have you been?"

"Don't go anywhere until I get there," he said.

"You don't need to—"

"Yes, I do," he argued. "Tell Brett to stay put until I get there. I should arrive around noon."

"Okay, but I don't think—"

The line began to buzz. He'd disconnected.

Tory followed Brett into the kitchen and handed him the phone. "He hung up."

Brett frowned. "That's weird. Didn't he say anything else?"

"Yes. To stay put. He'll be here before noon."

True to his word, Ryan Hooker pulled into the driveway at a quarter to twelve. But neither of them realized it was Ryan until he parked and got out. The Chevy four-by-four that he normally drove had been replaced by a brand-new, self-contained motor home. Brett whistled beneath his breath and went to the door.

"Have mercy, brother. That's some set of wheels."

Ryan dropped the keys in Brett's hand and then slapped him on the back.

"Yeah, and if you put a dent in it, I'll take it out of your hide."

Brett stared at the keys and then up at Ryan. "Why would we need—"

Ryan saw Tory standing in the doorway. "You're going to Arkansas, aren't you?"

She nodded. "But how did you know?"

"Because if that was my mother, I'd be going, too. As for the motor home, you'll be needing a place to stay. And I looked Calico Rock up in my atlas. It's a pretty small town, so housing will be limited. Add to that the media that's bound to converge on the place, and you've got yourself a mess. Besides, I figured you'd rather be on-site. With that rig, you can be." He looked away, unwilling to talk about why they were going. "It's a real nice motor home. I think you'll be more comfortable in it than in some motel."

Tory's chin began to quiver, and her eyes filled with tears as she moved to where they were standing.

"Ryan Hooker, how can we ever thank you?"

Slightly embarrassed, he still managed to grin as he hugged her. "Hell, Tory, don't make such a big deal out of it," he said. "Don't you know yet that's what families are for?"

Tory looked at Brett over Ryan's shoulder, and the smile on her face was one he'd never seen.

"No," she said. "I didn't, but I'm learning."

Ryan patted her on the back and then turned to Brett. "Give me the keys to your car."

"But—"

"I need a way to get home, remember? When you guys start home from Arkansas, just swing by Enid and we'll trade vehicles then. Okay?"

Brett handed his brother his keys. "Had it all figured out, didn't you?"

Ryan grinned. "Somebody had to get you two in gear. Be glad it was me and not Mom."

A short while later, Ryan left. He hadn't been gone more than a few minutes when the phone began to ring. Brett answered, already leery of who else might be calling.

"Hooker residence."

"Brett, Don Lacey. Is there anything my office can do for you and Victoria?"

Relieved that it was his boss and not some reporter, Brett dropped into a nearby chair. "At this point, Don, I don't know what to tell you. Our main objective is to start the ball rolling with the

Arkansas authorities so they'll investigate the site.''

"If it would help, I'd be more than happy to make a few calls. I know some people up that way."

Brett exhaled slowly. One less hurdle he would have to clear himself.

"Thanks, Don. That would be great."

"No problem," Lacey said. "Oh, and give Victoria my regards. Tell her we're with her all the way."

"Yes, sir, I'll do just that." He disconnected and went outside to look for Tory. She was coming out of the motor home with a smile on her face.

"You won't believe what's in there."

Brett took her in his arms. "Lacey sends his regards and says to tell you that everyone in the office is behind you all the way."

She couldn't hide her surprise. "That's really nice." She turned to look at the motor home once more. "I never knew people could be so thoughtful."

Brett put his arm around her as they started into the house. "That's because you didn't know the right people." He kicked the door shut and took her into his arms. "Sweetheart, what do you say we get packed and get out of here? I keep expecting some camera crew to show up any minute, and frankly, that's the last thing you need to deal with, okay?''

She nodded. "It won't take me long."

"Just pack comfortable clothes. Stuff you won't mind getting dirty. It's bound to be—"

When Brett realized what he'd been about to say, he stopped himself in midsentence. This wasn't just anyone they were going to dig up. It was her mother. And from the look on Tory's face, she was remembering it, too.

"I'm sorry, sweetheart. I didn't think."

"It's okay, Brett. I'm just glad I don't have to face this alone."

Brett wrapped his arms around her, rocking her gently as they stood. And yet in spite of his presence, Tory felt a tiny little pain digging itself deeper into the middle of her chest. She wouldn't ever know peace until this was over.

Thirteen

They crossed the border into Arkansas before dark, parking for the night at an RV campground just across the state line. It was a new experience for Tory and a renewal of an old one for Brett. As he completed the hookups, he kept thinking of the wonderful memories he had of traveling like this. Of camping out with his parents in state parks and roasting wieners over an open fire. Of sharing a bed with Ryan and scaring Celia just enough to make her scream, but never enough to make her cry. Of waking up to the smell of fresh-perked coffee and frying bacon. Of hearing his father's laughter and his mother's soft giggles.

While he might have good memories of traveling in an RV, this was Tory's first trip, and when it was over, the memories she would take with her would not be good. He couldn't control what might happen after they reached Calico Rock, but he could make the trip there as pleasant as possible. Although they'd packed plenty of food to cook, there was a restaurant just across the road.

That would be good. The best thing he could do for her tonight was to keep her mind off where they were going tomorrow.

He opened the door and poked his head inside. "Hey, sweetheart, I'm cooking tonight."

Tory emerged from the back of the bus with a smile on her face. "Great! What are we having?"

He pointed to the café across the road. "I don't know yet, but from what I can smell, it's been barbecued."

She laughed and let him help her down the steps. "Did you pack any antacids?"

"Very funny," he said, and swatted her on the seat of the pants. "Just put a hustle in that pretty little butt of yours. I'm starving."

The highway beyond the RV park was all but silent. Now and then a car would pass by, but it would be gone long before the sound had time to wake Brett up. And while the quiet was peaceful, Tory was used to the sounds of the city. To her, the silence was deafening. It gave her too much time to think, and way too much time to remember.

She tossed restlessly, trying to find a comfortable spot in the bed, but it was hopeless. Not even the proximity of Brett's arms could calm her tonight.

It was late September. But she remembered another September night many years ago, and the nights that followed before she was found. She shuddered and turned toward Brett, needing to see his face, to know that she was not alone.

Outside, the night air was cool. Crickets moved through the grass, chirping their passing. Frogs croaked in the little pond below the hill where they were parked, and if she listened real close, she could hear a tree limb scratching against the roof.

The wind must have come up.

Weary beyond words, she closed her eyes, praying for sleep. But sleep wouldn't come. She kept seeing herself hiding in that empty house and waiting for a mother who would never come back.

Don't think about it, Tory. It's been over twenty-five years. She isn't going anywhere.

But the urgency to find her mother's body and put it to rest was growing.

I will find you, Mommy, and I will take care of you. Just like you took care of me.

Outside, the wind began to blow in earnest, and she scooted beneath Brett's outflung arm, drawing comfort from his presence. She couldn't believe their misfortune. The inclement weather that Oklahoma had been suffering seemed to have followed them. Sure enough, a short while later, rain began to fall, pattering down upon the metal roof of the motor home and lulling Tory into a restless sleep.

* * *

The woman knelt before the Christmas tree, then lifted a small red package from beneath the branches. Her eyes were filled with love as she turned to the child beside her, who was dancing with anticipation.

"This is for you," she said. "Merry Christmas."

The little girl took the package, tearing into it and tossing aside the small bow and the bright red paper with no thought of how carefully it had been wrapped. At the age of three, her priorities were firmly in place. But when she lifted the lid of the box, she stilled. Her eyes widened, and her tiny mouth formed a small O as she reached inside.

"Look," the woman said. "Your very own baby doll. And see...she has long blond hair and blue eyes, just like you."

The woman smiled at her daughter's reaction, then took the doll out of the box and laid her in the little girl's arms.

"There you go. Now Mommy's sweet baby has a baby all her own."

The little girl bent to the doll with all the inborn nature of a true nurturer, cuddling it close to her chest and rocking it back and forth in her arms.

"Sweet Baby," she crooned, immediately bonding with the big button eyes and the embroidered red lips frozen in a timeless smile.

As the woman watched her baby daughter rock-

ing the doll, her heart swelled with love. She
thought of all the rest she'd sacrificed while sew-
ing in secret after Tory had gone to bed, but now,
seeing the joy on her face made it all worthwhile.

".Well, Tory, what do you think about her?"

The little girl's expression was solemn as she
gazed down at the doll in her arms.

"I love her."

The woman smiled. "She's going to need a
name. What do you think we should call her?"

The child's answer came swiftly, as if she'd
known it for years.

"Sweet Baby. I gonna name her Sweet Baby."

The woman laughed and caught her child up in
her arms, hugging her tightly against her breasts.

"But you're my sweet baby, remember? We
can't have two little girls with that name."

The little girl giggled, then pointed at herself.
"I your sweet baby. This my sweet baby."

The woman laughed again. "Okay, okay. You
win. Sweet Baby it is."

Tory woke up just as a gust of wind splattered
rain against the window near her head. There was
a sadness inside of her that she couldn't shake. She
knew that the dream she'd just had wasn't a dream
at all but an old memory that had decided to come
home—just as she had. She glanced through the

curtains. Although it was still dark and raining, she knew morning wasn't far away.

Brett sighed in his sleep and then rolled over, pulling her up against him, then kissing her ear before settling back into a soft, uneven snore.

She closed her eyes, savoring the feeling of being safe and loved, and in that instant she remembered that she'd felt this way before—on a Christmas morning, many years ago, in her mother's arms. A tear slid out of the corner of her eye as she scooted closer to Brett. The next few days weren't going to be easy, but, as her mother's daughter, it was the least she could do.

When they drove into the outskirts of Calico Rock, it was just after 9:00 a.m. They'd driven in and out of showers until a short while ago, but from the looks of the sky, the possibility of another rain was likely.

The prospect of getting out and stretching their legs was inviting. Yet when they pulled up to the local police department and parked, Tory suddenly panicked. This was such a final step, but it had to be taken. It was past time to finish something long left undone.

Brett had been watching Tory's reaction for miles. The closer they'd come to their destination, the more tense she'd become. Her hands were in fists, and her face was pale. There was a stiffness to her posture that wasn't normal, and her breathing had become shallow. Sure signs of panic.

She'd been through so damned much hell in her lifetime. He wanted it all to be over. He wanted to hear her laugh and see her smile and know that all was right with her world. But until they found her mother's body, that wasn't about to happen.

"Well, sweetheart, I guess we'd better check in here before we go any farther. We need to make sure that all the proper authorities have been notified and see what they might have planned."

She nodded, then glanced out the window, tensing even more as she spied a white van parked across the street. The logo painted on the side was impossible to miss. KEIO, Channel 5. She turned. There was another van farther down the street and parked just off an alley. KTIA, Channel 4, was here, too.

"Brett, look," she said, pointing to the vans.

"I saw them," he said. "Unfortunately, at the moment, you and your situation are news. It will pass."

She sighed. "I know. But this is so awful. People I don't know are digging into things about my personal life that I've only just begun to remember myself. It's like undressing in front of a room full of strangers. Whether you like it or not, everyone's about to get an eyeful."

Brett leaned over and kissed her square on the mouth. "And what an eyeful it would be."

She grinned, which had been his objective.

"Okay?" he asked.

She reached for his hand. "Okay."

"Then let's get this show on the road. The sooner we begin, the sooner it will all be over."

Denton Washburn, the police chief of Calico Rock, was up to his eyeballs in Feds. This morning, agents from the Arkansas State Bureau of Investigation had beaten him to the office. A half hour later, two FBI agents from national headquarters had arrived with their own agenda, all but confiscating his men and his desk. It was fortunate that he was a patient man. Yet when he heard a commotion outside his office and went to investigate, his patience came to a quick end.

He recognized the two men blocking the doorway to the station. They were from a local television affiliate. And he was pretty sure that the woman in red with the microphone and the hat was part of the Oklahoma television crew who'd arrived last night. What he didn't know, and at that point didn't care, was what they were doing upsetting his department.

"What the hell's going on out here?" he shouted.

The crowd parted, like the Red Sea at God's

command, and then he saw her, caught in the midst of the melee and trying to hide her face against the jacket of the biggest, most pissed-off man he'd seen in years. Denton understood the man's anger. He'd been stifling some of his own ever since this mess started. But what aggravated him most was that the shit Victoria Lancaster was having to endure was happening in his office. His first instinct was to run off everyone within a forty-mile range, and his second was to find himself a stiff drink. He took a deep breath and did neither.

Twenty-five years ago this month he'd been a rookie with the Calico Rock police force. There had been plenty of long days since when nothing much had happened, and enough days in between when he didn't think life would ever calm down again. But every now and then, when he let himself think about it, he would remember going out to the old Lancaster place to pick up that kid. At the time, he'd been gung ho and so certain he could handle anything. And then he and the chief had driven up to the house. They'd heard her screaming before the car had stopped. The sound had stayed with him for days.

Now and then, there were nights when the wind blew just so between the hills. And on those nights, the wild, restless shriek reminded him of her cry—high-pitched and keening, like a cornered and dying animal.

In spite of his presence, the news crews continued to press toward the couple, shoving microphones in their faces and shouting questions above the noise to be heard. Denton shifted his gun belt, giving ease to the buckle that rode against his belly, and then put his hand on his gun. Enough was enough.

"Hey!"

His shout got results. Everyone hushed. "I'm giving the lot of you exactly three seconds to start toward that door, then I'm going to start hauling you in for disturbing the peace."

"But Chief, the public has a right to—"

Denton reached for his handcuffs and started walking toward the newsman who'd chosen to argue.

"Don't tell me about the public," he growled. "I work for the public. And right now you're impeding the progress of an ongoing investigation."

Then he shoved a cameraman aside and stared straight into Brett Hooker's face.

"You with her?" he asked, pointing to Tory.

Brett nodded.

"Then step on back to my office," he said. "I'll be with you as soon as I get rid of these blowflies."

His analogy of the media that always swarmed

around a story as flies on carrion was too pointed to miss. Brett moved Tory toward the back office. Grateful for the respite, they slipped inside and closed the door, leaving the chief to tend to his business his way.

Brett grasped Tory by the shoulders. "Baby, are you all right?"

She thrust a hand through her hair, combing the tangles away from her face, and then nodded.

"Thanks to you and that bulldog of a policeman, I'm fine," she said. And then she tried to smile around a shaky breath. "I can't believe that just happened."

Just then Denton Washburn burst into his office as abruptly as he'd come out of it, slamming the door shut behind him. His face was flushed, his eyes sparkling with anger, but there was a calmness about him that made Brett think there was more to the man than just a badge and a gun.

"Chief. I'm Brett Hooker, and this is—"

Denton nodded. "We've met," he said gruffly, meeting Tory's startled gaze. "But I doubt she remembers me." He extended his hand toward Tory. "I'm Denton Washburn, Police Chief of Calico Rock."

Tory blushed. "I'm sorry, but I'm afraid I don't remember you."

He nodded. "It's been a while. About twenty-five years ago, I suppose. And I wasn't chief then.

I was only a rookie, and you were in pretty bad shape when we took you out of that house.''

Startled, Tory's eyes widened. Here was another man who'd been a part of the past she couldn't remember.

"I'm sorry. I don't remember much of that time.''

Denton glanced at Brett, then back at Tory. "Just how much of that day *do* you remember?''

Tory didn't give in to the frustration she was feeling. "Nothing.''

Brett put his arm around her. "Up until a couple of days ago, the only thing she remembered about her childhood was being jerked from one foster home to another.''

Washburn frowned. "That's too bad. Your mother was a real nice woman. Everyone in town liked her and Danny. We were all real sad when he died.''

Tory frowned. "Who's Danny?''

Denton's eyebrows rose. "He was your daddy. I think you all better have a seat. Looks to me like we need to visit a spell before we get down to plans.''

They'd just taken a seat when a knock sounded on the door, and then a man entered without waiting for permission. Washburn frowned at the interruption.

"Miss Lancaster. Mr. Hooker. Meet federal agent Rickshaw."

Darrel Rentshaw didn't break a smile as he corrected the chief's mispronunciation.

"It's Rentshaw," he said, offering his hand to both Brett and Tory.

"Whatever," Denton said. "Is there something *else* I can do for you?"

No one missed the less than subtle emphasis Denton had put on the word *else*. Brett stifled a grin. It wasn't the first time he'd seen local law enforcement tangling with state and federal authorities.

Rentshaw ignored the chief's thrust. "I thought it best we set things straight with Miss Lancaster as to what we expect of her."

This time, Brett was the one who got pissed. There was a smile on his face that never quite reached his eyes as he interrupted the conversation.

"Look, Rentshaw. Sounds to me like the only straightening out needs to come from you. Miss Lancaster is here for a purpose. As distasteful as it may be, we all know what it is. She doesn't care who's in charge. She doesn't give a flying you know what who steps on whose territorial toes. All she wants is to locate her mother's body and give her a proper burial. She will be on-site until Ruth Lancaster's body has been found, and she will make any and all decisions as to where it will be taken afterward."

Rentshaw did a mental reassessment of Hooker and made a bet with himself that the man was an ex-cop, and a tough one at that. But he was getting tired of having to reassert the authority he'd already assumed.

"I'm sorry, Miss Lancaster, but you have to understand our position. We aren't certain that there is a body to be found. According to my information, the doctor who witnessed Oliver Hale's confession isn't totally convinced it was valid. He's leaning toward the theory that the old man was just out of his head from the drugs he'd been given."

Denton Washburn drew himself up to his full height of five feet, eight inches tall. "Then what the hell..." he glanced at Tory "...pardon my French, ma'am..." he glared back at Rentshaw "...are you doing here messing with my town if you think it's all a big hoax?"

Rentshaw's face was beginning to flush. "It's not my place to sit in judgment. I'm here on orders. It remains to be seen whether there's a body or not. If there is, the proper procedures will be followed, no matter how old the corpse. And the case will go through the system, just as any murder would."

Tory was tired and hungry, and she'd heard

enough. She stood, pushing Brett to the side, to speak for herself.

"Then you tell me something. Who are you going to prosecute when you find her? Oliver Hale's confession eliminates the need for a trial. He's dying, and he's already in prison. Explain the sense of claiming a body when you have no one to prosecute."

Denton Washburn interrupted. "Actually, Miss Lancaster, Hale's not in prison...at least, not anymore."

Tory turned to face the chief and knew what he was going to say before he finished. "He died, didn't he?"

"Yes, ma'am, he did. About six-thirty this morning."

Tory sighed. For Hale, justice had already been dealt. She turned back to Rentshaw.

"Then you have no need to hold a body when you no longer have a killer, am I right?"

Rentshaw's shoulders slumped. Damn, but he hated not being in control.

"Look, Miss Lancaster, if we find a body—and I say *if* then we'll deal with what comes."

"I won't get in your way, but I don't intend to leave until we find my mother."

Rentshaw threw up his hands. "I have no problem with that, but I don't know where you think you're going to stay. All the rooms have been taken for a thirty-mile radius."

"That's not a problem for us," Tory said. "Like the tortoise, we travel with our shell on our back."

Rentshaw remembered that fancy, self-contained motor home parked out front, and just for a moment, he thought of asking if they had a spare bed. And then he glanced at Hooker's face and amended the thought.

"That's fine, then." He glanced at the chief, then back at Brett and Tory. "When you've finished in here, I'll be glad to direct you to the location."

"Thank you. We won't be long." Tory turned and sat down.

Rentshaw had the feeling he'd just been dismissed. He glared at the police chief, nodded to Hooker, then left as abruptly as he'd entered.

Denton frowned as the door slammed shut. "That man needs to take himself a vacation." Brett grinned. He was liking the chief more by the minute.

"Let's see," Denton muttered. "Where was I when we were so rudely interrupted?"

Tory leaned forward. "My father. You were going to tell me about my father."

Denton sat down with a grunt. "Yes, ma'am, that I was."

"Chief?"

"Yes, ma'am?"

"Considering our history, I think it would be fine if you called me Tory."

He almost grinned. "As I was saying...your daddy was a hell of a man. He rodeoed a little and drove a truck for one of the oil companies. He died when his truck slid off an ice-covered road and rolled down a mountain. You were born about a month later."

"Then I never knew him?"

"No."

"I have a vague feeling that Hale lived in our house. Is that so?"

The chief nodded. "No one much approved of him. We didn't think he was good enough for your mother, if you know what I mean. But she'd been alone a long time, almost five years, when Hale stepped into her life. He sweet-talked her into letting him move in. After that, it's anyone's guess as to what happened." Denton frowned. "Everyone here in town thought she ran off with Hale and left you behind. I'm real sorry to say I was one of those people."

Tory's eyes teared, but her voice remained firm. "You have nothing to apologize for. I thought the same thing, and she was my mother."

Brett reached for Tory's hand, then threaded his

fingers through hers, giving her comfort in the only way he could.

"Is there anything else we need to know before we meet Rentshaw?" he asked.

Denton shrugged. "Not that I can think of. But if something comes up, I know where to find you."

Brett held Tory's hand tighter. "We'll be going now, and thank you for your help out there."

This time there was no mistaking Denton Washburn's grin. "It's my pleasure," he said. "Besides, Lacey would have chewed me up and left me for fish bait otherwise."

"Don Lacey...from Oklahoma City?" Brett asked.

"Went to school with the man. He always was a hardhead. Once he had a notion fixed in his mind, it was plain hell to get him to turn loose of it. He asked me to look after you. I told him it would be my pleasure." Then he glanced at Tory. "Real sorry about your mother, Miss Lancaster."

"Thank you."

"And I'm real sorry about the way you got shuffled through the system."

"I'm not the first child who fell through the cracks, and I doubt I was the last."

Denton Washburn nodded. "Still, we should have been more concerned when it happened to one of our own. In a way, we let you down worse than the system did.''

Tory just shook her head. "The best way you could pay me back is to make sure it never happens to a child you know again."

"Miss Lancaster, that's a promise."

Rentshaw hadn't wasted his time by waiting. He'd cleared out the media with a single order to his men and then made sure the present owner of the old Lancaster property would be on-site and waiting for their arrival. When he saw Hooker and the Lancaster woman come out of the police department, he got out of his car and went to meet them.

"Are you ready to proceed?" he asked.

Brett nodded.

"Then follow me," Rentshaw ordered.

"I need to get gas before we leave town."

Rentshaw sighed. "There's a station on our way out. I'll lead the way."

"Thanks," Brett said, and they were on their way.

Brett was filling the gas tank as Tory strolled up and down the four-aisle quick stop. She had a pop in one hand and a couple of candy bars in the other. Every now and then she would put one of them back in lieu of one she'd just seen. Then, when she couldn't make up her mind, she would take them both. Right now she was deliberating between a Milky Way and a Snickers bar to go with the Baby Ruth and the Payday she already had.

"Hey, don't I know you?"

Startled, Tory looked up. The cashier behind the counter was pointing at her, which in turn had called her to the attention of three other customers. The fiasco at the police department was too fresh in her mind to ignore, and she glanced out the window at Brett, wishing she'd waited for him before coming inside.

"Uh, I don't think—"

"Yeah, I do! I know you!" the man said. "You were on the TV the other day. You're that woman. The woman who used to live here, ain't you?"

Tory stared at the man from across the aisles. She was closer to the door than he was. If she had to, she could always make a run for it.

"Yes, when I was a child."

He nodded. "I knew it. I don't forget a face."

Tory reached for the Snickers bar.

"I told my wife, I bet I'll be seein' that woman when she comes to Calico Rock. Everyone who comes to town usually winds up here before all's said and done."

Tory glanced out the window and then picked

up the Milky Way, too. If Brett didn't hurry, she was going to run out of hands and money.

"Is it true what they said on the TV? Did that fella really kill your—"

"Well for the good Lord's sake, Clarence, why don't you just hush and leave the poor girl alone?"

Tory looked up. A new face had come upon the scene. She didn't know who it was, but she was heartily glad she was here.

"Now, Tootie, I just wanted to know if—"

Tootie slapped the man on the arm and then shoved him out from behind the counter.

"Your food's gettin' cold. Get on outa here and go eat what I fixed you before I throw it to the dogs."

Clarence did as he was told, giving Tory a last, lingering look of regret as he ducked out the back door of the store.

Tory hid a smile. Tootie must be "the wife" to whom he'd referred.

"You'll have to excuse Clarence," she said. "He's just naturally nosy. He don't mean nothin' by it."

Tory nodded. "That's all right," and then she saw Brett coming and began to relax. She added a Butterfinger to her stash as he stepped through the door, and when he got out his billfold to pay for the gas, she laid her candy on the counter.

He looked at the assortment and then arched an

eyebrow. "Doesn't pay to leave you alone too long, does it, baby?"

She grinned.

And then Tootie chose to step into the conversation.

"You know what? You sure do put me in mind of that actor fellow, Mel Gibson." She looked at Tory. "Don't you think?" She looked back at Brett. "Yes, you sure do look like him." Then she squinted. "You aren't...are you?"

Tory laughed, grabbed her candy bars and made a break for the RV, leaving Brett behind to deal with the female version of Clarence.

Fourteen

It was obvious from the dust boiling beneath Rentshaw's vehicle that last night's rain at the RV camp had not passed through Calico Rock. The thick growth of trees and bushes on either side of the road was coated with a layer of good Arkansas earth. While it was impossible to see the houses from the road, every now and then they would pass a dusty mailbox at the end of a lane, a marker for the people who lived up in the hills.

Tory was silent, her gaze fixed on the scenery as they passed, and Brett could tell she was searching for anything familiar. About three miles outside of Calico Rock, she suddenly straightened and pointed toward a winding road off to their left.

"I think some people named Wiggins used to live up there. They had a daughter named Mary Ellen. She was my first best friend." *And my last.*

Tory sighed. Moving from one foster home to another had not been conducive to making or keeping friends. But she didn't have to say it.

There was no need repeating something Brett already knew.

"You know what, baby?"

"What?"

"Aren't you glad you can remember her now?"

Tory sat there for a moment, a little surprised by his insight, as well as the fact that she hadn't thought of that herself. She'd been so wrapped up in the bad, she'd forgotten to give thanks for the good. She smiled.

"Yes, Brett, I am."

He chuckled aloud as he remembered something from his first year at school.

"My first best friend was a boy named Charlie. His mother let him keep a snake as a pet, and he could burp louder than any kid in first grade. For a kid who was only six, Charlie was ahead of his time."

Tory laughed, which was what Brett had intended, and the moment passed. They continued to follow Rentshaw's dust trail without comment and were unprepared when he suddenly braked and turned off the road. Brett felt himself tensing. If Rentshaw was stopping, then they must be there.

Tory leaned forward as Brett followed Rentshaw's lead, her gaze fixed on a small, run-down house at the far end of the lane down which they'd driven. A wide metal gate had been hung across the drive, and cattle could be seen grazing in what used to be the yard. But it was the house that caught her eye. Something beckoned at the door of her mind, begging to be let in. And the longer she sat there, the louder it knocked.

A bus. She'd been riding home on the school bus! She could almost feel the heat against her skin as she'd stepped down from it to go home. A flash of color moved through her thoughts, as ephemeral as the butterfly she'd raced so long ago, and in her mind, she skipped blithely toward the house, unaware of the devastation that awaited her there. Tory held her breath, waiting for the panic that had followed, but the only emotion she could feel was an overwhelming sadness for what she'd lost.

"Oh, Brett."

Brett reached toward her, touching her face, her arm, then her hair, wishing that his love was enough to make everything bad go away and knowing the task was impossible, even for a love as strong as his. Her eyes were wide and fixed on the scene before them, and she was blinking furiously to hold back the tears.

"I'm here, Tory. Just hold on to that thought."

She clutched at his hand, willing the pace of her heartbeat to slow down to its normal rhythm. But it was impossible. Somewhere in the idyllic scene before them, her mother's earthly remains lay in an unconsecrated grave. Of that she was convinced. And what loomed most in Tory's mind was the three days she'd spent in that house, unaware that the mother she was waiting for had already begun to rot.

As they sat staring at the house and waiting for Rentshaw to make a move, a pickup truck suddenly swerved off the road behind them, parking near the passenger side of their RV. Tory watched in the sideview mirror as the driver emerged. He was redheaded and tall, and his belly was pushing toward a slight paunch. Something made her reach for the door, and without a word to Brett, she went to meet him.

When the woman stepped out of the RV, Art Beckham came to an abrupt halt. His stomach knotted, and his throat went dry. When she smiled at him, he belatedly yanked off his cap. It had been years since he'd seen her, and if her picture hadn't been flashed all over the tube for the last two days, he wouldn't have known her. But it had, and now he did, and in his nervousness, the irony of it all was lost upon him.

"Victoria? Victoria Lancaster?"

Tory heard a door slam and knew Brett would be right behind her, but this time she didn't need his protection. This man's face was too open for guile.

"I know you, don't I?" she said.

He ducked his head, reluctant to meet her gaze, and then took a deep breath and looked up.

Trying to grin, he nodded. "I reckon so. I used to give you hell on the school bus." And then the grin slid off his face. "And for that, I'm sure sorry."

The tension went out of Tory in one fell swoop. "Arthur Beckham!"

He grinned. "One and the same. And it's Art now."

"Then, hello, Art Beckham."

His grin widened. "Hello, Tory Lancaster."

Brett was hurrying to her side, the memory of the media fiasco in the police chief's office too fresh in his mind to ignore, when Tory turned toward him and smiled.

"Brett, this is Art Beckham. When we were children we used to ride the same school bus."

The two men shook hands, and then Art began to fidget, looking down at his feet and then at a spot on the horizon just over Tory's shoulder. Finally he looked her square in the face.

"Tory, something's been weighing on my mind for years, and I'm thankful I finally get a chance to apologize."

"What's that?" she said.

"That day you got off of the school bus…"

Tory shrugged. "I'm sorry, Art, but my memory's not so good about my early years. What day are you referring to?"

He began picking at a speck of dried mud on the brim of his cap, needing something on which to focus in order to finish what had to be said.

"You know...the last day you rode the bus."

Understanding dawned. "You mean the day I went home and found everyone gone?"

He looked up at her, judging the tone of her voice against the look on her face. When he was satisfied that she was holding her own, he continued.

"Yeah. You know, I was a little older than you, but I was still just a kid. I didn't mean anything by it, but it's bugged me for years that I teased you that day. Later, when I heard my folks talking about what had happened to you, and how some people came and took you away to some home in the city, I felt guilty, like I'd been a part of it."

Tory laid her hand on his arm. "Why, Art, that's silly. Besides, as you said before, we were just children."

"Still, I'm sorry I did it. And I'm sorry about what happened to you." He took a deep breath and then grinned. "I had a crush on you, you know. That's why I picked on you all the time." Then he gave Brett a nervous look, startled that he'd revealed something personal in front of her man. "I'm happily married."

Brett laughed, then winked at Tory. "I have plans in that direction myself."

Tory blushed, and the tension that had been between them was gone. But before they could continue, Rentshaw came around the corner of the RV.

"Are you Beckham?" he asked.

Art nodded.

"Good. I'd appreciate it if you would let us in. And do something about those cows," he added. "We need to be able to leave this gate down until we've finished."

Tory frowned. "What's going on?"

Art sighed. One last thing to admit. He wondered how she was going to take the news. He waved his hand toward the house.

"This is my place now," he said. "I bought it about six years ago. The cattle you see are mine, and I've been using that old house you grew up in for a barn. Unfortunately, before anyone can start poking around inside, I've got to move about two tons of hay and a ton of sweet feed."

Startled, Tory looked back at the old house, only now aware of the hay just visible through the missing windows.

"Oh, my," she said.

"Exactly," Rentshaw said. "It will take a good day to clear all of that out before we can start."

"Then let's get at it," Brett said. "I'd be glad to help."

Art frowned. "No, sirree. I wouldn't hear of it. I've got some men on their way out now." He nodded toward the RV. "You planning to stay in that while you're here?"

Brett nodded.

"You're more than welcome to hook up to the utilities down at the house. There was an old trailer house out back when I first bought the place, so the hookups are there. And I keep electricity on at the barn, uh, I mean the house. All we'll have to do is throw a switch for the water well."

"That's awfully generous of you," Brett said. "And we really appreciate it."

Art gave Tory a last, apologetic look. "It's the least I can do."

A temporary fence had been strung between the old house and the road, penning Art's cattle out of the yard but still giving them free rein to graze the rest of the place. The square bales of hay that had been inside the house were now out in the yard, stacked as high as the roof. Art hauled the sacks of sweet feed back to his home. Although it was early afternoon, everyone was gone except for a couple of state agents, who were still taking pictures and mapping off roads and outbuildings. It would be tomorrow before the real stuff began.

Brett watched from a chair in the shade while Tory meandered about the property, picking up sticks and poking about in the weeds. He knew what she was doing. She was looking for memories. And as long as he could see her, he didn't worry. This was something she needed to do alone.

But while she had prowled and walked over almost all the area, she had yet to go inside the old house, and he thought he knew why. There were ghosts in there that she wasn't ready to face, and that was okay. But when she *was* ready to go in, there was no way in hell he was going to let her go alone.

A short while later the two agents drove away, with promises to return in the morning. Now Brett and Tory were alone.

Within the hour, a car turned in the driveway and then stopped several yards from where they were parked. Brett saw it from the window, and his first thought was that some reporter had gotten brave enough to try getting past the guard Denton Washburn had left at the gate.

He could see the guard lean down to the car window, talking to the woman inside, but when she got out and began gesturing toward the RV, Brett went out to look for Tory, anxious that she not be harassed.

Tory was on the far side of the house when she heard a woman calling her name. Before she saw her, her first instinct was to panic. Another reporter? Another stranger with whom she couldn't cope?

And then she saw the short, chubby redhead in black culottes and a black-and-white checked T-shirt standing at the end of the drive. She looked more like a referee than someone who'd come visiting.

"Tory Lee. Tory Lee."

Whether it was the sound of the woman's voice or that she was calling Tory by both of her given names, a fact very few people even knew, something clicked. She started up the driveway, forgetting to be worried or afraid.

When Brett saw her, he yelled for her to wait, but she kept moving, as if she hadn't even heard him.

"What now?" he muttered, and started up the road after her.

As she neared the end of the driveway, she kept thinking that she'd done this all before. A lizard darted across her path, and she paused in midstep, staring down at the tiny little tracks that it had left in the dust.

"Tory Lee. Yoo-hoo. Tory Lee."

She looked up and started walking again. The sensation of déjà vu was intense. Somewhere before, she'd heard that same voice calling her name.

Seen a lizard cross her path. Felt the heat on her face and the wind in her hair, just like this. Heard her own heartbeat and felt alive in a way that can only come from knowing your inner self.

She drew nearer, and the chubby face wreathed in smiles hurt her heart. Dear God, but she knew that face. She'd slept with her. Laughed with her.

"Mary Ellen?"

"See!" the woman crowed, pushing at the guard's arm and sailing on past. "I told you she'd know me."

She wrapped her arms around Tory's waist and hugged her, all but jumping up and down with delight.

"It *is* you!" Tory said, and returned the hug as fiercely as the one she had just received. Then she heard Brett calling her name and spun around.

"It's okay," she called. "She's a friend."

Brett stopped a distance away. "Are you going to be okay?" he yelled.

She nodded. "We'll be there in a few minutes, okay?"

He waved and then headed back to the RV, willing to give her all the space she needed.

"It's okay," Tory told the guard, who was still looking anxious. "We went to school together. Would you mind watching her car while we walk a bit?"

"No, ma'am, I sure don't," he said, and tipped

his hat, smiling with relief as the two women started back down the drive.

"How did you know I was here?" Tory asked.

Mary Ellen giggled, and it was the sweetest sound Tory had ever heard.

"Shoot, honey. Everyone knows you're here. You're a celebrity, don't you know?"

Tory shook her head. "I'm not a celebrity, and this is a nightmare."

Mary Ellen's giggle faded, and she unconsciously slipped her hand into Tory's, just as they'd done when they were children.

"I'm so sorry about everything," she said. "I cried for days after they took you away. Momma and Poppa wouldn't tell me a thing. All I knew was that you were gone." She sighed and gave Tory a bashful glance. "You were my first best friend," she said softly.

Tory squeezed her hand. "And you were mine."

Mary Ellen smiled. "I missed you, Tory Lee."

Tory sighed. "I missed you, too, more than you can know."

They had reached the RV now. Tory tugged at Mary Ellen's hand. "Come in and meet Brett."

"Is he your husband?"

Tory shook her head. "Not yet."

Mary Ellen giggled. "From what I saw, I wouldn't dither. That man is a hunk of gorgeous."

Tory grinned. "I'll tell him you said so."

"Oh, no!" Mary Ellen shrieked. "You can't do that! Why, what would he think?"

Tory's grin widened. "Why, probably that you were the most intelligent woman he'd ever met."

Mary Ellen giggled again. "That's a man I've got to meet."

Brett stuck his head out the door. "Did I hear someone calling my name?"

Tory shook her head. "You were eavesdropping, and you know it."

Brett grinned. "Guilty." Then he smiled at Tory's friend. "How about coming in for a cold drink?"

Mary Ellen took Tory by the hand. "I have a better idea...and a confession to make," she added. "Come to my house, instead. Some of your old friends are there, waiting to greet you." She glanced toward the dilapidated house, well aware of why they'd come. But she wasn't going to be swayed by her need to reconnect with an old friend. "It's not a party or anything like that. I know this isn't the best time in the world for you. But we all loved you dearly, Tory Lee. Let us help you through this in our way."

Brett stepped out of the RV. "Do you want to, sweetheart?"

Tory looked at Brett, and then back at her

friend. "I can't think of anything I'd rather do," she said softly.

"Oh, goody," Mary Ellen said. "Come with me. I promise I'll bring you back as soon as you're ready."

A few minutes later, they were gone. And except for the guard at the end of the driveway, the old Lancaster place was, once again, on its own.

Mary Ellen's chatter was endless. Some things never change, Tory thought. But her heart was racing with anticipation. She kept looking in the back seat at Brett, drawing reassurance from his presence while looking forward to what lay ahead.

When Mary Ellen began slowing down, Tory looked up in surprise. "Isn't this where you used to live?" she asked.

Mary Ellen's smile widened. "I inherited the farm after Mother and Daddy passed away. David, that's my husband, works at the feed store in town. We have three children, who by the way are at their Grandma Miller's. We won't be bothered by rug rats."

Brett laughed. He already liked this little woman, even if she didn't know when to hush.

"Sounds like my family," he said. "Never a dull moment."

Mary Ellen nodded. "You said it." And then she braked to a stop. "Well, we're here. Hop out and come say hi."

The yard was filled with cars. Nearly a dozen, from what Tory could see. Even though she was anxious to go inside, she was shivering with nerves, and her stomach felt as if a cloud of butterflies had taken up residence. And then Brett took hold of her hand and everything settled.

"Ready?" he asked.

She looked up at him and smiled. "Yes."

He grinned. "Then ready or not, here we come."

Mary Ellen led the way, opening the front door and then stepping inside ahead of them.

"We're here," she called, and more than a dozen people turned to look.

Some were smiling. Some were in the act of getting up from their chairs. And some of them looked nervous, which, under the circumstances, was understandable.

"Everyone, this is Tory's fiancé, Brett Hooker. Tory, I know you won't remember us all, but we have sure remembered you."

"I saw some of your pictures in the Sunday supplement," one man said, and then grinned. "You're a real good photographer."

Mary Ellen added her own aside. "That's Edward Bailey. You remember him...the Halloween we were five, he put that goat in Mr. Pilzner's car."

Tory grinned, not so much from what Edward

Bailey had done all those years ago, but that she remembered him doing it.

"We were all real sorry to hear about your mother."

Tory's gaze moved to the woman who'd just offered her sympathies.

"Thank you. I don't remember your faces. You're going to have to help me."

She smiled. "I'm Mavis Candy—use to be Ellis. My daddy ran the grocery store next to the movie theater."

And so it went, one after the other, the people who'd had a share of a six-year-old's life had come to pay their respects and to say hello.

Tory's face mirrored her joy as they gathered around her, each offering her solace in the only way that they could...with their presence.

Brett wanted to hug them all. They had no way of knowing how unusual it was for her to be mingling comfortably in a crowd. He'd spent four years watching her withdraw from situations exactly like this, but now, seeing her with her eyes alight and a smile on her face, was something rare.

Mary Ellen played hostess as if she'd been born to the job. The conversation never faltered, and she'd prepared a buffet of food that seemed to have no end. Purposefully, Brett stayed on the outer rim of the group, ever watchful of Tory for signs of stress. But they didn't come, and for that he was grateful.

"Okay now everybody," Mary Ellen suddenly announced. "Your bellies are full and your jaws are bound to be tired from talking. If they're not, they should be. I know mine is. It's getting late and Tory and Brett have a hard day ahead of them tomorrow. However…" And then she giggled, and because it was so infectious, everyone laughed with her. "However," she repeated, "we have something special for Tory before she leaves, don't we?"

A chorus of yesses and you bets went around the room.

"Okay, Tory Lee. You sit here," Mary Ellen ordered, pointing to a recently abandoned love seat. "And you, you good-lookin' thing. You sit right there beside her."

Brett grinned and did as he was told, sliding in beside Tory and then giving her a quick hug before the impromptu ceremony began.

Tory felt as if she were flying. She couldn't remember a time in her life when she'd felt so accepted. She smiled at Brett and then back at the crowd, wishing she could bottle this feeling and make it last forever.

"Now! Mavis, where did you put that package? Run get it. Hurry. I can't wait to see Tory Lee's face."

"You didn't need to buy me anything," Tory said. "Renewing our friendships was the best present anyone could give me."

"Oh, we didn't really buy it," Mary Ellen said. "Except for the album. Oh, now I've gone and given it away." She rolled her eyes and then giggled again. "Well, that's what you all get for telling me what it was. You know I can't keep a secret."

They laughed as Mavis produced a box, which Tory proceeded to open. Her smile widened as she ran her hand over the fine leather with which the enclosed album had been bound.

"A picture album. Considering the fact that I'm a photographer, you couldn't have chosen a more perfect gift."

"Oh, silly, we didn't get you one to fill up. This one's already got stuff in it," Mary Ellen cried, and then opened the cover for her, unable to wait for Tory to do it herself.

"We figured since all your things disappeared when you were little that you wouldn't have any of these. And you know how clannish we all are here in Calico Rock." She looked at Brett, assuming he would need an explanation. "Family is a real big deal down here."

"If you don't have any, it's a real big deal anywhere," Tory said.

The room got still. Her quiet reminder as to why

she'd come home was enough to settle their high spirits.

Mary Ellen was close to tears and needed to head them off before they cut loose.

"Well now, you've got us. And you've got that good-looking thing sitting there beside you, too, so don't expect me to feel too sorry for you. Now, see what we made for you."

Tory looked and then had to blink away tears to be able to focus. It had been twenty-five years since she'd seen that face, but the moment she saw it, she remembered. It was her mother.

"That's your momma and daddy," Mavis Candy said. "We got the picture from the newspaper. It's just a xerox copy and all, but it ran in the paper when they got married. I thought you'd like to have a copy."

Tory traced the shapes of each of their faces, lingering longest on the tender curve of her mother's cheek. Her heart hurt, but in a good way. When Brett's arm slid around her shoulders, she leaned into him, needing his strength, because she was shy of her own.

Brett pointed to the picture. "You look like your mother, but I think you have your daddy's hair and eyes."

Edward Bailey spoke up. "That's true. My momma said Danny Lancaster had the bluest eyes and the lightest blond hair you ever saw on a man.

Why, she said in the summer it would bleach out so much that it almost looked white. But he wasn't no sissy. When it came to work, he was as tough as they came. It was a real shame about him dying like he did. I bet he would have made a real good daddy.''

And Mommy would still have been alive.

Tory didn't say it, but the knowledge was there. And when she looked up, she could tell they all shared her thought.

"Remember my slumber party?" Mary Ellen asked. "Remember how Momma kept running around the house taking pictures of us with that old Brownie camera? I had copies made for you to keep. You're even in a couple." She pointed. "Look. There you are. You can't miss Tory Lee and her long blond hair."

One after the other, Tory went through the album with each of her friends, listening as they shared the memories behind the pictures they'd donated, afraid that she was going to cry. But when Mary Ellen suddenly leaned down and kissed her on the cheek, it dawned on her that she didn't need to maintain control. These were her friends. They would accept her no matter what. So she let go of the joy and the pain.

Long after Mary Ellen had taken them home, Tory sat with the album in her lap, poring over the pictures. Thanks to a handful of people who'd known her when, she had recaptured a part of her life that had been lost.

"Sweetheart, I made us some supper."

"But I just want to—"

He took the album and laid it on the table. "It will be here in the morning. Why don't you eat a bit, and then we'll go outside and take a walk? We've been cooped up in here long enough."

She nodded.

It was nearing sundown as Brett sat on the front doorstep, watching Tory walking about the yard. He shoved his hand through his hair, rubbing at a knot in the back of his neck. Ryan's motor home was great, but the bed was too damned short. It would feel good to get back home and into his own king-size bed.

He looked up, centering his focus on Tory, and then relaxing again. As long as he could see her, he didn't worry. He glanced out toward the road. There had been a changing of the guard, but thanks to Denton Washburn, someone was still there. Just beyond the fence, three news vans had already set up shop, and he squinted, trying to read the logos. Then he whistled beneath his breath. One of those vans belonged to a cable news channel. Tory's trouble had hit the big time.

He thought back to the party at Mary Ellen's and the fun that Tory'd had. Her reason for coming back here was hell, but the fact that she'd gotten to reconnect with old friends was the best thing that had ever happened to her.

Unaware that she was being observed, Tory paused at the side of the house and laid the flat of her hand against the old, weathered wood. Although the house was in shade, the wood still held some of the day's warmth. A fleck of color near the foundation caught her eye, and she knelt, poking in the dirt with her stick until she had dislodged the object she'd seen. As she looked, a spurt of excitement hit her belly-high. It was a tiny white cup from a child-size tea set. And she knew, before she picked the dirt from inside, that there would be a small pink flower in the bottom of the bowl.

"Tory?"

She spun around, the cup still clutched in her hand.

"Did you find yourself a treasure?"

The fact that he had not once interfered with her meandering had not been lost on her. She'd known that he would understand what she felt compelled to do. But she was also thankful that he was there for her when she was ready to share. She opened her hand.

"Look."

Brett leaned closer, eyeing the tiny bit of dirt-covered china. "Was it yours?"

Her eyes were alight. "If there's a pink flower in the bottom, I'd definitely say yes."

Brett looked at her, at the hope and the expectation in her face, and wanted to hold her. Instead, he lifted the little cup from her hand and tilted it toward the fading light.

"Want to find out?" he asked.

"Oh, yes!"

"Then let's go wash it off and see what we've got."

Tory clasped his hand and off they went, her heart lighter than it had been in years. Things were happening here that she hadn't expected. She'd been braced for despair but unprepared for the rest. With each passing hour, she became more and more aware of a settling within her, as if she'd come back into her own.

Inside the RV, Brett held the little cup beneath the flow of water, gently rubbing at the years' accumulation of dirt, then using a toothpick to dislodge the dirt packed inside the bowl. When the lump suddenly turned loose and fell out, Tory crowded near his elbow, anxious to see.

He ran the cup beneath the water once more to wash off what was left of the grime, then handed it to her.

"There you are, baby. A small piece of home."

She looked inside, and the tension within her

began to relax. Faded to a near white, the pale pink shadow of a hand-painted rose was just visible.

"Oh, my."

There was a wealth of meaning in those two little words. Brett had nothing to add but a hug. And while they stood in an embrace, sunset came, followed by a three-quarter moon night.

The ground was covered with a new fall of snow, and more was still coming down. Outside, the wind whistled as it whipped around the eaves of the house, but inside, the old walls held the heat from the wood-burning stove just fine.

The little girl was at the kitchen table, on her knees on a chair, diligently putting raisin eyes, noses and belly buttons on the tray of gingerbread men that had yet to be baked.

Outside it was winter, but inside, spring had already come. The woman rolled and cut out the last of the dough, knowing that when she gave her daughter this tray to decorate, she was going to be delighted. This one was filled with bunnies and tulips and Easter egg shapes, just waiting for a little girl's touch.

"I thwough, Mommy."

"Good girl. One more tray and we're through."

When she saw the new cookie dough shapes, the little girl giggled and clapped her hands, convinced that her mommy was the most fun ever.

Her mother was standing in front of the cook-stove. Tendrils from her hairdo had come loose and were falling down around her forehead. Her face was pink and flushed from the heat, and the front of her dress had a slight dusting of flour.

"Mommy, will I be pwetty as you when I gwows up?"

The woman smiled and then popped a raisin in her daughter's mouth. "You already are, Sweet Baby, you already are."

Tory awoke with a knot in her stomach and a pain in her heart. She turned to look at Brett, who lay sleeping beside her. Moonlight shone through the part in the curtains, slicing across his belly in a thin, white glow, and highlighting the scar from the bullet wound high on his chest.

She rolled toward him, needing to feel the warmth of his body to take away the chill in her soul. She'd walked over every inch of the yard and up and down the driveway a dozen times this afternoon, and with every trip she had purposefully ignored the yawning doorway of the house. The thought of going inside had been terrifying. But she couldn't ignore it forever. Tomorrow they would start the search for her mother's body. They would ask her things she didn't want to remember. They would expect her to go in that house. And she would. But not with them. The first time, she needed to do it alone.

And so she lay wide-eyed and shaking, waiting for first light to complete her journey. Brett had brought her back to the place of her birth, but she was going to have to take the last steps toward home all alone.

Dew-stained grass dampened the hem of her blue jeans as she moved toward the house, clutching the flashlight in her hands as if it were a Jedi sword. Although the air was still night cool, she was sweating beneath her jacket. Nerves. That was all. Just nerves.

A whippoorwill called from a nearby tree, and somewhere off to her right, its mate answered. At that moment, the urge to go back for Brett was overwhelming. But she kept on walking, her eyes focused on the darkened doorway of the house. The air was still, empty of motion and sound. Everything around her seemed to be waiting. But for what? For old ghosts to be laid? For the last of old memories to resurface? For old wounds to open—or maybe to heal?

And then she was there, standing at the doorway to the house and staring into the darkness. Something skittered across the flooring inside, and she switched on her flashlight, catching the last glimpse of a scurrying mouse as it disappeared through a hole in the floor. She took a deep breath and relaxed.

I can understand your fears, little fellow. You scared me, too.

Then she tilted her chin and stepped into her past.

There was a light switch on the wall near the door. She flipped it. The sudden illumination of a forty-watt bulb, hanging from a dangling fixture in the ceiling, shed more light on the place than it could bear.

Outside, the air suddenly stirred as a morning breeze began to swell, pushing a draft through the old house and lifting the hair from Tory's neck. She shuddered and then moaned beneath her breath as the ghostly fingers of air moved past her face.

Oh God, oh God, please help me get through this.

She moved farther into the room, then closed her eyes, letting herself remember—letting herself go.

Brett didn't know what woke him, but the moment he turned over and realized he was in the bed alone, he knew where Tory had gone. He rolled out of bed and, in a panic, began grabbing for his jeans and shoes.

He bolted outside, only then aware that the first

light delineating differences between trees and shadows had come and gone. All the way to the house he kept telling himself to relax, that Tory was a strong woman. She had come this far on guts and nerve. She could make it the rest of the way on her own, too. But the closer he got to the doorway, the more nervous he became. Although he heard nothing that could give him alarm, he kept remembering the fragile hold she'd had on reality only weeks earlier.

As he rounded the corner, he saw light spilling out of the doorway and told himself to calm down. The last thing he needed to do was burst in and scare her. But anxiety got the best of him, and he cleared the first step, calling her name.

"Tory?"

His only answer was the wind, wailing through the window openings like a woman in mourning. The hair on the back of his neck suddenly crawled as he thought of a six-year-old child coming home to this emptiness.

"Tory? It's me, Brett. Where are you?"

Something scooted off to his right, scratching against the old wood like a boot on a sandy floor, and he thought of his Glock, locked in the glove box of the RV.

"Tory, baby, is that you?"

And then he heard a sigh, like the last gust of escaping air from a birthday balloon, and he turned, only then aware of the small closet to his right. The door was slightly ajar. As he stared into the opening, he thought he saw movement beyond.

In that moment, his mind flashed on Tory, and of coming back to their old apartment to find her huddled inside the bedroom closet and clutching that doll. His heart sank.

God, please let her be all right.

As he started toward it, dread of what he might find weighted his steps. The rhythm of his heartbeat shattered, rocking from one side of his rib cage to the other in an erratic, pulse-pounding throb.

Please, God, please.

He heard her choke, and his own breath stalled. With trembling fingers, he grabbed the doorknob and pulled, letting light into the darkness of Tory Lancaster's mind.

Tory walked through the house room by room, and was startled by its size. In her memory, the rooms had been huge and the space endless. Now it felt tiny and cramped. As she stood in the hallway, looking into her room, she had to accept that the only thing that had changed was twenty-five years' worth of perception.

She moved back from the doorway. It was unnecessary to go farther. Whatever of herself she'd left behind wasn't in there. A small doorway beckoned at the end of the hall, but she refused to move toward it. It was obvious from where she stood that the bathroom fixtures had long ago been removed. And later today, the floor would follow. After that...

She shuddered and spun sharply, heading back toward the front of the house. Tory's ghost didn't lie beneath the bathroom floor of this house. If it was still here, she knew where it would be. In that closet.

Moments later, she stood before it, debating with herself as to the wisdom of what she was about to do. And while her good sense kept telling her to get back to Brett, old memories wouldn't let her go. With a resigned sigh, she reached for the doorknob and opened the door.

A small cobweb hung high in a corner, and there was a pile of old feed sacks on the floor. They'd been folded neatly together and then wrapped and tied with a length of baler twine. Art was nothing if not neat.

She moved the beam of the flashlight up one wall and then down the next, mapping each inch of the coffin in which she'd buried six years of her life. The urge to run became stronger. To get out before the old fear came back. But Tory stood firm, refusing to give in, refusing to leave. Instead, she took a tentative step forward, then another, and another. When she was all the way inside, she turned, staring back into the room beyond. Then she took a deep breath, turned off the flashlight and reached for the door.

She was crouched in a corner with her head on her knees, and when Brett first saw her, his heart skipped a beat. Afraid to move, he called out her name.

"Tory?"

She lifted her head and looked up.

"Brett. I knew you would come."

He exhaled on a shaky groan and then extended his hand. When she curled her fingers around his wrist, his heartbeat resumed its normal rhythm.

"Come on, sweetheart. I bet you're starved. How about I make you some pancakes?"

Using his strength as her own, she pulled herself upright, then walked out of the closet and into his arms. Brett wrapped his arms around her, resisting the urge to take her and run. "Are you all right?" he asked.

She sighed. "Not just yet…but I will be. I really think I will be."

His vision blurred as he looked down at her face, then he leaned forward and kissed the edge of her lower lip where it trembled the most.

"That's my girl."

The pain behind Tory's heart kept easing with each breath that she took, but what she'd found in that closet had been more than she'd expected. Now that she'd faced it, she wanted to leave it behind. And to do that, she knew she needed to tell.

"I saw him when he came in the door," she said.

Brett froze. He didn't know exactly what she meant, but he wasn't going to interrupt her by asking for explanations. If need be, that would come later.

"I knew who he was. I didn't like him. He was Ollie's friend. He'd been here before."

She shuddered, then sighed, taking strength from the warmth of Brett's embrace.

"I was inside the closet, and I thought if I didn't move he wouldn't find me. The door was slightly ajar, and I could see him moving back and forth. He kept cursing about Ollie owing him money. And then I saw him stop. I saw him look toward the place where I was hiding." She looked up, needing to see Brett's face when she said it. "When he saw me, he grinned."

No! Sweet Jesus, no! Something inside Brett began coming undone. There was a growing horror within him that he couldn't ignore. He wanted to stop her from uttering the words he knew he would hear. But there had been too many years of denial already. It was time to face the past, no matter what it had been. He leaned down, resting his forehead against hers and feeling her breath on his face.

"It's okay, baby. Just say it."

Tears spilled out of her eyes and ran down her cheeks. Her voice shifted into a softer, higher pitch, like that of a child.

"I wet my pants and started to scream." She drew a shuddering breath. "And then he said he would take what Ollie owed him out of my hide."

Oh God. Brett picked her up and then held her, unable to move.

"He raped me, Brett. I was just a little girl, and he raped me."

"I love you, Tory."

She choked on a sob and hid her face.

Anger for what she'd endured made him sick, but he couldn't give in to his feelings without injuring hers. And she'd been hurt far too much in her life as it was.

"Don't turn away from me, baby. Don't ever turn away from love. I'm so sorry for you, but it doesn't change the way I feel about you. Nothing could do that, do you understand?"

She wrapped her arms around his neck and slid her head beneath his chin.

"Brett, thank you."

His voice was deep with emotion as he kissed the crown of her head. "For what?"

"For being faithful."

He shifted her in his arms and then started toward the door. "You're welcome...and thank you," he added, as they stepped out into morning.

This time it was her turn to be puzzled. "For what?"

"For coming back to me, time after time."

She sighed. "You were all I had. I was afraid to let go."

"Thank God for small favors."

He put her down just outside the door to Ryan's RV, dug a handkerchief out of his pocket and began mopping her tears.

She stood without moving, absorbing the tenderness of his touch and the love in his eyes. And then he kissed her.

"Tory...sweetheart?"

"What?"

"Did you ever tell anyone about what happened to you?"

She shook her head. "No."

He cupped the side of her face, tilting her chin until she was forced to meet his gaze.

"Why not?"

Her shoulders slumped.

"Because I didn't remember it until this morning."

Brett's face flushed. He kept remembering what he'd read in her file. Of her days of hysteria and then months of being mute. No wonder. It wasn't enough that her world had been destroyed. Her body had suffered as much or worse. Anger boiled, spilling out between them in a short, but succinct curse.

"Son of a bitch." When she flinched, he took a deep breath and hugged her to him. "I'm sorry, baby. I'm just angry *for* you, not *at* you."

"I know."

"Do you remember his name?"

She shook her head. "I never knew it."

Rage boiled. "I'll find out, and I'll find him, and when I do—"

Tory pressed her fingers against Brett's mouth, gently stifling a promise he could never fulfill.

"Don't," she said. "There's no need. God deals with people like that in His own time. Remember Oliver Hale. He didn't escape justice, and neither will that man. I accept that, and so can you."

Brett caught her hand before she could take it away and then threaded his fingers through hers.

"You, my love, are one hell of a lady." He lowered his head and pressed her hand to his lips.

She gazed down at the dark swirl of hair on the crown of Brett's head. She remembered how close she'd come to losing him, and her heart tightened with love.

"Hey, you. How about those pancakes?"

Brett lifted his head. "Yeah, how about them?"

he said, and then opened the door and helped her up the steps and into the motor home.

"Let me wash up, and I'll help you make them," Tory said, and headed for the bathroom.

Brett watched her until she was out of sight. Without thought, he turned the lock on the door, shutting them in and the rest of the world out. For now, it was all he could do.

Fifteen

Tory was standing in the hallway when they ripped the first board out of the floor. As the crack of wood split the air like a gunshot, splintering and sharp, she flinched. And with each succeeding board, she kept hearing Oliver Hale's voice.

I put her under the tub.

She shuddered. Her poor mother. Twenty-five years waiting to be put to rest. And then Brett stepped up behind her, wrapping her in his arms.

"Tory, baby, are you all right?" he asked.

The urgency in his voice was impossible to miss, and after what she'd revealed this morning, she couldn't blame him. He was probably waiting for her to come apart at the seams.

She felt Brett's chin at the crown of her hair, felt his thumb rubbing at the pulse point at her wrist. All right? As long as he walked beside her, she would always be all right.

"Yes, Brett. I'm fine."

Men in orange coveralls were all over the place, pulling nails, moving boards, taking pictures.

Twice she had to move aside to let one of them pass, but each time she resumed her watch, unwilling to relinquish her space. This had been her home—and her nightmare. More than anyone else, she had a right to be here.

As the demolition of the small room continued, Denton Washburn leaned in an open window to their right to greet them.

"Morning, Miss Lancaster. Mr. Hooker. Hell of a mess."

"Yes, sir, it is," Tory said.

At that point, Rentshaw stepped out of the bathroom, and waved her down. "Miss Lancaster, may we speak with you a moment?"

The urgency of panic stayed with her, but she made herself relax. If they'd found something, they would have said so.

"Want me to go with you?" Brett asked.

She shook her head. "No. I'm fine."

He touched her hair and then kissed the side of her cheek, watching intently until she reached the end of the hall and began conversing with Rentshaw. Satisfied that she was going to be all right, he headed to the window where the police chief was standing, then squatted on his heels so that he was eye level with the chief.

"Got a minute?" he asked.

When Hooker lowered his voice, Washburn's

interest was piqued. Obviously, whatever Hooker was about to say, he didn't want advertised.

"What's up?" the chief asked.

"You told us yesterday that you took part in Tory's rescue."

Washburn nodded. "If you can call it that. I always consider a rescue as a save. We didn't save that little girl from anything." He frowned as he remembered the condition in which they'd found her. "Everything was over before we got here, but yes, I was one of the officers who took her out of the home."

"Okay," Brett said. "We know you came after her, but what we don't know was how your people were notified. Who called you? Who told you she was here?"

A curious expression crossed Washburn's face. "You know, that was some years back. I'd have to do some thinking."

"Then think," Brett said. "It matters."

Washburn turned and spit, his eyebrows knitting as he stared down at the ground for some time. Finally he looked up.

"You understand that to verify this, I'd have to dig through some really old files, but I'm thinking we got an anonymous call. Seems to me like someone claimed to have been driving by and heard screams, or something like that."

"Damn." Brett stood abruptly. He'd been afraid of something like this.

Now Washburn was more than curious. Without waiting for an invitation, he headed for the front door, joining Brett moments later in the empty room off the hall.

"Now you answer me a question," he said.

Brett wouldn't commit himself. "If I can."

"What I just told you fits into something I don't know, doesn't it?"

Brett nodded.

"What was it? What did we miss?"

Brett inhaled slowly. "When you took her back to town, was she ever examined by a doctor?"

"Oh, yeah," Washburn said. "In fact, I took her to the hospital myself. Even had to help hold her down while the doctor looked her over." When he realized how terrible that sounded, he looked apologetic. "You have to understand...she was hysterical. In fact, when I saw her that day, I wouldn't have given a plug nickel that she'd ever be right again." And then he shook his head and sighed. "Except for a couple of old scratches on her knee and the fact that she was partially dehydrated, she was physically okay. But it was a bad situation. I didn't think we'd ever get her calm."

"And how did you?" Brett asked.

"As I remember, it was a nurse who worked the miracle. Finally she told all of us men to get out, even the doctor. Then she took Tory into her arms and started to rock her. It didn't stop her from crying, but it stopped the shrieks.'' He shuddered. ''Damn, but they were awful. She'd screamed until her little throat was all hoarse.''

''So she stopped screaming when the men left, is that what you're saying?''

Washburn nodded. ''Yep, that's about the—'' And then it hit him, right in the gut where he lived. Years ago he would have missed the clues, but he'd been to too many awareness seminars on child abuse not to get the connection. He paled as he took a step back.

''Oh, shit.'' He broke out in a sick sweat, imagining what that child must have endured. ''What happened to her?''

Brett sighed. This was all so complex. Would Washburn understand? But he wanted answers, and to get them, he had to trust someone.

''You have to understand that, until recently, Tory hasn't remembered anything of her childhood except being shunted from one foster home to another. A few weeks ago she started having nightmares, but when she would wake up, she never remembered what they were about.''

Washburn nodded. ''That makes sense. It's a delayed reaction due to extreme trauma. Sort of like the post-traumatic stress disorder that vets suffer.'' His voice began to shake, and he lowered it until it was barely above a whisper. "What happened to her, Hooker?"

"Evidently Hale owed some man money. He came looking for Hale, and all he found was Tory hiding in a closet. He took what was owed him out on her." And then Brett's voice started shaking in anger, and he began to pace the floor. "What keeps going through my mind is how close she probably came to being murdered. If someone was sick enough to rape a child, it's a miracle he didn't kill her to keep her from telling."

Someone paused outside the doorway, glancing in at them, then moving on toward the dig. Washburn waited until the sound of footsteps had disappeared before he continued.

"Considering her condition, he probably figured she wouldn't be making any sense for the rest of her life, and whatever she'd known, she wouldn't be capable of telling. In a way, he was right. Whoever he was, he's damn sure long gone."

"That's my guess, too," Brett said.

Washburn felt sick and, in a small way, responsible. But he'd been so green. At that point in his career, all he'd known how to do was take orders.

"If there's anything I can do to help, just ask," he said.

Brett shook his head. "With no more than what we have to go on, it's impossible to guess who it could have been. The only people who might have known were Tory's mother and Hale, and they're both dead. Tory's willing to let it go. I have no choice but to follow her lead. This one is her call all the way."

And as he was thinking of her, he heard her shouting his name.

"Brett! Where are you?"

He spun around. There was just enough panic in her voice to make him jump.

"In here," he yelled, and bolted.

She met him in the doorway, apologizing before he could speak. "I'm sorry," she said. "It's just that when I didn't see you, I——"

He hugged her. "Hush, baby. You can yell your head off at me whenever you feel the need. So, what's going on in there?"

She saw Washburn look at her and then look away, and in that moment, she knew without asking what they'd been talking about. Oddly enough, she no longer cared.

"They've run into a slight snag," she said. "Except for a couple of boards at the threshold, the entire floor is now gone."

"And...?"

The pupils in Tory's eyes widened, as if she were suddenly staring into a black hole.

"She's not there, Brett. They've taken the entire floor out, and she's just not there."

His stomach knotted. Hell. Back to square one.

"Well, sweetheart, it's been twenty-five years. Surely they didn't think a body would just be lying there. Between decomposition and animals, it would have been a miracle if..." He left the rest unspoken.

She nodded. "That's what they said. They plan to start digging after lunch. The forensic expert is setting up a place to screen all the earth they remove. He says if there are even bone fragments, he'll find them."

"Then that's that," Brett said. "Come on. Let's get out of here. We both need some fresh air and sunshine, okay?"

Tory nodded, then looked at Chief Washburn. "If you'd like to come to the RV with us, you'd be welcome. We have plenty of food."

Washburn was pleased that she'd offered, but there was a knot in his throat that food wouldn't pass. It was all he could do to look at her and not cry. After what he'd just learned, he might never be hungry again.

"No, but thank you kindly. I better make a run back to town and check on things at the office. And if you decide to picnic outside your RV, I'd advise setting up on the far side. Those damn news crews are camped out on the road, hovering like hungry vultures. They just might have one of them long-distance lenses trained right on you."

"I'm not afraid of pictures," Tory said. "But I don't like having my space invaded."

"We'll be careful," Brett said. "And thanks for the warning, but I'm giving you a warning of my own. If they get in Tory's face again, someone's going home with a black eye, and it won't be me."

Washburn grinned. "I'll pass them the message as I go by."

Tory's sandwich was all but untouched. She'd taken less than half a dozen bites before picking up her camera and wandering off toward the cows in the pasture behind the makeshift fence.

Brett watched her take shot after shot, but when she crawled between the wires and started walking toward the herd, he decided to intervene. The last thing he needed was to have to rescue her from some pissed-off bull.

"Tory! Wait!" He headed toward her at a lope.

She paused and turned, waiting for him to catch up. And when he came to the fence, she grinned and lifted her camera, taking pointed aim at the way he came over the three-barbed wire fence. He was too old to crawl under and too long-legged to crawl in between. With mere inches to spare, he slung one leg over the top wire and then, ever so carefully, the other. And she got it all on film.

Brett looked up just as she snapped a shot, and the grin on his face was worth another.

"Am I going to regret this in the morning?" he asked.

She grinned back. "Probably. But I promise I'll still respect you."

Startled by her unexpected humor, he threw back his head and laughed. The sound spooked the cows. They threw up their tails and took off to the back of the pasture in a dead run.

"Now look what you did," Tory moaned.

He pointed to the big Angus bull who was bringing up the rear of the herd. "Better that than having to put you up a tree ahead of that bull."

Tory looked startled. "I didn't think."

Brett put his arm around her shoulder and turned her toward the house.

"We'd better get back. They're about ready to start digging."

Tory followed his lead, suddenly quiet after the moment of delight.

The afternoon breeze was a terrible tease, like a back seat babe who never followed through on her promises. Sweat was running down Tory's back as they reached the fence. Just as Brett started to crawl over, she grabbed his arm.

"What if she's not there?"

He'd had the same worry himself. But hearing her voice his own doubts was worse, because he didn't have an answer she would want to hear.

"What if the doctor was right?" she continued.

"What if Oliver Hale was just out of his head? What if my mother is still out there somewhere?"

Brett cupped her cheeks with his hands, tilting her face until she was forced to meet his gaze.

"Is that what you think? Is the mother you remember capable of walking out on you?"

In that moment, the last of her uncertainty ended. She looked up at him, her eyes wide and fixed upon the man who'd anchored her world.

"No. The mother I remember would have died before she would have given me away."

The old cliché came out of her mouth before she'd given thought to its meaning, but the moment she said it, she knew she'd answered her own question.

Brett's smile was gentle, as was the kiss he placed on the side of her mouth.

"There you have it," he said softly.

She sighed. "I will be so glad when this is over."

Brett hugged her, then lifted her up, setting her down on the other side of the fence and then climbing back the same way he'd come.

No one was willing to look at Tory Lancaster and tell her what they'd been thinking for hours. By four o'clock, all they'd taken out from beneath that house was a mountain of dirt, an arrowhead, two pre-Civil War coins and an old Mason jar containing two rocks and a petrified lizard. There wasn't a man among them who believed they would find even a remnant of Ruth Lancaster, let alone her body.

Rentshaw was ready to pull up stakes, but his orders were specific. A man had confessed to a killing and then to hiding a body. It was his responsibility to see that the flooring was removed from every room in the house before he called it quits. He was a thorough man. Tomorrow they would finish the job. Then, and only then, would he dismantle the dig.

Tory was morose to the point of withdrawal and had given up watching for miracles. She'd gone into the RV, closing the door and pulling the shades behind her.

Brett was frustrated on two counts. He was still locked into the hell of knowing the woman he loved had been raped. Granted, it had happened twenty-five years ago, but for him, it had just happened today. Coupled with that was the fact that they were coming up empty with each shovel of dirt. He didn't want to think it, but the possibility that Hale had been out of his mind, or just out-and-out lying, had crossed his mind. And then he would ask himself, why would a dying man lie? If Hale had believed in a greater power, then he would have had nothing to gain and everything to lose.

No. Brett was convinced that Oliver Hale had not been lying, although the possibility that he'd been hallucinating was real. And if that was so, it had been fate at her most cruel, giving hope to one person and taking another into death on a dream.

For now, all they could do was wait.

"Now, sweetheart, bring Mommy the flowers."

The woman pointed to the flat full of seedlings she'd bought at the store, then smiled as she watched the concentration on her little girl's face, juggling the doll under her arm against the small pots of flowers that she needed to carry.

"Maybe if you put Sweet Baby down you could carry them better."

The little girl frowned. "Oh no, Mommy, no. Sweet Baby helpin' me. We gonna plant 'em inna tub and watch 'em gwow."

The woman rescued the flat of seedlings just as they would have toppled to the ground. Then the little girl stood by as, one by one, the woman transferred the flowers into the old wooden half barrel, filling the space with yellow and orange blossoms on tender green stems.

"Is we done?"

The woman gave the soil around a small marigold a final pat and then rocked back on her heels, viewing her work with delight.

"Yes, sweet baby, we're done. What do you think?"

The little girl shifted her dolly to her other arm and then frowned, as if giving the question much thought. A bee was already dipping into the nectar of a nearby bloom, and there was a butterfly hovering just above another. She pointed.

"They likes it...and so does I."

"So do I," her mother said, gently correcting the lingering remnants of her daughter's baby talk. But the point was lost as the little girl looked up and smiled.

"If we bofe likes it, then we's done."

The woman's face mirrored her surprise, then delight. She reached for her daughter and pulled her into her lap, hugging her close.

"You're the best little girl a mommy could ever want, did you know that, Tory Lee?"

"Yes, I knows that," the little girl said, and then giggled.

The woman brushed a stray strand of hair from her little girl's eyes, then kissed the sweat of her brow.

"And who told you that you were my best little girl?" she asked.

The child leaned over, whispering in her mother's ear.

"Sweet Baby told me. Her knows ever'thing."

* * *

A cow lowed in the pasture behind the RV. A
distance away, a calf answered with a plaintive
bawl. A few minutes later, the pasture was silent
as the old cow had relocated her calf.

Brett rolled over in bed and then sat up, wondering what it was that he'd heard. Tory was
asleep on her side near the wall, and from the
looks of her, she hadn't moved since he'd covered
her up.

The air was still, the night muggy, and he
thought about closing the windows and turning the
air conditioner on. But that would likely wake her,
and that was the last thing he wanted to do. She
was restless and distraught enough without losing
sleep, too.

He slipped out of bed, making his way through
the dark to the refrigerator. Maybe something cold
to drink would cool him off, and then he could
relax enough to get back to sleep. He opened the
door, took out a can of pop and then put it back,
settling for some orange juice, instead. The last
thing he needed was caffeine.

After draining the carton, he tossed the empty
in the trash and then opened the door to look out.
Dew on the grass gleamed bright in the moonlight,
like white diamonds on velvet. He leaned outside,
pausing on the step and inhaling deeply. Peace
came in that moment, easing the tension with
which he'd awakened and giving him ease to ap-

preciate where they were. And then, like a whisper on the wind, the scent of newly turned earth drifted to him, reminding him of where it had been and why it had been disturbed.

He looked toward the old house, and not for the first time considered the wisdom of just throwing a match to it, effecting a cleansing in a way she could not. He couldn't help her get rid of her demons, but he could demolish the reminders. And then sanity returned before the thought became deed. He turned his back on the past and stepped inside, locking the door behind him.

A bedspring squeaked as he moved through the RV and he hurried, suddenly afraid that Tory would wake and find herself alone. He paused in the doorway, listening. Her breathing was even. Good. She was still asleep.

As he moved toward the bed, Tory rolled onto her back, one arm outflung, the other tucked beneath her breasts. He stood at the foot of the bed, watching her sleep, and wondered how one person could so drastically change another one's life. He couldn't imagine his world without her.

Anxious now to touch her, he crawled back into bed, easing down beside her and then slipping his arm beneath her neck. As he did, she rolled again until his chest became her pillow. Brett smiled to himself, looking down and gazing at her in the moonlit darkness. Then his smile froze and faded, his heart jerking painfully as he reached for her cheek, tracing with a fingertip, the quiet path of her tears.

Jesus.

It was a prayer, rather than a curse. Brett pulled her to him, wanting to take away her pain, yet knowing all he could do was be there if she called.

Rentshaw looked as nervous as he felt. They had one room to go, and then it would all be over. If Ruth Lancaster's bones weren't shining when they pulled up that floor, he was calling a halt to the whole procedure.

Art Beckham wasn't too happy with what they'd done to the floor of his barn and had already garnered an agreement with Rentshaw's superior that a new one would be in place before the end of the week.

Calico Rock's police chief had made himself scarce, leaving Rentshaw to play boss man as well as handle public relations. The media was pressing for answers he didn't have to give, and Tory Lancaster was staring at him with those big, haunted eyes. At that moment, he wished to hell he'd gone into the appliance business with his father-in-law. Right now, selling dishwashers seemed a lot more appealing than the place he was at.

Tory had taken to her camera, regressing to old behaviors by looking at the world through a third and impartial eye. She wouldn't let herself believe that they had failed. She couldn't deal with the truth, because the truth put her back where she'd started.

A butcher-bird lit on the barbed-wire fence, a red worm dangling from its beak. She lifted her camera, focusing on the bird and clicking the shutter just as it impaled the worm on the barb.

That's a sure sale, she thought, and forwarded the film for the next shot.

Something rustled in the grass to her left, and she spun, looking through the camera's eye as a small brown rabbit leaped out of sight.

"Too fast for me," she muttered, and then swiped at a bead of sweat as she moved toward the shade.

The grass was cooler there, and she kicked off her shoes, feeling the blades slipping between her toes and tickling at the arches of her feet. She slipped the camera from around her neck and leaned against the tree, squinting her eyes against the glare of the sun. It was like looking at the world through a crack in the blinds, focusing on a thin slice of life and seeing all that was before her, but nothing else.

And that was when she saw the old half barrel, lying on its side against the stack of Art's hay. Several staves had gone missing, and the middle ring of iron had rusted away. But there was enough of it left for her to remember...and she remembered where it had been.

Her heart started racing as she stood.

"Brett!"

Her voice broke on his name as she started to run; ignoring the pain in her bare feet, she darted across the yard toward the hay.

"Brett!"

Now she was screaming his name, and men were coming out of the house, some of them curious, others wild-eyed and nervous, looking for a target that wasn't there.

Brett was inside the house when he heard her, and in the moment it took him to turn and run, it seemed as if his heart had stopped and started a dozen times. He bolted out the front door, his gaze immediately on the crowd by the road, and when he didn't see her there, he headed toward the back, calling her name as he ran.

There was a group of men at the haystack, staring at a woman they were convinced had gone mad. She was on her knees and clutching at an old wooden tub as if she'd just found the proverbial pot of gold at a rainbow's end. And she kept muttering the same thing over and over beneath her breath.

"The tub. He buried her beneath the tub."

Brett shoved the men aside, dropping to his knees beside her.

"Tory. I'm here. Tell me what's wrong."

Her voice broke as she looked up at him with a tear-stained face.

"The tub. It was Mother's flower barrel. We've been looking in the wrong place. He didn't put her under the bathtub. It was this tub. Oh, God, Brett, she's in the well."

Everyone froze as Tory got to her feet, urging Brett to follow her. It was as if she'd forgotten the others were even there. She moved past the hay toward the border of trees, and then stopped so suddenly that Brett almost walked on her bare heel. When she began pulling at weeds, Brett grabbed at her arm, stilling the fever with which she was working.

"Tory, you're not making sense. What did you—"

And then he saw it, too. All but hidden by a waist-high stand of noxious weeds that cows wouldn't eat. Something that concealed the concrete cover of what had once been a well.

Oh, God...could this be?

"Tory, tell us what you remembered!"

She looked up at him, then back at the men. The scent of crushed weeds and heat was thick in her nostrils, and the bottoms of her feet were beginning to sting. But she could take care of herself later—after she showed them where her mother would be. She pointed to the concrete slab.

"That tub. We always planted flowers in that tub. And it sat here…on top of an old dry well. Oliver didn't lie. We just misunderstood."

Rentshaw shifted gears, ordering everyone in place. Within moments, a crew of men were down on their knees, pushing in unison and holding their breath as the slab began to slide.

Brett reached for Tory, but this time she was beyond anyone's help. Inch by inch, the pit beneath began to reveal itself, and when there was more than a foot of space open to view, Tory pushed her way to the edge, peering inside.

Someone turned on a flashlight, and so did another, and then another, until there was a wide, steady beam shining down in the hole. The beam moved like a beacon, slicing through the darkness and illuminating the small, perfect skeleton at the bottom of the pit. What was left of a leather belt was around the waist, and there was one small shoe on and another shoe off.

A gasp went up from the men around her, but Tory didn't hear and couldn't see. She was staring at the world through a veil of tears. When she started to rock back and forth on her knees, weeping with the quiet of a heartbroken child, there wasn't a dry eye left among them. She leaned forward, unaware that Brett was holding on to her tightly. In a sweet, high-pitched voice, she called out to the woman below.

"Mommy…Mommy…I'm home."

Epilogue

Brett lay stretched out on the bed. Except for the shirt hanging on the back of a chair near the door, he was dressed and ready to go. His blue jeans were old, his tennis shoes clean. And his T-shirt, the one he had yet to put on, was almost as old as the child straddling his knee.

Dark curls tumbled around her face, and the little hair bow Tory had clipped in only minutes earlier was hanging down around her ear. She crawled from one leg to the other, begging for another ride on the "horsey," and every now and then pausing to see what her mother was doing. At three and counting, she'd reached a fascination with all things of a feminine turn. Be it perfume or a ribbon, lipstick or pearls, Bonnie Ruth Hooker had the face of an angel but the spirit of an imp.

He glanced up at the wall, to the framed magazine cover and the caption beneath the photo. A Face in the Crowd. He kept remembering the pride that he'd felt when it had hit the stands. Someone else had the byline on the story inside, explaining how the picture Tory had taken was instrumental in solving a twenty-five-year-old mystery regarding her past, but the picture was credited to her. His wife had become a celebrity in her field.

His focus centered when Bonnie kicked the inside of his knee as she crawled across his lap. He reached down and lifted her high above his head, laughing as he dangled her just out of reach.

"Have mercy, Tory. Aren't you about ready to go? Miss Priss is making me black-and-blue."

Tory looked into the mirror, smiling at the reflection of what was going on behind her.

"She just ate a Popsicle," she warned him. "Be careful you don't get it back in your face."

Startled, Brett quickly lowered his daughter back down to the bed and then grinned at her little red face. "And you would, wouldn't you?" he muttered, trying without success to reposition the bow in her hair.

"I'll fix it in a minute. Just as soon as I braid my hair."

Brett gladly relinquished his task, watching instead as Tory pulled the hair away from her face and then separated it into three long sections.

"Memorial Day at Mom's is fun, but it will be hectic. Remember last year?"

Tory arched an eyebrow. Bonnie had barely been two, and she'd let Cynthia's house cat out into the yard with the neighbor's dog. As the old saying went, there had been hell to pay.

She grinned. "Between Celia's pair and Bonnie, hectic is putting it mildly."

"Well, it's Mom's fault for spoiling them. After Celia and her family moved to Tulsa, nothing would do for her but selling the house in Denver and moving here to Oklahoma to be close to all of us."

"Nanny," Bonnie said, and turned a somersault on the bed. Brett grabbed her just before she went off on her head.

"Careful," he muttered, and set her down between his legs, once again trying to clip the bow back in place.

"Don't worry about it," Tory said. "I said I'll fix it in a minute."

Bonnie leaned against her daddy's tummy, suddenly aware that her mother was doing something interesting to her hair.

"Do me," she begged, pointing to the twists Tory was making of the long lengths of her hair.

"I can't, sweetheart. Your hair's not long enough yet," Tory said.

"It might have been if she hadn't taken the you-know-whats to it last month."

Tory grinned. "Yes, and if you hadn't left the you-know-whats where she could reach them, it wouldn't have happened."

Brett made a face. "They weren't exactly within reach," he reminded her. "They were on the cabinet."

Tory rolled her eyes. "And so was she."

Brett grinned. "That's my dainty little daughter. The way she climbs, we should have named her Tarzana, not Bonnie."

Bonnie wasn't finished talking, but her focus had moved from her mother's hair to the old doll sitting on a corner shelf.

"Mommy's doll?" she asked, pointing to the shelf.

Tory reached for a band to tie off her braid. Bonnie had asked the question a thousand times, and Tory figured it would be asked a thousand more before she became too old to care.

"Yes, that's Mommy's doll," she said.

"Her's dirty," Bonnie said.

Tory smiled. Bonnie's questions never wavered from a set routine. "Yes, she's dirty, because she got lost from me."

"Buts you found her," Bonnie said.

"Yes, I found her," Tory said.

"Then you found me," she cried, and threw up her arms in a winning gesture, as if she'd just crossed a goal line and won the game.

Brett rolled her out of his lap and set her down on the floor, chuckling as he gave a gentle swat to her little behind. "Yes, in a manner of speaking, then we found you."

"I gonna get my flowers," she yelled, and bolted out of the room before anyone could object.

When Brett would have gone after her, Tory shook her head. "It's okay. I already loaded the ones we're taking to the cemetery. I gave her one to carry...and it's plastic. What can she hurt?"

Brett took Tory in his arms, cupping her hips and pulling her close. When she wrapped her arms around his neck, his world settled. She smelled sweet and tasted sweeter.

"I love you, baby," he said softly. "So much."

Savoring the rhythm of his heartbeat as it pounded beneath her ear, Tory sighed, wishing they could stay this way forever. "I love you, too," she whispered. "More than you will ever know."

A crash shattered the last of their moment. They looked at each other, then broke apart and ran.

Tory got out of the car and stretched as Brett unlocked the trunk. The cemetery was crowded and she glanced toward Bonnie, making sure she was in sight before letting her thoughts wander.

The months after they'd found her mother's body had been crazy. The paperwork needed to have her parents disinterred and then reburied in Oklahoma had been endless. It seemed as if no one liked change. But Tory was different. She relished it. And thanks to Brett's insistence, the rape counseling she'd gotten had healed the remainders of old wounds. Now she thrived in every way.

She felt a touch on her arm and turned. Brett handed her a bouquet of roses and a smaller one of assorted marigolds.

"You okay?"

"I'm fine," she said, and saw relief on his face before he walked away. Impulsively, she called out. "Brett."

He turned.

"I love you."

His dark gaze raked her face and she saw the truth in his eyes, even before he spoke.

"I love you, too."

And then their daughter interrupted and the moment was gone...but not forgotten.

"Mommy, why we puttin' flowers onna ground?"

Tory handed her daughter a handful of roses. Bonnie was at a need-to-know age, and to a point, Tory was willing to tell her anything she needed to know, but no more.

"We're decorating the grave."

"What's a grave?"

Brett heard the question and gave Tory a careful look. "Want me to take her back to the car?"

Tory shook her head. "No. She's just curious."

Luckily, Bonnie had already forgotten her last question and moved on to another.

"What's that?" she asked, pointing to the engraving on the tombstone beside her.

"That says 'Ruth Ann Lancaster.' And the other name says 'Danny Lee Lancaster.' They were my mommy and daddy. They went to heaven when I was a little girl like you."

Bonnie frowned. "I don't like heaven."

Tory knelt and hugged her, understanding instantly what was wrong.

"I'm not leaving you, sweetheart. I'm right here, and so is Daddy." Then she stood and turned to the nearby tombstone.

Bonnie looked up at her mother's face and frowned as they laid the flowers on the grave. "Are you sad?"

"A little," Tory said.

"I hold your hand," Bonnie said.

"And so will I," Brett added.

"Thank you, my dears," she said gently, and took what they offered.

As they returned to the car, Tory glanced back at the flowers she'd just laid on the grave: roses for her father, the others for her mother. The yellow and orange blossoms were small compared to some of the other more elaborate arrangements around them. But it wasn't the size of the flowers that counted, it was the thought behind them.

Year after year, Ruth Lancaster had marked the coming of spring by planting those same little flowers in the old wooden tub. It seemed only fitting that they should mark her passing, as well.

shocking pink

THEY WERE ONLY WATCHING...

The mysterious lovers the three girls spied on were engaged in a deadly sexual game no one else was supposed to know about. Especially not Andie and her friends whose curiosity had deepened into a dangerous obsession....

Now fifteen years later, Andie is being watched by someone who won't let her forget the unsolved murder of "Mrs. X" or the sudden disappearance of "Mr. X." And Andie doesn't know who her friends are....

WHAT THEY SAW WAS MURDER.

ERICA SPINDLER

Available in February 1998 at your favorite retail outlet.

The Brightest Stars in Women's Fiction.™

MARY LYNN BAXTER

*S*HE'D DO ANYTHING FOR HER BROTHER....

Desperation drove Paige Morgan to contact her estranged husband, Lane. She regretted it immediately. All the pain, the love and the passion of their failed marriage came flooding back. But she had no choice— her brother was in trouble.

Paige wasn't surprised when Lane made her an offer she couldn't refuse. He offered Paige her brother's freedom—but the cost was her own.

TEARS OF YESTERDAY

Available in February 1998 where books are sold.

The Brightest Stars in Women's Fiction.™

Look us up on-line at: http://www.romance.net   MMLB417